D0847885

CROSSINGS

a
novel

LEONARD CHANG

BLACK
HERON
PRESS

ISBN 978-0-930773-92-2

Published by
BLACK HERON PRESS
Post Office Box 13396
Mill Creek, Washington 98082-1396

For my mother

Books by Leonard Chang

Crossings

Dispatches from the Cold

The Fruit 'N Food

The Allen Choice Trilogy:

Over the Shoulder

Underkill

Fade to Clear

CROSSINGS

PART I

A BROKEN ENGAGEMENT

1

A young Korean woman glided into the United States on a bicycle. This woman, Unha, had her hair cut ragged-short right before her journey so that where it was once long and shiny, it now hung unevenly over her neck, her bangs slashed crookedly over her forehead. She was pale and sweating. She was trying not to appear as terrified as she really was. She was in Tijuana and everything—the language, the people, even the sweltering, dusty weather—was foreign and strange, and she was overwhelmed with a multitude of fears.

She feared being abandoned in Mexico. She feared crossing the border illegally, her imagination exaggerating the stories she had heard of illegals being imprisoned for years. She feared Han, Mrs. Bung's grossly overweight son who rarely spoke but looked at all of them through puffy slits for eyes, sweat bubbling over his acne-scarred forehead. Unha prioritized her fears, ranked the most urgent one getting stopped at the border.

They had explicit instructions. They each had a California Driver's License. Unha's was for a Julie Kim, even though the photo looked nothing like her. Julie was chubby and cheerful, Unha skinny and exhausted. Julie had long hair, Unha short. But Mrs. Bung had told the girls to study and memorize the information, to be able to speak it in English if asked. The other four girls were stricken with test anxiety. They had to learn the words—the address, even the names—phonetically. Unha, though, had a good memory and she knew enough English to sound out the words.

The "L" consonant was difficult for Koreans. "Julie" could sound like "Jurie" or "Judie," but Unha had learned the way to say it from her English lessons with Mrs. Chun in her village outside of Taeshin. Mrs. Chun had called it the buck-teeth sound, because the tip of the tongue pressed against the front teeth. La. La. La.

Unha practiced her name, address and birthdate. Mrs. Bung told them to know how old they were supposed to be, just in case they were quizzed. They were waiting for Han to return from the border crossing. Unha had overheard Mrs. Bung tell him to gauge how busy it was.

They were in a small, dirty motel in Tijuana, the carpets stained and the paint peeling off the walls in long, diseased strips. Dust coated the windows, and outside, on the street below, sat restaurants, clubs and more small motels. The air conditioner blew lukewarm air that smelled of fish. Mrs. Bung explained how they were going to do this. As soon as it was busy enough, they would rent bicycles to ride through the special bicycle gate.

Bicycle, Unha asked, alarmed. Why a bicycle?

Mrs. Bung was a short, stout woman with thick fingers and folds of skin under her neck. She said in a sharp, impatient voice, A bicycle is faster. They do not check as many people.

I cannot ride a bicycle, Unha said.

Of course you can, Mrs. Bung replied. Everyone can.

Mrs. Bung continued her instructions: ride through the border crossing; drop off the bicycles at the rental stand on the U.S. side; get into the waiting van. They will then drive up to San Francisco.

Let me do the talking if you are stopped, Mrs. Bung said.

Unha wasn't listening. Her back had broken out into a sweat, and not just from the heat in this hotel room. The last time she had been on a bicycle, over ten years ago, she had tried to pedal a few times and lost control of the handlebars. She tumbled to the side and crashed to the ground. Her friends laughed at her. She skinned her palms, scraped her knees. She hadn't been back on a bicycle since then. She hadn't needed one in town; she always walked everywhere.

What if the border police saw her falling off her bicycle? Would they know she was illegal? She tried to remember what had gone wrong ten years ago. She had lost her balance and hadn't known how to recover. How could she ride without practicing? She was about to tell Mrs. Bung that she couldn't do this, but there was a knock at the door. Han opened it and filled the doorway. Mrs. Bung asked if it was time.

He nodded his head slowly.

Unha's story really began with a broken engagement, and what annoyed Unha was that it was a broken engagement with someone she didn't particularly love. Her fiancé, Woo Chul, the son of a family friend whom she'd known since she was a child, had actually broken up with her, and this had shocked her. *He* broke up with *her?* This was a man who had a beak nose and a habit of picking his teeth with his bony, crooked pinkie, a man who was going to spend his life working at his father's machine repair shop, and had never shown any signs of ambition other than buying a new car. They had dated for five years, first through the end of high school and then as Woo Chul worked for his father and Unha helped her grandmother make imitation handbags and wallets that Unha's cousin sold in Seoul. Woo Chul's proposal had been expected and unenthusiastically accepted. She liked Woo Chul, she had become used to him, but she certainly didn't love him in any thrilling and romantic way.

When Woo Chul sat her down for an important talk, she had suspected what he was going to say. He couldn't meet her eyes. He talked to the ground, and shifted on his feet. He said he wanted to go to Seoul and find work there. She said cautiously that she had always wanted to live and work in Seoul.

I want to go alone, he said.

Although she knew what he meant, she pretended to be confused. She said, I'll follow later? You want to set up an apartment? Do you want to have the wedding there?

She watched him squirm. He grimaced, and she thought what a coward he was. He said, I am sorry. I am too young to get married.

She almost smiled. She said, So you want to postpone the wedding until you've established yourself in Seoul? That is a good idea.

He picked his teeth and shook his head. No, he said. We should not get married.

Now?

Ever.

Then she realized that everyone would know that he rejected her, and she became angry. She said, Was this your mother? She always believed she should get a dowry.

No. My mother knows your mother and grandmother can't afford a dowry.

Unha's father died when she was young, and her mother worked in a rice noodle factory. They couldn't afford the traditional dowry of buying wedding clothes and gifts for all of the groom's family. Unha said, Your mother thinks you can get the three keys from someone else?

Woo Chul said, That is a custom for the rich.

Another dowry—keys for a new car, a new house, and an office for the groom—was becoming more popular in Korea. Unha said, You know that the women in Seoul will laugh at you.

He hesitated.

Unha said, You have made a very big mistake.

She turned and left without looking back. She was feeling both elated and frightened. She was free, yet didn't know what to do. But she was impressed by Woo Chul's decision to leave their small town for the city. She should do something as bold. She realized that she needed to get out of here too. There would be the smell of failure around her; she had somehow lost her man, and she knew her mother and grandmother would be disappointed.

She remembered a girl from her town named Munya, who had no money yet managed to emigrate to the U.S. and find a factory job. Her mother had told Unha's mother how Munya was beginning to send money home. Almost immediately after leaving Woo Chul, Unha went to talk to Munya's mother. There was nothing left for her here.

The bicycle rental stand was just a wooden trailer and a fold-out table. Unha stood in line, worrying. A deeply-tanned, bearded Mexican man in a sweat-stained T-shirt stood behind the table and told the crowd of American tourists to form one line, that they would get through the crossing much faster by bicycle. Unha remained tense, watching a group of young college-aged men rent bicycles and speed away, laughing, swerving and racing each other. They had crew cuts. They made riding look effortless. Unha's heart beat rapidly, her breath quickening. The border police in their short-sleeved uniforms stood casually at the large gate, thick lines of cars and people crowding the narrow entrances. The mid-morning sun was hot, and Unha's shirt stuck to her body.

Mrs. Bung spoke with Han, telling him to divide up the group—two with him, three with her. They would ride through separately and meet at the rental pick-up stand. Mrs. Bung's face had rivulets of sweat dripping down off her cheek. Unha cleared her throat and said, I don't know if I can ride one.

Mrs. Bung said to her, All you have to do is ride through the gate.

I don't know if I can.

You will.

What if I fall? Unha asked.

Get back on and keep riding, Mrs. Bung replied.

And if I fall again—

Enough, Mrs. Bung said, wiping her face with a sopping handkerchief. If you fall and get caught, we will leave you behind.

Unha bit her lip. They joined the line to rent the dusty, rusting bicycles from the bearded man. Mrs. Bung pulled out a wad of cash, counting off five-dollar bills. She separated two of the women, sending them with Han, and herded Unha and two others to another section of the line. She said in English, You are American tourists. Okay?

They nodded their heads, though Unha knew the other two could barely understand a word of English. Unha wiped her sweaty palms on her jeans. Maybe she could walk with the bicycle. No, they wouldn't allow that. Maybe she could coast, using her toes on the ground to keep her balance. But what if the bicycle was too big? She looked for a child's bicycle, but they were all one brand, one kind. The big kind.

What happened if she was caught? Detained? Interrogated? Arrested? She would be deported back to Korea, and everyone would know she had tried to smuggle herself in like those Mexican workers they had seen in pictures, jumping the fences and running from the Border Patrol. Her mother would be disgusted, because Unha had lied to her, told her that everything was legitimate, that her job as a waitress was already set.

The line moved forward quickly. A blond-haired American family stood in front of her. Their faces were sunburnt and peeling, and they smelled of mint lotion. The bearded man explained to them that sometimes the border police stopped riders to ask for identification, so have their identification with them, but usually the guards just waved them through. Just bring the bicycles to the stand at the other side.

A truck with a trailer clattered toward them—more bicycles arriving. As the truck pulled onto the shoulder, dust billowed up and swirled around them. A group of skinny Mexican boys filtered through the long line of people, selling tourist trinkets, churros, bottled water. Unha felt dizzy. She inhaled dust and coughed out grit and phlegm. The other girls looked at Unha with concern. They were nice girls, a little young, and just wanted to get out of Korea, like Unha. One of them, Singme, a pretty, tan girl with severe cheekbones, asked Unha if she was all right. Unha nodded her head quickly.

It was their turn. Mrs. Bung paid the bearded man and led them to the row of dusty, dirty bicycles leaning against the trailer. She climbed onto one, her thick leg easily swinging over the seat and pushing onto a pedal, gliding her forward. She stopped and turned, waiting. The other two girls chose their bicycles, and even though the seats were too high and their balance was wobbly, they pedaled forward and joined Mrs. Bung. How did they do that? Unha grabbed the handlebars of the next bicycle, and straightened the front wheel. Everyone was watching her. In line behind her, the two other girls with Han whispered to each other.

Unha's hands shook. She straddled the seat and planted her feet on the ground. The handlebars were rusted, the rubber handgrips cracked and hard. At least she could stand up with her feet planted on the ground. Mrs. Bung told them in Korean to follow her and to act like they were having fun. She began pedaling, swerving easily around a pothole and heading for the bicycle gate.

Unha walked the bicycle forward, shifting left and right, trying to gain momentum, but she couldn't keep the handle bars straight. She locked her elbows and leaned forward. Her feet slipped and she hit her shin on one of the pedals, sending a shock of pain up her leg. She heard someone on line behind her say in English, She can't ride that.

She stopped, and tried to catch her breath. She looked down and saw that she had torn her jeans. Sweat dripped down her forehead and stung her eyes. Mrs. Bung and the two other girls were coasting ahead, the distance growing between them. Singme called back, Hurry up!

Any child can do this, Unha told herself. She stepped up onto a pedal and pushed down, but this forced her too far to the side, and she realized with a gasp that she was falling to the ground, the bicycle caught in her legs and the handlebar digging into her ribs. She cried out as she clattered to the pavement, her limbs entangled. Her elbow sent spasms of pain through her arm.

Han ran to her, his heavy body jiggling, and he grabbed her roughly by the arm and pulled her up. He yanked the bicycle up with his other hand. He said in Korean, Get on and ride or we will leave you here.

This was the most she had heard him speak in the past three days, and she was surprised by the high pitch. She said, I am trying.

Try harder, he said, and he held the bicycle still. He waited, keeping it steady for her. She climbed back on, her ribs and elbow aching, and clutched the handlebars tightly.

Put your feet on the pedals, he said.

She did, shifting back and forth unsteadily.

He said, I will push you forward. Pedal slowly. Look straight ahead. Go in a straight line.

She asked, You will push me through?

No, he said. I will push you to get you moving.

He held the back of her seat, and walked forward. She swerved the handlebars and he said sharply, Keep them straight!

He sped up, pushing her faster, and she tried to keep the handlebars straight. He said in between heavy breaths, Pedal.

She pedaled, her thighs burning, and found that the faster she went, the more balanced she was. Hot wind blew in her face. Then she saw that Mrs. Bung and the two other girls were on the other side, watching. To her horror she also realized that the border patrol guards were watching her too. Han yelled, Now keep pedaling!

He gave her an extra push and let go. She wobbled for a moment, but kept pedaling, and her heart was beating so fast that it hurt her chest. If the guards stopped her, she'd fall again. She had to keep going fast. She approached the gate, and the guards watched her. The handlebars wobbled again, and she almost lost her balance. The guards pointed to her and laughed. One of them clapped his hands, saying in English, Go, go, go!

She glided though the gate, and entered the United States of America.

2

A heavy-set Korean man trudged up to the second floor of a Korean club in San Francisco, preparing himself to meet the gangster to whom he owed $20,000. Sungmo, or "Sam," believed he might actually die here tonight because of the stories he had heard about Mr. Oh, stories that his younger brother Joonhan, or "Jake," had recounted to warn Sam away from Mr. Oh. But Sam had little choice. He needed the money. He had already borrowed over $13,000 from Jake. His wife Sunny had been dying; she had needed more medicine and a nurse. His health insurance had reached its cap.

Club Saja was loud and thumping with music. The tables were filled with young Korean men drinking too much soju and trying to talk over the Korean pop songs with electronic beats and high-pitched, soulful singing. The guard at the bottom of the stairwell, a huge bald man with folds of fat underneath his chin, blocked the doorway. Sam told him his name and that he was supposed to meet with Mr. Oh. The man grunted and pointed up the stairs. He said in a hoarse voice, Last booth.

Sam moved slowly up the carpeted stairs. It was quieter here, the walls lined with acoustic tiles. He paused with each step. All he could do was ask for Mr. Oh's leniency and mercy. Sam just did not have the money, and couldn't foresee getting it any time soon. He would explain how sick his wife had been before she had died. He would talk about his son David and hope he could create sympathy. And yet he should expect nothing but what a gangster would provide: threats and violence.

He arrived at the top, where thick, red curtains barred his way. He glanced down at the guard, who was watching him, and the guard motioned him forward. Sam pushed his way through, appearing at the foot of a long corridor, doors to the right, curtains to the left. The music was even more muffled, only a faint thudding beat.

One of the curtains had been left open, and Sam saw the booths with a view of the floor below. He heard voices coming from some of the booths, men's voices speaking in Korean. Some were loud and animated, others quiet and serious.

One of the doors on the right opened, and some staccato laughter spilled out. A man in a wrinkled business suit, his tie askew, stumbled into the hallway. Sam caught a glimpse inside—a small party room, with red sofas and brown lounge chairs, dozens of bottles and glasses crowding the low wooden table in the center. A few women in short skirts and heavy make-up sat intertwined with other men. The door closed. Sam continued walking. The man wiped his shiny forehead and staggered down the stairs.

At the end of the hallway Sam knocked on the wall next to the closed curtain. Voices stopped. A deep, older voice asked in Korean who was there.

Sam announced himself, and the curtains opened. He stepped back. There was a large, round, mahogany table with

19

three people, drinks and food in front of them. Sam recognized Mr. Oh immediately—the oldest man here, in his sixties, his face creased with deep wrinkles, large bags under his eyes, dark misshapen age spots covering his neck. The man who opened the curtains was a younger, skinny man whose face was skeletal. His skin looked as if it was being pulled tightly back, a bony grimace confronting Sam. His suit hung loosely on him.

The third man said, You are Joonhan's brother?

Sam, surprised that his brother was known to them, nodded his head. The third man had on wire-rimmed glasses and gave Sam an amused smile.

Mr. Oh asked, So what are we going to do here?

Sam looked at the others, not sure if the question was for him or them.

Mr. Oh introduced the man with the eyeglasses as Koman, and the skinny man as Im.

Koman said pleasantly to Sam, You owe quite a bit of money.

I know, Sam said. He tried to keep his breath calm, but his chest tightened.

Im sat down without speaking. He still had on that strange grimace. Sam added, I am working for my brother, and am doing everything I can to—

Mr. Oh waved his hand, quieting him. He said, Because of our relationship with Joonhan, we have been very lenient, but it is time to do something about this.

Sam thought, Relationship?

They waited for his reply. He cleared his throat. I understand. I will do whatever it takes to pay you back.

Koman said, Would you be willing to work it off?

Yes, Sam replied quickly, a faint surge of hope tingling his neck. Absolutely.

Mr. Oh studied him. I am sorry about your wife. I understand you have remarried?

20

Yes, Sam said. I brought over a new wife earlier this year.

It was cancer?

Yes.

Mr. Oh sighed. Did you know I lost my wife five years ago to cancer?

No, I did not.

Mr. Oh said, The work you will do is unpleasant.

Sam kept his expression neutral, though he grew uneasy. He looked Mr. Oh in the eyes. I will do what I have to.

Good, Mr. Oh said. You will work with Im.

Sam turned to Im, who studied him without blinking.

Koman said, Come by here tomorrow night. You begin then. You will work off your debt to Mr. Oh.

Thank you, Sam said. Thank you very much.

He bowed low.

Im stood up and closed the curtains.

When Sam returned home everything was quiet. His wife Yunjin snored quietly in their bed. His son David was sprawled under his sheets, his Kung Fu instructional book by his head. Sam sat on the living room sofa, a large glass of whiskey and ice clinking in his hand. He stared at the TV news, the volume on low. Tomorrow he would have to tell his brother about his new job. He finished his whiskey in two gulps.

Yunjin appeared from the hallway, her eyes puffy from sleep. Where were you? she asked.

Sam said, Dealing with my debt.

Mr. Hendricks wants his rent.

I will write a check tomorrow.

A good check, she said.

Sam let out a slow breath and put his glass down on the coffee table.

Yunjin said, He will evict us.

Sam looked at her dark face, her dark eyes, her matted hair. He had never gotten used to how strange she could look in different lights. She was of mixed blood—a Korean mother and a black American soldier for a father—and her features were so...odd Her lips were big, her nose flat, and yet she had narrow, slanted eyes.

She repeated, He will evict us.

He said sharply, Leave me alone.

But what if he—

Leave me alone!

She stepped back, her face hardening. She was about to argue, but then stopped. She walked back to the bedroom. Sam cursed to himself, regretting his tone, but she nagged him too much. They had been together for only seven months, and he knew that this marriage had been a mistake. He had needed someone to take care of his son, and his aunt in Seoul said she knew of a young woman, a honhyol, a mixed race, who wanted to get out of Korea.

It is too late now, he thought. I am stuck with her.

Yunjin then checked on David as she did every night. She opened his door, peered in, and stared for a minute. David pretended to be asleep because he didn't know what to make of it, and only later would he realize that she was doing this not just to make sure he was all right, but to confirm the reality that she was indeed a mother, something she had never thought was possible.

She was only twenty-two, yet was suddenly a mother to an eleven-year-old; she was a new wife and an immigrant in a country she knew almost nothing about. She spoke a little English and was teaching herself more from TV and books, but even after seven months she still hadn't ventured farther than the corner grocery down the block.

They were living in Oakland, near Lake Merritt, in a small two-bedroom apartment above a dry cleaners and across from a Mexican restaurant. David's mother had died a little over a year ago, and he still couldn't understand how his father could replace her so easily and so quickly. He was worried that the memories of his mother were fading, in part because his father had thrown out everything of hers after she died. He was obsessed with removing all evidence of her, including the photos. David couldn't understand this, and watched with growing alarm as her clothes, books and collection of porcelain figurines filled boxes in the living room. When he saw his father carting them to his car, he grabbed one book from a box called *House Plans*, and hid it in his room. It was just pages and pages of architectural plans his mother used to study, imagining the house she and his father would build some day. Some of the page corners had been folded, with notations in her handwriting added on the plans—arrows, "washer/dryer here," large "x"s. Coffee stains covered a few of the pages.

David kept the book in the space behind his bookshelf and wall, and occasionally took it out when he wanted to touch the writing from his mother's hand.

3

Unha woke up when the van hit a bump and rattled the floor. She had been dreaming of making handbags with her grandmother, the imitation Gucci leather patterns strewn around them as they worked on the sewing machines. Her grandmother had an old-fashioned manual machine, with a foot pedal, but Unha used an electric one. They worked quietly, her grandmother's pedal squeaking.

As Unha realized where she was, she suddenly missed her grandmother who had said goodbye and rested her gnarled arthritic hands on Unha's head, adding, You are very brave.

Her grandmother smelled of kimchi from making it in the backyard, burying the pickled cabbage in jars underground to help the fermentation—the pungent red pepper oils seeped into her fingertips but had a comforting, lingering scent that made Unha think of her grandmother's work ethic; she rose at dawn to start cutting the handbag material slowly, painfully, the intermittent shearing waking up everyone in the house.

It was dark out, and the other girls were still asleep on the floor of the van. They were on blankets, huddled near each other, but Unha was closer to the rear door. She sat up and squinted out the back window. The landscape had changed from a few hours ago—long stretches of barren hills had been replaced by concrete freeways and malls lit up with bright signs written in English.

The van hummed along steadily, other cars passing them. Unha's back ached from sleeping in a curled-up position. She still smelled the French fries they had eaten earlier—they had stopped for dinner at a McDonald's. The hamburgers here tasted different—meatier, heavier.

One of the other girls, a young one, Minji, woke up and rubbed her eyes with small, child-like fists. She hunched her narrow, bony shoulders,as if she were cold, and squinted. She asked Unha quietly in Korean, Where are we?

I don't know, Unha replied. Closer to a city.

Minji moved up next to her and peered out the back window. Her smooth, pale skin glowed and she leaned closer to Unha. She whispered, I am worried.

Unha knew she needed comforting, and said calmly, There is no need to be.

What happens when we get to San Francisco?

Unha said, We work.

I have heard stories, Minji said.

I know, but my friend came here through Mrs. Bung and now she is working at a garment factory in Los Angeles.

Was she pretty? Minji asked.

Pretty? Why?

Because the ugly ones get those kinds of jobs, Minji said. The pretty ones work as waitresses and sometimes as…prostitutes.

Unha remembered Munya being plain-looking, neither ugly nor pretty. She didn't know how to reply to this except to say, I never heard that.

Minji's face broke out into an unexpected smile, her eyes bright in the darkened van. She whispered, I can't wait to see the Golden Gate bridge.

Unha patted Minji's arm, and Minji moved up against her.

Han mumbled something to Mrs. Bung, waking her up. She asked in a clotted voice, Where are we?

Han replied, San Jose.

Their voices awakened the other girls. They crowded next to Unha and Minji at the window, and Unha smelled their sweat and grime from their two days of travel. That and the lingering scent of the French fries in the air made Unha nauseous. She hadn't slept much in the past two days and had trouble focusing her thoughts. She wanted to take a hot shower and sleep in a real bed. She wanted to eat a cold, fresh apple.

Mrs. Bung called to them, We are almost there. Sit down.

They sat on the floor, leaning up against the sides of the van. Unha smiled at Minji, who was playing with her long hair, curling it around her fingers.

Tall buildings surrounded them, the streets narrow and crowded with cars and trucks. Unha and the others peered out of the back window at the dirty sidewalks littered with fluttering newspapers. At a stoplight they saw two black men in rags pushing each other and yelling in deep, frightening voices. Minji moved closer to Unha, who was surprised by this. Minji whispered, This is San Francisco?

Singme pointed up to a sign. Look. Hanja.

They saw Chinese lettering over a grocery store. They soon began spotting more and more Chinese signs, and Han drove the van down side streets, the buildings even more cramped together. They pulled up to a small, dirty motel, the front light flickering. Mrs. Bung climbed out and opened the side door. She said to them, Follow me.

They stepped down. Unha's legs were stiff, her knees cracking. Apartment buildings with rusty fire escape cages surrounded them. A small donut shop sat across the street, the lights on inside, but the tables empty. Exhaust and gasoline fumes billowed up from underneath the van. A car alarm beeped in the distance.

Mrs. Bung led them into the main lobby where an old Korean man with gold front teeth stood up from behind the check-in desk and said in Korean, Room three hundred. He looked the girls up and down. Unha and the others followed closely behind Mrs. Bung as she walked up a flight of stairs.

In room three hundred—a cramped twin bed in the center that the five girls stood awkwardly around—Mrs. Bung told them to wash up and wait here for her return. She said, Do not go out. You are here illegally and can be arrested. Do not answer the door or talk to anyone. Understand?

They nodded their heads. As soon as Mrs. Bung left, Minji turned on the TV and flipped through the channels. The American TV shows quickly drew everyone's attention, and they sat on the bed, staring. The English was disorienting, and there were too many choices; Minji kept changing the channels, and Singme said, Leave it on one.

Minji stopped at a music video. Unha watched for a moment, then walked to the bathroom. She looked at herself in the mirror and was startled by her short, greasy hair. She regretted cutting it. And her cheeks were drawn. She was losing weight quickly. She washed her face, and was impressed by the fluffy towels. She looked down at the small shampoo bottles and considered stealing them when she heard voices outside. Men's voices.

The TV sounds stopped. Unha heard Mrs. Bung speaking, and a man replying. Unha left the bathroom and saw two Korean men, both in casual blue and grey suits, standing by the door while Mrs. Bung told the one wearing eyeglasses that only one of them spoke any English. She studied Unha and said in English, How much can you speak?

Very little, Unha replied in Korean.

The man with the eyeglasses said to her, Speak in English.

Unha said, Little English.

He asked, But you can understand what I'm saying?

She replied, Yes.

Can you work as a waitress? the man asked. Can you take food and drink orders in English?

Unha thought about this and said, Yes.

The man said to Mrs. Bung in Korean, She goes to the club.

Mrs. Bung nodded her head.

The man looked over the other girls. He pointed to two of girls who had been quiet the entire trip and said to Mrs. Bung, These two to the factory. The other two I will bring to the massage parlor.

Minji and Singme glanced at each other.

Unha tensed. What did he say? *Maechun-gul?* Brothel?

Mrs. Bung said to Unha, Go downstairs to Han. He will drive you to the club.

She asked, Right now?

Right now, Mrs. Bung said.

Unha stared at Minji. She and Singme seemed frozen on the bed. The man with the eyeglasses said to them, Come with us.

Mrs. Bung said to the other two girls, You will stay here tonight. Tomorrow we will go to the garment factory in Daly City.

Unha hesitated, wanting to ask where Minji would be going. Minji gave Unha a frightened look. Mrs. Bung said to Unha, Go. Han is waiting.

Unha walked slowly out of the hotel room, her mind

tumbling with questions, and she heard Minji say something, but Mrs. Bung cut her off with, You go with those men. Now!

In the hall Unha turned around to see Minji and Singme walking rigidly out of the room, their eyes darting, and Minji was breathing rapidly. The two men were behind them. Unha had the wild impulse to grab Minji's hand and flee. All she had to do was push past the men and pull Minji toward the stairs and out of this hotel. She slowed her steps, thinking, Do something. But then the elevator door opened. The men were watching her. She walked in and held the door as Minji and Singme approached. Singme's soft, young face was red and terrified.

The man behind them told Unha to go ahead. They would take the stairs. Unha hesitated, then slowly let go of the doors. Minji kept blinking her eyes rapidly. The doors closed.

Unha was too confused and tired to untangle her concerns. She stood in the tiny descending elevator that shuddered and almost stalled as it passed each floor, and the single light above had a dull yellow tint that barely illuminated the panel in front of her. She thought, What is happening? Why are they being split up?

Divide and conquer. Separate and confuse. She wondered why Minji and Singme didn't protest. Even if it was really a massage parlor, Mrs. Bung hadn't mentioned that as a possibility. It was either waitressing or factory work. But they were both young and, like Unha, they were exhausted and confused. And scared. As the elevator reached the ground floor Unha tried to calm herself. She knew her English helped her. She would be all right—

The doors opened to the sound of crying. She saw Singme on the floor, holding her face and shaking her head. Minji stood near the wall, her hands curled up at her chest, her eyes wide. The two men reached for Singme, who cried out, I changed my mind! I don't want to do this!

Shut up, one of the men hissed. Singme twisted away from him.

The other man reached down and grabbed Singme by the arm and yanked her up onto her feet. She tried to shake free, and the man slapped her face. The sound shocked Unha. Singme withered. Everyone was quiet. The man said to her, Don't be foolish. Come quietly.

Singme nodded her head. The man continued holding her arm and pulled her out of the lobby. Minji followed.

The elevator door started to close again and Unha stepped out. She saw Han sitting on one of the benches by the front desk. Han stood up slowly, sighing. He asked, Are you ready?

Unha didn't know what to say. She couldn't believe that man had slapped Singme. Did that really happen or was she just so tired—

Han said, Come on.

Where am I going? she asked.

Club Saja. Let's go.

David woke up to the sound of his father yelling at Yunjin. His father had always drunk, but it wasn't until his mother began getting sick that the drinking took on a steady, predictable, excessive pattern, beginning with a few beers after work, building to whiskey with ice, and then ending with whiskey straight from the bottle. Before Yunjin came, David's father would sit in the living room and talk to himself, having strange conversations in Korean with someone who might have been his dead mother. David was never sure.

Yunjin's arrival was very bewildering for him. One day his father announced that he would be bringing over a new wife from Korea. He quickly added that she wasn't going to replace David's mother, but they needed someone to help. She arrived the next week, and David immediately saw how nervous she was. Her mixed-race features weren't that unusual here in Oakland—in fact she fit in well here in their neighborhood where there were many African Americans—so when he first saw her he registered her darker features and curly hair quickly, but then focused on what kind of stepmother she would be.

She was clearly anxious. She spoke haltingly in Korean, and when David pretended not to understand her, she tried in English. She had trouble meeting everyone's eyes. She almost spilled her drink of water. David's father told him she was tired, having traveled all day. Yunjiin then asked David what he liked to do. When he told her he was learning Kung Fu, she said she used to watch people practice at the local tae kwon do studio.

This immediately got his attention. Despite his wariness David began asking her about tae kwon do, and she told him about how Korean churches often taught kids for free. She was supposed to find a local Korean church to make more friends. David's father told her that they didn't go to church, and when she asked why, he said in Korean, Because there is no God.

This stopped her. Later they would fight more about going to church, but at that moment they both fell silent, and David found himself eager to talk about tae kwon do. But Yunjin was tired, and he had school the next day.

The fights they had usually began with money, but then David's father would harass Yunjin for the many faults he found with her, often with the implicit comparison to David's mother. Yunjin would take this at first, but as she began to feel more comfortable here, she fought back.

Most of David's memories of his father around that time were of him sitting on the sofa, holding his glass of whiskey on the armrest, the condensation staining the pale brown fabric. His mumblings were usually incomprehensible, but occasionally Korean or English words broke through the garbled haze. He often seemed to be justifying himself, saying things like, I am doing the best I can.

The night when he agreed to work for Mr. Oh, Sam fought more loudly and more vehemently with Yunjin than ever before. He had been drinking all evening, triggered by his new relationship with Mr. Oh and the sense that no matter what he did, he would be dragged deeper and deeper into trouble. His face was deep red, his breathing shallow. He rocked back and forth in his chair, trying to catch the rhythm of his dizzy spells. He dreaded having to tell his brother about Mr. Oh, but he had to, since he wouldn't be able to work on the new restaurant. Jake would see this as another chance to look down on him. The prospect of his younger brother's further disapproval sent Sam back to the kitchen for another refill.

When they were children Sam had the advantage of age and size over Jake, but by the time they entered their teens, Jake was excelling at school and showing a shrewdness that Sam lacked. Despite being younger by two years, Jake was looked at by their parents as the more responsible one, the more mature one, and Sam hated it. Yet he couldn't seem to do as well in school as Jake, couldn't seem to focus on anything, and when he almost failed his college entrance exams, he was relieved to apprentice to a carpenter. The competition with Jake was over.

Jake had emigrated to the United States first, studying business administration at Bay College, then getting a work visa by having a Korean food distributor sponsor him. From there he eventually earned his green card and sponsored Sam to immigrate. That Jake was more successful didn't bother Sam at that point because he had just married Sunny and was in love. They planned to have a big family and own a house. She got pregnant with David after two years here, and when he was born they were happy that he was an American citizen. Sam found a job with a contractor, and because the real estate market in the Bay Area was strong, they were offered more work than they could accept.

But the first sign of trouble was Sunny's second pregnancy and miscarriage, and the complications that followed. At the time they hadn't known that the miscarriage was related to what would become ovarian cancer—they hadn't even known she had cancer—but she was unable to get pregnant after that. They thought they were destined to have one child, which was fine. But then the pains started, the swelling, the nausea, and soon she could barely straighten up, the pain shooting through her insides. That was when she was first diagnosed, and they removed one of her ovaries. Then the cancer spread, and they removed the other. It kept spreading, and soon it had traveled into her lymph system.

The memory of her suffering deepened Sam's depression. He thought, I have nothing.

Yunjin suddenly appeared in the kitchen and said, You are making too much noise.

Sam looked down at the counter. He had knocked over and broken one of the glasses and hadn't even realized it.

Yunjin said, You are drunk again.

Sam felt the day's frustration bubbling up, and he said more sharply than he intended, Why do you always nag me!

Yunjin yelled, Because you are going to get us kicked out onto the street!

And that was how their fights began.

4

When Minji and Singme were brought to Yang Acupuncture and Massage in North Beach, they found themselves in a small massage room with two other girls. The room, barely large enough for a low massage table and an end table, was stifling hot and smelled of fruit oils. They had been directed up here by a small Korean woman whose hoarse voice had frightened Minji—it sounded as if the woman's vocal chords had been sandpapered.

Minji kept telling herself that this wasn't what it looked like, that she had the wrong idea. She kept tugging at her long, slender fingers. Her piano teacher had once said that she had perfect fingers for the piano, if she would only practice. But she hadn't. She quit her lessons when a boy, Wikung, said that no one played the piano anymore and that the guitar was the best instrument.

Most of her bad decisions were because of a boy, and when Jin, her boyfriend whom she met at an Itaewon club, told her he was going to the states to study chemistry, she decided impulsively she'd go as well. She told him she would find a way to meet him, since she didn't have any money or

U.S. relatives to sponsor her. Jin could barely afford his own plane ticket, and his uncle was housing him. The easiest way for Minji to get here was to answer an ad in one of the weeklies for waitresses and hostesses.

She had Jin's uncle's phone number memorized, but was waiting to call. She wanted to be sure where she would be and what she would be doing. But now, as she and the three other girls waited in this small, cramped massage room, she began to realize she was in trouble.

A thin man with high cheekbones and a shiny black leather jacket walked in. He eyed them one by one, his expression blank. Minji held her breath. He closed the door behind him slowly. He pursed his lips, then said in Korean, You all owe ten thousand dollars for bringing you here. You must work this debt off. The only way to do it is to massage customers and have sex with them.

Minji kept perfectly still, the words sinking in. What did he say? She must have misheard him. She waited for one of the girls to say something, but none of them did.

The man said, For this you will be given a place to stay and fifty dollars a week for make-up and clothing.

One of the other women began to cry.

The man shook his head and said, There is no use in that. You do what you are told and you will pay off your debt and be free. If you do not, you will either end up in jail or dead. It is up to you.

Minji thought, Wait, wait. This cannot be right. She had trouble breathing. She couldn't seem to get enough air and inhaled quickly. The man turned to her. She said, I have to…I have to get out of here.

You cannot leave, the man replied.

Singme said, I…I will tell the police.

The man took a quick step forward and backhanded her across the face. She cried out, and collapsed to the floor. Minji and the other girls stood there, frozen. The man said to them, We know where you came from. We know your families. If you tell the police or anyone, we will kill you and then send people after your families. Once you pay off your debt you will be free to go. But you must pay off your debt.

Minji thought about her parents, who had been worried about her going to the U.S. by herself. Her father had met with Mrs. Bung and asked questions about what kind of job Minji would get. Mrs. Bung had assured him that a good factory job was almost guaranteed, but a higher paying waitressing job was a possibility, depending on her skills.

Yes, they knew where her parents lived.

The man asked Minji, You want to say something to me?

Minji looked down at the floor.

The man stepped forward and grabbed Minji's arm, pulling her. He said, You come with me.

She tightened her body, keeping her feet planted.

He pulled harder, wrenching her forward and hurting her shoulder; she stumbled after him. She had trouble forming thoughts. He pulled her out into the hall and closed the door. She found herself hypnotized, walking without any idea of what to do. She stared at the grungy wallpaper, faded flower prints under a sheen of grime. She heard the man's heels clicking on the floor. Her head felt stuffed, like she had a bad cold.

The man opened another door, and motioned her in. She walked into a small room with a massage table on one side and a small mattress on the floor. The man followed her and closed the door behind him. He said, Take off your clothes.

She stood there, uncomprehending.

He frowned and said, Are you stupid?

He unbuckled his belt.

Slowly, her hands and arms began to shake. She couldn't look at him, and gazed down at her feet. She saw a

36

new hole in her shoe. A sob almost burst up from her chest, but she kept it stifled.

He unbuttoned his pants, unzipped his fly, and let his slacks fall to the floor. He pulled down his underwear, exposing his erection. Minji stared in shock as he moved toward her, touching himself. The skin around his pubic hair was white. He stopped.

Come here, he said.

Please, she started to say, but nothing came out. She couldn't get her voice to work. She tried again. Please.

He said in a low, chilling voice, Come here or you will not walk out of here alive.

She shivered.

Come here!

She didn't know what else to do. She stepped forward.

The morning after David's father's and Yunjin's fight, when he told Yunjin that he would no longer be working for his brother and would in fact be working off his debt for Mr. Oh, David found the tension between them unbearable. His father sat stoically at the kitchen table, eating his eggs, bacon and toast, while Yunjin stood at the sink and washed the dishes from last night. The air was dense with the smell of bacon and residual anger. His father asked him what he was going to do today, and he lied and told him he was going to a summer program at the library. Yunjin glanced at him, but didn't say anything.

As David's father finished his breakfast and got up to leave, Yunjin asked him for the check. He said, I will take care of it.

Yunjin started to reply, but his father gave her a hard, cold look. She stopped. She watched him put on his leather jacket and close the door behind him.

She said to David, Where you go all day?

He said, To the library.

He grabbed his *Kung Fu for Beginners* book and fled the apartment.

It was only partially true. David did spend hours at the main Oakland library, reading books about martial arts and sometimes reading novels in the children's section, but he also wandered through the neighborhoods and even took BART into San Francisco. This was the summer that he realized he could do whatever he wanted, and was limited only by money and time. He found ways around the money problem, like figuring out which turnstile entrances to slip under on BART—ones that were usually the farthest from the ticket booth window—and which movie theaters were the easiest to sneak into—the Grand Lake had a second employee entrance that was connected to the hot dog and burrito restaurant next door—and which karate studios occasionally let him watch the students practice—Lee's Tae Kwon Do on Piedmont.

He was teaching himself kung fu because he liked the animal styles, but there were no kung fu studios near him. One of his goals that summer was to find a studio that would allow him to sit and watch. He continued his search that day.

He knew that Yunjin suspected his wanderings since they had seen each other at Lake Merritt a few times. She rarely ventured far from the apartment. She would clean in the mornings while watching TV, practicing her English. In the afternoons she would bring one of her Korean novels and read at the lake.

Her history, which came out in small bits, was convoluted and startling to him, and the first inkling he had that she was happy to have left Korea was when he heard her and his father arguing, and his father called her a *tuigi*.

Later David asked her what it meant, and she kept very still.

She said, Where did you hear that?

My father—

38

Never use that word.

Why? he asked.

It is a bad word.

What does it mean?

She shook her head. It means...It is because I am mixed blood.

Oh. What does it mean?

It's bad word. Curse. Like I am animal.

My father called you that?

She nodded her head and said, Everyone call me that in Korea.

Everyone?

She said, When I was your age other children think I am ugly monster.

David didn't know what to say. She patted him on the head and told him to go and play. As he walked out of the kitchen he glanced back at her and suddenly imagined her as a scared little kid.

5

Sam wanted to tell Jake in person that he'd be working for Mr. Oh, but could already anticipate his brother's reaction. Jake had a disapproving frown that also wrinkled his forehead, the skin on his smooth bald head folding up in small ridges. That his brother was bald but Sam was not pleased him, and this was one of very few advantages Sam had had over the years. Sam's size and strength was another. Sam had always been bigger and stronger, and he was amazed that Jake's frail and skinny body came from the same two parents. Jake had inherited their mother's genes, Sam their father's.

Jake's second restaurant was off Geary in the Richmond district, in an area where there were a few small Korean restaurants, but he was remodeling this one to become more like a lounge. Sam had already helped him tear out part of a dividing wall and add booths. Jake wanted to reopen in a few weeks.

Sam parked his car and walked along Geary, passing the tiny Korean barbecue places with hazy windows and handwritten signs of nightly specials. Fancier Japanese and Burmese restaurants dotted the area, though this neighborhood during the day had a tired, empty feel to it, most of the bars closed until later. A large hospital administration building sat across the street. At night, Sam hardly noticed the building because the surrounding restaurants were all lit up. Jake's restaurant had a new glittering sign—Seoul Silver— that cast bright white light onto the sidewalk below, but right now the sign was as gray as the concrete.

Sam walked through the front door and found Tim, one of Jake's managers, studying menus at a table. Tim peered up with tired, bloodshot eyes, and told Sam that his brother was in the kitchen.

Sam asked, Is that the new menu?

Yes, Tim said, sliding a single-page laminated menu across the table. In both Korean and English the anjoo, the appetizers, were listed on the left side, and the soju drinks on the right.

Sam asked, Is this all?

There will be specials every night, Tim said.

Sam read through the drinks and said, I have not heard of these.

We have a bartender who made many of them up.

A soju Martini?

Yes, Tim said. We avoided the twelve-thousand-dollar liquor license by serving only soju. We already have a beer and wine license for the restaurant.

How much is a beer and wine license?

Three hundred.

Sam nodded his head. His brother was tricky like that. Tim returned to studying the menu. Sam inspected the main dining room floor, the new semi-circle booths shiny under the lights. When he entered the kitchen, he saw Jake standing over one of the countertops, papers spread out before him. He had on a sharply-pressed white shirt and blue tie, his sleeves rolled up and exposing his thin, girlish wrists. His gold watch hung loosely, and he had a habit of shaking it while thinking. Even though Sam was only two years older than his brother, when he looked at Jake's boyish face, and his quick and aggressive movements, Sam felt much older and tired.

Jake saw him and said, Did you clean out the vents at Shilla?

No, Sam replied.

Why not?

Sam paused. His brother shook his wrist impatiently. Sam motioned out into the dining room and said, I saw the menus.

What did you think?

Is that enough food?

You make more money when you have smaller plates. They keep ordering them with the drinks. What about the vents?

Sam cleared his throat and said, Mr. Oh wanted to talk to me.

Jake stood up straighter. He narrowed his eyes at Sam and asked, About what?

The money I owe, Sam said.

Jake frowned, his forehead wrinkling. I told you not to get involved with—

In order to pay it off, Sam said, I am going to work for him.

What? Are you crazy? Do you know how dangerous he is?

You work with him, Sam said. Don't you? What do you do for him?

Jake pressed his fingers against his forehead and shut his eyes. He said quietly, Why don't you ever listen to me?

Sam said, I didn't have a choice. I do not have the money to pay him back.

You should not have borrowed—

I had to! Sam stepped closer. You know I had to. I was not going to let Sunny die in pain.

Jake inhaled and exhaled slowly. He asked, What kind of work?

I will find out tonight, Sam said. I am meeting Koman and Im—

Im? He's crazy.

Sam said, I am meeting with them tonight.

This is how Mr. Oh operates, Jake said. He gets you in his debt and you never get away.

Are you in his debt?

Jake said, I work with him, not for him.

How?

That is not your concern.

Sam shook his head. You are always so secretive.

Jake said, Be careful with Im.

Sam remembered that the apartment rent was late, and wondered if he should ask his brother for another loan. He said, Money is very tight right now.

Jake said, Money is always tight with you, even as kids. You could never hold onto anything.

Sam didn't want to hear about how he wasted the little money he had made working at a tool factory while his brother had saved enough for college. Sam checked his watch and told his brother he had to go.

What about the vents at Shilla? Jake asked.

I will get to them.

Jake said, I was going to make you manager of the Shilla.

I have to pay Mr. Oh back.

You have to pay me back too.

Sam thought about this, and said, But Mr. Oh is more dangerous.

When his brother left, Jake walked out into the back alley

and smoked a cigarette. He had made a promise to himself not to interfere anymore in Sam's life. No matter how hard Jake tried to help him, Sam only managed to make things worse. And he never appreciated what Jake did for him. Jake knew he'd never see the fourteen thousand dollars he had lent him. It was probably more than that if he included the money to help bring him and Sunny over. Jake had paid for the immigration lawyer, all the immigration fees, and even helped get Sam started working with contractors.

Yes, his brother always had bad luck, but it was more than that. His brother was fundamentally lazy. His brother had no real ambition or drive. But what annoyed Jake more than anything was the fact that despite his bad luck and laziness, Sam still managed to find a woman like Sunny. She had been too good for him, and from the moment Jake met her at their wedding in Seoul he knew that Sam, without even trying, would soon have something that Jake just couldn't seem to find—a family.

Jake hadn't had time, and the few women with whom a matchmaker had arranged meetings weren't right. Yes, he was very picky, and he wasn't in any hurry. It was also pretty obvious to him: he couldn't help comparing every potential wife to Sunny.

She had been beautiful in a casual, unselfconscious way. She was shy and tended to dress down and wear hats that hid her face. She tolerated Sam's moods and his tendency to be forgetful about anything not directly concerning him. When Jake thought about Sunny he did not picture her pale, drawn-out dying face as she lay in bed, but remembered the day she came to his restaurant on Telegraph shortly after they had moved here.

The Shilla was still struggling, and Jake was losing sleep from worrying. He was growing bald, and he believed it was because of stress. He had invested almost all of his personal savings in the restaurant, and after seven months the take-out business was generating more than the sit-down, which meant that his labor and overhead was draining him. He needed more customers and more turnover. Advertising wasn't helping. The location, on Telegraph, sandwiched between a karaoke bar and a hairdresser, was in the heart of this tiny Koreatown, this strip of Korean-owned stores and restaurants with both English and Korean signs in front. The Shilla was one of a dozen restaurants on the strip. The largest, Koryo, down the street, with free parking, was attracting the most business. He needed more word-of-mouth, but because he was relatively new to the Oakland area, he wasn't sure where to begin.

Sunny walked into the restaurant on another slow night. Sam was working late on a renovation job in Marin, and although Jake had often invited her to come in for dinner, this was the first time she had come in alone. She was wearing a dark grey and black dress with small white flowers on the shoulders. This was when she had long, shiny hair that fell to her shoulders. Her cheeks were flushed from the walk, and he sat her down at the best table by the front window. She looked around and said, Not crowded.

No, he sighed. It has been too slow all week.

You need to tell more people about it, she said.

He smiled. I know. I'm not sure how. I put ads in all the Korean and American papers.

What about the Korean churches?

The moment she said it, he realized she was right. The Korean churches had their own tight-knit community, the Sundays extending into social gatherings and Korean culture classes for the children. He wasn't religious and hadn't considered networking at the churches. There were probably a few of them in the East Bay.

It turned out there were dozens of them, and over the course of the next few months Jake began frequenting them, slowly getting to know more of the local Korean community.

45

He joined the local Korean Restaurant Association and Korean Businessmen Council, and began networking with San Francisco Korean restaurant owners, who planted the idea of a larger club in the city. The Shilla began to turn around soon after that, and he owed it to Sunny.

But that night when he had the cook make Sunny her favorite meal, mandu-guk, a dumpling soup, he wasn't thinking about his business. He was thinking about how lovely she appeared with her cheeks pink and her hair messy from the wind. She had a small crooked front tooth that kept her from smiling too broadly, unless she forgot about it, and then she would remember afterwards and cover her mouth. She would speak to Jake as she would her blood brother, joking with him about his thinning hair and how much weight he was losing from overwork. She said, Sam doesn't have any trouble eating. Maybe you two should switch places for a while.

He knew she had meant switching places at the dinner table, but he wondered if there was more to the remark. He sat with her at the table and tried not to fall in love with her, but it wasn't easy.

Then she told him the news that sank his hopes. She was pregnant, and Sam had wanted to tell him tonight with her, but he had to work late. Jake pretended he was happy for her, and congratulated her. He brought her more food, since she was now feeding a baby, but deep inside he mourned the loss of her as a possibility. With a child she and Sam were complete. They were a family.

The despair he felt that night was second only to what he felt when he learned of her illness.

The clues of Jake's affection were there for others to see. David certainly noticed it. When his mother was still alive, he knew that his uncle liked her, liked talking to her, liked everything about her, but he didn't really understand the extent of it until after her death.

He remembered, when his mother was alive, Jake coming over to their apartment, smoking cigarettes but blowing the smoke out a window, and talking to his parents about one day buying a big house on a beach. Jake told David's mother a story about how as kids he and Sam once vacationed at Chejudo, an island resort off the tip of Korea, and they wandered away from the resort pretending they were on a deserted island by themselves. They wanted to build a shelter, so they stole wood from a nearby construction site and put together a small lean-to. Their parents and a group of hotel workers found them a few hours later; they had fallen asleep in the lean-to.

David's mother laughed at this story. David's father shook his head and said they were stupid kids, and when David turned to his uncle he was staring at David's mother with a pleased, almost joyful expression on his face.

There were other small clues. Jake almost always took sides with David's mother when his parents had an argument. Jake brought gifts that were supposed to be for both of them, but were usually appreciated only by David's mother, such as animal figurines, which she collected. Once Jake brought home a jade turtle, and David's mother told him that her father, a merchant seaman who traveled all over the world, had seen the oldest living creature on earth, a tortoise in Bengal, and had brought home for her a wooden replica from the Bengal zoo. She had lost the turtle during one of her moves, and Jake had said, That's why I got this for you.

David's mother looked up at him, startled. She said, You remembered?

Of course.

She smiled and even blushed.

Once, when David was eating dinner at the Shilla during a slow afternoon, Jake studied him and then sat down. He asked Daivd if he thought about his mother. David stopped eating and said, Yes. Sometimes.

Do you miss her?

Yes. Do you?

Jake looked down at the table and touched a scratch in the varnish. After a long pause he sighed and said, Every day.

6

Sam spent the morning cleaning out the vents in the Shilla, the grease and smoke residue from the barbecue grills oozing thickly down the aluminum shafts and overflowing the capture bins. He should've emptied these weeks ago. The grease could've caught fire. But this was a dirty, sweaty job, and now he was going to have this oily, meaty, burnt smell on him for days afterwards. He would have to wash his hair with vinegar, even though he was wearing a plastic head cover. Everything would taste of barbecue, even his toothpaste.

But he was doing this to keep Jake happy. Otherwise Jake would bring it up whenever they saw each other, nagging him like an old woman. It would be another item on the long list of disappointments, and since Sam had a few hours before he had to meet Mr. Oh again, he might as well do this now.

The Shilla wasn't much to look at, with its rickety chairs and fading red carpets, yet it had become a moneymaker for his brother, who had bought a house a few years ago in the Oakland hills. It was so easy for Jake to be disapproving. He was practically rich. Of course he sent money back to their parents in Kuro-dong, taking on the role of the elder brother. He could afford to.

Sam finished the vents, and hurried home to shower. No one was around, and he wondered what everyone did during the day. He ate some of the leftover bulgogi he had taken from the restaurant, and considered having a beer, but then decided not to. He wanted to be clear and alert when he met with Mr. Oh again.

Based on what Koman and Im had been wearing, Sam dressed better this time, putting on slacks and a button-down shirt and tie. His sport coat was threadbare and too warm for this weather, so he put on his thin leather jacket. He checked himself in the bathroom mirror, surprised by how ruddy he seemed. He had put on weight, his cheeks were fuller, his stomach bulging, and even his hands and fingers seemed thicker. He no longer did as much carpentry work, so he was getting fat.

He vowed to cut back on the big dinners, on the free food he took from the Shilla. He combed his hair and left the apartment.

Club Saja wasn't open, but Sam knocked on the door. The large man who had been guarding the stairwell last night opened the door and nodded to him. He said, Im is upstairs.

Sam thanked him and walked inside. Without its patrons and in the light of the afternoon, Club Saja looked shabby. The bright overhead track lighting revealed the dingy upholstery and chipped tables. The walls were streaked with smoke damage. He stopped and stared at the walls, wondering where the smoke had come from.

There were voices coming from the kitchen area, and two women walked out and glanced at him. They were in jeans and sweatshirts, and headed for the stairwell, still talking. Sam heard one of them say, The new girl is pretty.

Sam walked up to the second floor and searched for Im among the booths, but everything was empty. He called out Im's name.

One of the doors on the right opened, and Im peered out. His clothes were rumpled, his eyes sleepy, his shirt untucked. He said, Wait downstairs. I will be there in a minute.

As Im closed the door Sam caught a glimpse of a woman lounging on a sofa.

Sam returned downstairs and sat at one of the tables.

More waitresses were coming in, going downstairs, and changing into their waitressing outfits—grey and white blouses and blue miniskirts.

A young woman walked out from the kitchen in jeans and a black and grey San Francisco 49'ers jacket. Sam sat up. For a moment he thought she looked exactly like Sunny, the same narrow face, the same thick eyebrows, the same small mouth and nose. She turned to Sam, noticing his stare, and peered curiously at him. His cheeks flushed with heat as their eyes locked. After a moment she continued downstairs, her short, fluffed hair bouncing on her head.

His chest tightened. His thoughts collided. Could she be a relative of Sunny's? A cousin? But Sunny didn't have any cousins that he knew of. Her only living relative on her father's side had been an aunt, unmarried, no kids.

He waited for the woman to walk back upstairs. After a few minutes she reappeared in the grey and white uniform, her hair now clipped back, and she glanced at Sam again. He couldn't stop staring. She had a slim, elegant neck. He watched her talk to an older woman who directed the other waitresses to set up the tables.

Then Im walked down the stairs and said, We have to head down to Santa Clara.

Why down there?

Im said, We have to convince an owner of a liquor

store chain to switch to Mr. Oh's distributor.

Who is that girl? Sam asked.

Im replied, She is new. Why?

She looks like someone I knew, Sam said.

Im shrugged his shoulders. Come on. We have a long drive.

Sam stood up.

Im asked, Do you have a gun?

Sam stopped. What?

A gun, a gun, Im said impatiently.

No, Sam said.

Okay, Im said. It is not a problem.

Do I need a gun?

Im said, I have one.

Sam watched Im head to the kitchen exit. Im turned and said, Coming?

Sam followed, telling himself that a gun was only a precaution. He glanced back, hoping to get another glimpse of the woman.

Although Unha noticed him, she had little time to wonder who he was, because she had to learn the computer system by tonight. She had never seen a touch screen monitor; there were color-coded blocks that corresponded to the tables and to the waitresses. The assignments were fluid, allowing the waitresses to float to different areas depending on how crowded it was. They could also work upstairs, and all the receipts and tips were saved on the computer.

It took Unha most of the afternoon to learn the system, but she liked the visuals, and when she demonstrated to Hyunma, her boss, that she understood it, Hyunma said, That was much faster than the other girls. Do you like computers?

Not really, Unha said. But I like the colors and blocks.

Hyunma smiled, her face wrinkling. She was Mr. Oh's sister, a small, compact woman with age spots on her forehead, similar to the spots her brother had on his neck, and her hair was very thin on top. She asked, Does the uniform fit?

Yes, Unha said.

And the shoes?

Even though they were tight, Unha said, They are fine.

Hyunma gave Unha a quick tour of the club, explaining how she and her brother had started it ten years ago with only half of the building. They soon managed to buy the entire building and expand the club to include private party rooms and an upstairs members-only dining area. The main club had a bar, a dozen small tables, six booths, and a small dance floor. Unha would be working the main club, serving drinks and appetizers, and occasionally helping in the kitchen during the early dinner hours when the club was quiet but the dining area upstairs was busy.

Hyunma said, You help the others get the club ready. Any more questions?

No, Unha replied.

Good. Go.

As Unha helped the other waitresses wheel in the extra trays of glasses, storing them behind the bar, Unha worried about Minji. She told herself that Minji was probably fine. That strange scene at the hotel had probably been made worse by how tired they had been. She thought for a moment about asking about Minji, but wasn't sure if she was supposed to acknowledge that they had arrived here illegally. What about Minji's family back home?

Then Unha remembered that she wanted to call home to let her mother and grandmother know she was all right. She hadn't had any free time to think about them. She wasn't sure how to call home. She wasn't sure about anything.

It struck her: she was here in the U.S., on the other side of the world, about to serve people drinks.

She was actually here.

And Minji? Minji was here too. She sat with nine other girls in the main lounge of Yang Acupuncture and Massage, watching TV and reading fashion magazines. When a customer walked through the side entrance, an iron door with an alarm system, and went to the front desk, Mrs. Shim asked the man what kind of massage he wanted, and then told him to choose a girl. Minji then sat absolutely still, trying not to attract any attention. But she often knew even before the man said anything whether or not she'd be picked. Sometimes they stared directly at her. Sometimes they were embarrassed and just looked at her quickly. But she could sense their interest— a fraction of a second lingering; a quick double-take; a scan of her body from head to toe while pretending to look at the dragon painting on the wall.

The man paid Mrs. Shim in cash. Mrs. Shim nodded twice to Minji, which meant a blow job. One nod meant a hand job. A wave of her hand meant everything else. Minji stood slowly and walked up the stairs to the massage rooms. The man followed. Their footsteps clunked on the wooden stairs. The voices from the Korean soap opera sounded hollow as they carried up to the second floor. She counted the number of steps every time. There were ten steps, and the higher she went, the more numb she became. She counted slowly in her head. By the third step she was turning off her thoughts. By the eighth step, her head was blank. By the tenth, she felt nothing.

Minji found an open room and held the door for the man. After he walked in, she closed the door behind him and told him to take off his clothes and lie down on the table, under the sheet. The room was small with just enough space for a low massage table and a roll-out mattress.

There was a secret panel in every room for the girls to hide in if there was a raid. The panel was just part of the wall behind the table, and opened from the bottom at the small crack. If the alarm bell went off, Minji had to hide. Mrs. Shim had said that if they were caught, they would be imprisoned and their debt would increase in order to get them out. They might be deported, and if that happened their families would have to pay back the debt. They must not get caught. During the lulls Minji had practiced running to the panel, opening it, and crawling in. Because she was small and quick, she could hide before the bells stopped ringing. The cramped space was just large enough for her to hug her knees and bow her head. Despite the mustiness, the cement grit sprinkling into her hair, she felt safe in there.

Minji averted her eyes when the man undressed and lay down on the table. He already had an erection poking at the sheet. She told him to turn onto his stomach.

A small cubby by the door contained massage oils, a roll of toilet paper and condoms. Minji took a bottle of massage oil and began massaging the man. Mrs. Shim had told her that this was a legitimate massage business, so they must begin with a massage.

After a few minutes, Minji asked the man if he wanted the extra treatment. He said yes, and she told him to roll over.

Minji could barely even feel the man in her hands. She was thinking about the Korean soap opera, about how she disliked her roommates, about the sunny but cool weather. If this man, for example, had been one nod, she would oil up her hands, oil up his erection with the sweet cherry oil, stroke him up and down, staring at the ugly penis but thinking about how tired she was and how she wanted to have a full night's sleep. But he was two nods. She closed her eyes and put him in her mouth. She tasted the cherry oil. She smelled the muskiness of his sweat, and felt his pubic hairs scratching her nose and lips.

The first time she tried to imagine it was Jin, her

boyfriend whom she still hadn't called. How could she contact him now? What could she tell him? No, it didn't work to imagine Jin. She had never done this with Jin. They had only kissed. No, she couldn't imagine anything.

She wondered why Sook in the soap opera had chosen not to marry the poor man who was in love with her, but instead had chosen the wealthy old mean man. Why would she do that? Didn't Sook understand that love was more important than money?

The man groaned and touched her head, trying to make her move faster. She sucked harder and felt his penis rub the roof her mouth. He tried to push deeper in, but she pulled back, not wanting to gag. He slowed down.

When the man climaxed, his penis pulsed in her mouth, and his semen squirted, and she had to fight her nausea. He tasted salty and slimy, the cherry oil gone. The disgust tightened her body then quickly subsided as she turned away and spit him out in the white bowl by the massage table. She wiped her mouth and hands, then the man's penis with toilet paper. They hadn't spoken. She never looked the man in the eyes. She spit a few more times to get the taste of the saltiness out.

The smell of his sweat mingled with the smell of the semen. She rubbed mint massage oil under her nose.

The man cleaned himself off, and dressed. He grunted a thanks as he left the room, and Minji took the white bowl into the bathroom. She washed out the bowl. She gargled and washed her face. She brought the bowl back to the room and checked the sheets and table, straightening up. She then walked back downstairs, and sat again in the lounge, watching the Korean soap opera, until the next customer arrived.

She saw Sook on the TV, begging her poor lover to forgive her for choosing the rich old man. Minji thought, I would've chosen the poor one.

PART II

MANY STARS, MANY SORROWS

7

When David wandered around his neighborhood he had no plan other than to explore. He started at his dingy apartment building on Perkins, the yellow façade gray and cracked, the brick trim crumbling, with a few thorny and dying rose bushes in front. The Lakeview Drycleaners took up a corner of the first floor of the building, and David would watch the long parade of plastic –covered clothes shudder and dance up and around the ceiling, then descend down behind the front counter.

There were two Japanese restaurants and one Chinese dim sum place along Grand Avenue. He walked along this busy street and peered into the hair salons, the bars, and the women's clothing stores. Eventually he'd work his way over to the small Koreatown along Telegraph Avenue, just a strip of stores with English and Korean signs. Recently he noticed a couple of Italian restaurants opening up down the block, but most of the places were Korean, and on the weekends he saw Korean families crowding the sidewalks, large cars emptying out kids and grandmothers.

Heading back to Lake Merritt, David sometimes thought about his mother, since this was where she took him to play. Children's Fairyland, a small amusement park for toddlers, was practically across the street from their apartment. The rides were tame and small, yet still frightened him as a toddler. His mother used to tickle the back of his neck whenever he seemed afraid of the rides. A few hundred yards from the Fairyland was the bird sanctuary, and David occasionally found Yunjin there, reading, her head bowed low and her eyes squinting in concentration. Next to the aviary was a small playground. Once Yunjin asked if he wanted to go with her and play on the swings and monkey bars while she read one of her Korean novels, but he told her he was too old for that. She looked at him with surprise, and said, You are?

Yunjin just didn't understand what to do with David, and she certainly didn't feel like she had the authority to be a parent. She didn't have any siblings, didn't have any experience with children. What did she know? She knew how to clean houses, how to wash laundry by hand. She knew how to make rice porridge.

Right before she married Sam she was living with her aunt and uncle, essentially working as their servant, preparing meals, cleaning, and taking care of her aunt, who was often in bed with headaches and various mysterious stomach ailments. They had taken Yunjin in when she was twelve, after the orphanage in Chuncheon finally located them.

Her mother had committed suicide. Yunjin had been nine years old and had lived with her mother in a small motel room near Uiam Lake in the northern province of South Korea. Her mother worked at the nearby Chuncheon Tourist hotel. The area was becoming a vacation spot for hikers during the summers and skiers in the winters. Her mother had originally come here because her boyfriend was stationed at

Camp Page, a U.S. Army base. The boyfriend left, and Yunjin and her mother returned home to Hoengseong, but when her parents disowned her, she went back to Chuncheon and found work as a maid.

Yunjin didn't remember too much of this time. She hated her life there because they were so alone. She had no friends at school since she was the only mixed-race child. Usually children of soldiers ended up in Seoul; they rarely stayed in the small towns near the bases. She was teased incessantly and spent most of her time by herself, reading religious comic books given out by the missionaries.

Her mother never smiled, never laughed, and Yunjin would often hear her crying late at night, trying to muffle her sobs with her pillow. Every morning her mother would have deep bags under her red eyes, her cheeks hollow and pale. She would shuffle across the street to buy rice cakes for breakfast, and sit quietly with Yunjin as she prepared for school.

The mood around them was always muted and sad. They were always so quiet. One morning her mother didn't come back from buying breakfast. Yunjin waited until she was supposed to take a bus to school and then went out to search for her mother. Along the banks of Uiam Lake were the morning fishermen, standing with their buckets and their poles lashed to the railing. It was summer, so the Taebaek Mountains were lush green, and she saw the signs for the upcoming Chuncheon Puppet Festival, when puppet shows and doll exhibits would line Jungang-no, the main street. She was looking forward to that. They had moved here shortly after the last festival, and Yunjin had seen the banners and posters. Her mother had promised her that this year they would watch the shows.

Then Yunjin saw a large group of people at the train station, many of them college students from nearby Hallym University, crowding on the platform, where a train had stopped before reaching the end. Conductors were running back and forth. Passengers were streaming out of the train cars. Someone hurried toward them from down the road, calling, The police are coming!

There were murmurs, and a few people on the platform peered down, turned away and covered their mouths. Yunjin suddenly had a frightened, sick feeling. She ran toward the train. She heard one of the conductors say, Clear the platform. Get off the train. Get everyone away from here!

Yunjin pushed past the crowd, jolted aside by bulky backpacks. As she neared the edge of the platform she saw a flip-flop on the tracks, and recognized the yellow plastic flowers on the strap. Then she saw a bare foot underneath the train, the pale skin bright against the dirty tracks. She stared.

One of the conductors noticed her and grabbed her arm, pulling her away. She tried to run back toward the train, but the conductor picked her up and carried her off the platform.

Yunjin told David this story one night when his father had come home drunk, and Yunjin sat with him as he tried to fall asleep. The light from the hall shone in and shadowed her face, but as she told him the story he could hear the sadness in her voice. She said, They take me to the orphanage after that. My grandparents didn't want me.

She sat on the edge of his bed. His mother used to do the same thing, though she would sometimes sing to him. He smelled bulgogi, because Yunjin had been preparing the marinade.

Yunjin fell quiet for a while. He tried to get comfortable.

She said, Can you sleep?

I can, he said.

His father mumbled to himself out in the living room.

She said, Your daddy have hard night at work.

At the restaurant?

62

No, he work for another man now.

What man? He asked, drifting off.

She replied, but he didn't hear her. Instead he dreamed of puppet shows and plastic flip-flops.

Earlier that evening, Sam and Im were caught in traffic on the way to Santa Clara, and Sam closed his eyes and conjured a vivid image of Sunny. The corners of her eyes had wrinkles that deepened with her smile, and Sam had been surprised to notice the creases were smoother when she got sick. It was as if her skin became more elastic. She looked younger when she was dying.

Sunny had a few grey streaks in her thick black hair; she had told him she started turning grey at twenty. During the first round of chemotherapy she lost all of her hair, including her eyebrows and eyelashes, and with the softening of her skin she seemed like an unfinished doll.

Im startled Sam when he honked the horn and yelled, Shibal nom, geseki! Fuck you, son of a bitch.

Sam sat up as Im swerved the car. I hate driving down here, Im said, and scowled, which made his skull-like face look more grotesque.

The sky had darkened and the red taillights blinked around them in stop-and-go traffic. They were in Im's low sports car, so they couldn't see beyond the cars surrounding them. Im tapped his long, bony fingers on the steering wheel. He cursed quietly to himself.

Sam asked, Can you tell me about what we will be doing?

Im told him that there was a man down there who had backed out of a deal with Mr. Oh. Im said, We will change his mind.

What kind of deal? Sam asked.

Mr. Oh owns a liquor supplier, Im said. This man has a chain of liquor stores.

They were quiet for a while. From the corner of his eyes, Sam saw Im's jaw tightening and relaxing, tightening and relaxing. A vein pulsed in his neck.

Sam asked him how long he had been working for Mr. Oh.

Im replied, Ten years.

Sam turned to him, surprised. Im couldn't be more than thirty, probably even younger. He said, Long time.

Im replied, He caught me stealing from one of his stores, and instead of calling the police he gave me a job.

How old were you?

Sixteen.

What were you stealing?

Im laughed. Batteries for my Walkman.

A convenience store?

A grocery, Im said. Mr. Oh started with groceries, then restaurants.

What about his brothels?

He has many businesses. His sister runs the brothel and club.

Is he rich?

Im nodded his head. Very rich.

He does not seem like it.

Im said, Mr. Oh has lasted this long without any trouble from the police because he is very quiet, very careful.

The traffic opened up, and Im slammed on the accelerator and raced into the fast lane. He muttered, Let's get this over with.

The liquor store owner was an old man. He had a gnarled, hardened body from many years of physical labor, his back was hunched, his arms and hands large and knotted with muscle. He walked with a shuffle. Grey stubble covered his face and head. When Im and Sam entered his large store, the man's lips curled in disgust. He said something to the young man behind the counter and walked toward the back. Im and Sam followed.

Rows and rows of shiny wine bottles surrounded them as they weaved through the narrow aisles and toward an office. The lights reflected off the bottles in symmetrical squares. The old man sat down at a bare desk and said in a raspy voice, Tell Mr. Oh that I am not changing my mind.

Im stood there with a blank expression and said, You know how Mr. Oh does things. That answer is unacceptable.

I know that Mr. Oh is a criminal in a suit, he replied.

Im said, You had a deal.

The old man shook his head. No. Mr. Oh said we had a deal, but I did not agree to anything.

Then, moving so quickly that Sam barely registered what was happening, Im walked briskly across the floor, grabbed a bottle of wine from an open crate, and swung it effortlessly into the man's chest. The thud was sickeningly loud, and the man was thrown back out of his seat and into the wall behind him. He let out a cry of pain, collapsing in a heap, then groaned loudly. Sam stared, slowly comprehending that they were here to beat the man into a deal.

Im said to Sam, If his son comes in, take him down.

Sam hesitated. Then, not knowing what else to do or say, he turned to the door.

The old man tried to pull himself up, and Im threw the chair aside and kicked him in the stomach. The man fell into the desk. A lamp crashed to the floor. The man grunted and curled up.

Sam heard the son call out to him, his running footsteps approaching. The door opened, and the son burst in. Sam reacted without thinking, and tackled him, throwing the boy's scrawny body easily to the ground, and clamped his hand over his throat. The son's eyes widened, and he gasped, unable to breathe.

Leave him alone, his father yelled.

Im kicked him again, and said to Sam, Bring him here.

Sam pulled the son up, twisting his arm behind his back, and forced him into the chair in front of the desk. Sam's heart beat quickly, the adrenaline rushing through him. He waited for more instructions from Im, surprised by how easily he took on this role as a thug.

Im reached under his jacket. Sam saw a shoulder holster, and when Im pulled out a gun, Sam tensed.

The old man said, You think that scares me? You tell Mr. Oh that—

Im pointed the gun at the son. His father stopped. Im said to Sam, Every time he says no, break one of his son's fingers.

No, wait, the son said in English, then he switched into Korean: I am a guitar player! Please!

Im said to the father, I will ask you again. Will you switch to Mr. Oh's company?

The man's face hardened.

His son said, Please, father!

The old man said to Im, Fuck you.

Im nodded to Sam, who wasn't even sure how to break a finger. He hesitated. The son let out a stifled sob and begged him not to. The son suddenly jumped up, trying to run away, and Sam grabbed his shoulder and forced him back down.

Im said, Do it.

Sam reached down, but the son struggled, trying to push Sam away, and his hands snaked out of Sam's grasp.

Im walked over to them and slammed the butt of the gun into the son's face. The son tried to protect his head, and Im grabbed his hand, caught hold of his index finger, and yanked it down, twisting it. Sam heard the crack, the finger bent back. The son screamed. Im hit him again with the gun. Sam flinched.

I will ask you again, Im said to the father. Will you switch to Mr. Oh's company?

The son was crying, saying in English, Motherfucking goddammit my finger, my finger...

The old man, still on the ground, stared at his son. He said to Im, I will kill you for this.

Is that a yes or a no?

Father...father, please, the son said.

The old man's face was red, his nostrils flared, and he said to Im, Coward. You have to hurt my son? You do not have the courage to hurt me?

Im said to Sam, That is a no.

Fuck, the son yelled as Sam reached down.

The old man jumped up and lunged for Im's gun. Im deftly stopped him, elbowing him in the mouth and yanking the gun up. The old man's head jerked back, and Im elbowed him again and pulled the gun away. He pushed the old man back down onto the floor. He said to Sam while pointing the gun toward the son, Keep him still.

Sam grabbed the son's shoulders and forced him tightly into the chair. Im said to the father, That was stupid. He then walked up to the son and lowered the barrel of the gun onto the back of the son's hand.

The son yelled, Wait!

But Im fired the gun, the sound loud and sharp, and hurting Sam's ears. Sam felt the son's shoulders jerk back as he howled in pain. The smell of gunpowder blew around them in the stunned aftermath. Im aimed the gun at the son's leg and turned to his father.

Well?

The old man looked up at his son, who whimpered in English, My hand... My fucking hand...

The son clutched his hand, blood seeping out from between the covering fingers. He rocked back and forth, shaking his head.

After a moment the old man said, All right. All right. I will use Mr. Oh's company.

Im nodded his head slowly. Good, he said. But this is for giving us trouble.

He moved quickly to him, and backhanded him with the gun, sending him sprawling across the floor. The old man lay there, unmoving.

Im stared down at the old man for a moment, then said to Sam, Let's go get something to eat. I'm hungry. Sam realized he had been holding his breath. He exhaled slowly, and followed Im out of the store.

David's father woke him up with his yelling. He called out, David! Come here! Where is David?

Yunjin shushed him, but David sat up quickly, disoriented, and when he heard his father call his name again he climbed out of bed and went into the living room. His father was swaying in the kitchen doorway, an empty glass in his hand, and his face was deep red. Yunjin said, See, you woke him up!

Be quiet, you stupid farm girl, he said. He went to lean against the doorway, but missed it, and staggered back into the kitchen. David heard the refrigerator door clatter open, bottles clinking, and then there was a pop and the sound of fizzing. Yunjin ran in and said, You are making a mess.

Be quiet!

David walked into the kitchen and saw a bottle of soda bubbling on the floor. Yunjin threw down a dishtowel but remained standing. His father said, David.

Yes?

I would never let anyone hurt you. Do you know that?

He glanced at Yunjin, then back to his father, who was swaying. His father was wearing a button-down shirt that had sweat stains under his arms. David said, I guess so.

You guess so? he said. You guess so? No. You should

believe me.

Okay, he said. I believe you.

Yunjin said, He has to get his sleep.

David's father asked him, You know I protect you, right?

Right, David said. He watched him try to focus. His father squinted and then took a deep, unsteady breath. David waited. Finally his father waved his hand and dismissed him.

As David returned to the bedroom he heard Yunjin urge his father to go to bed.

His father replied in Korean, You are always nagging me.

I am sorry, but it's late—

You are always sorry! I am sorry I married you!

You are always getting drunk! I can't stand this!

Without me you'd still be a slave to your aunt and uncle!

David closed his bedroom door and lay there as they continued fighting. Eventually Yunjin stormed into the bathroom and slammed the door. His father got another drink and sat in the living room, mumbling to himself.

David remembered when the mumbling started, when his mother got too sick to return home. His father often left him in the apartment while he spent the evenings with his mother, and sometimes he'd come home late, smelling of alcohol, and sit in front of the TV, the sound on low. David heard the mumbling as a one-way conversation with his mother, his father talking quietly as if she were sitting right across from him. He called her yubuh, or honey, and at first David didn't understand whom his father was talking to, until he heard his father say in Korean, You will get better. You will soon get out of the hospital.

8

Working at Club Saja was exhausting. Unha took drink and appetizer orders in both Korean and English from young men with spikey hair and garish gold jewelry. The soju menu was confusing, with over twenty different kinds of soju, including special blends made by Lee, the bartender, and a long list of mixed soju drinks that the women liked. A few times she confused the soju orders, the loud music making it hard for her to distinguish between similar sounding names, some of the customers using both English and Korean phrases, so she had misheard "pear" soju for "bek seju," an herbal soju with ginseng. She had to take back a few drinks, annoying Lee.

A young man with dark sunglasses and tattoos on his arms played music in the corner of the dance floor. He had a laptop computer connected to different kinds of equipment, and wore large headphones on his glistening, shaved head. A waitress told Unha that this music was Korean hip-hop; it was giving Unha a headache. More young men kept coming in. It was only ten o'clock on a weekday night, and already the club was crowded.

Hyunma escorted a group of older men through the club and to the doorway leading upstairs. Unha noticed that there was a large man guarding the stairwell. She hadn't learned the names of the other waitresses yet, but the thin one with her hair tied back in a small, neat ponytail quickly left her station near the bar and followed the older men upstairs, pulling out her pad and pen. The large man stepped aside, looking her up and down.

Agashi, one of the young men called to her. We need more Chamisul soju.

Unha bowed quickly and hurried to the computer, pressing the screen for their table and then scrolling down for the order. Her fingertips hurt from so much pressing. The computer at the bar would automatically print this out, and Lee the bartender would have it on a tray in a few minutes.

The music suddenly grew louder, hurting her ears. She turned to the DJ, and saw a few couples dancing; everyone in the club watched them. More customers flagged her, and she rushed over to them.

By midnight she could barely walk, her toes scrunched in the high-heeled shoes and tingling with pain; her knees hurt, her back ached, and she was just so tired. She had trouble concentrating. She almost fumbled a tray of drinks, but steadied herself. One of the other waitresses told her to take a break, which she did.

Although there were "No Smoking" signs posted by the entrances, she smelled cigarette smoke coming from somewhere, making her nose itch. Then she noticed the other waitresses' attention drawn to the front door. Hyunma walked quickly from a side office to the front to meet her brother, Mr. Oh, and two other men. It seemed as if all the employees suddenly snapped to attention and worked harder. Lee wiped down the bar, then folded the rag up neatly. The waitresses straightened their uniforms.

But Mr. Oh didn't notice them as he walked toward

the back stairwell, and the large man in the doorway bowed low and stepped aside. Mr. Oh stopped, and asked Hyunma something. She nodded and pointed directly at Unha, who quickly averted her eyes. Mr. Oh stared at her, listening to Hyunma, and he nodded his head. He said something and went upstairs, the two men following him.

Hyunma approached Unha, who straightened her skirt and blouse. Hyunma said, He wants to talk to you.

Mr. Oh? Me? Why?

Just to see how you are doing. Bring up their drink orders.

Unha stood there, worried about making a mistake, about spilling a drink or worse. Hyunma said, Well? Go.

Unha bowed quickly and hurried to the bar where Lee had already filled a tray with empty glasses of ice and a bottle of whiskey. She grabbed the tray too quickly and almost toppled the bottle. Lee yelled, Careful!

She stopped. She took a breath. Her arms were weak, her vision blurry. She held the tray carefully with both hands and lifted it slowly, surprised by the weight of the bottle. Walking slowly toward the back stairwell, she got a better look at the large man who had acne scars along his cheeks. His forehead shone under the lights from above.

He said to Unha, You are new.

I am, she replied.

He stood there, unmoving.

She said, I have to bring this up to them.

Do you know which room?

She shook her head. It's for Mr. Oh.

I know who it is for. He is in his private booth. It is the one farthest down the hall.

Unha nodded. The man didn't move. Her arms were getting more tired. He said, My name is Choon.

Thank you, Choon.

What is your name?

Unha.

He stepped aside.

She walked up slowly and steadily, making sure her high heels didn't miss the edge of the steps. The music below hollowed out and became more muffled the higher she went, and when she reached the top she pushed through a thick curtain on large wooden rings. Two doors to the right led into a dining room that was empty. To the left were the booths, recessed with tinted windows looking down over the club. She heard voices from the booth down the hall.

When she appeared at the booth, Mr. Oh was with two younger men. He said to her, Hyunma tells me you are doing well for your first day.

Surprised by this, Unha thanked him and bowed quickly, but forgot that she was carrying the tray, and the bottle of whiskey tipped over. She straightened up and grabbed the bottle, but then the glasses slid off the tray and bounced onto the carpet. One of the glasses broke, and ice scattered under the table.

Everyone stopped. Unha apologized quickly and bent down to pick up the glass, but one of the men said, Clumsy girl. Don't use your fingers.

She straightened up, her hands trembling, and she said, I am very sorry. I will get a dustpan and broom—

No, Mr. Oh said. Just get more glasses and pour our drinks.

She was about to hurry off with the bottle of whiskey, but the third man said, Leave that here.

She did, and hurried down the stairs. Hyunma saw her and asked what happened. When Unha told her Hyunma shook her head and motioned to another waitress. She said to Unha, You stay down here. We add the cost of breakage to your debt.

What?

How many glasses did you break?

One, Unha said.

We will add that.

Can I see the debt? How much do I owe?

We will tell you when you've paid it back.

How do I know you haven't made a mistake?

Hyunma just shrugged. You don't.

But then how...

Hyunma walked away.

Unha had to work ten- to twelve-hour shifts at Saja. She shared an apartment nearby with four other girls and had one night off a week. Minji, however, was essentially on call twenty-four hours a day, and lived in the basement of Yang Acupuncture and Massage, crowded on a cement floor with a dozen other girls. They slept on roll-out mattresses, and had small suitcases with all their belongings ready to go at the first sign of a raid.

Most of the girls laid their mattresses near the dusty brown water heater, despite the loud clicking, because it radiated warmth, but Minji couldn't get used to the clicking and the way the girls would have to step around everyone to get to the bathroom. Minji had a corner to herself and tried to keep warm at night by rolling herself into her blanket and laying her extra clothes on top.

Singme didn't last long. She wouldn't stop crying and even after she was beaten to the point of not being able to walk she refused to have sex with the customers. Finally Mrs. Shim sent her away, and the other girls said she was probably dead. Minji couldn't believe that they would actually kill her, but the few girls who had been here for a while said it had happened before. If you didn't cooperate, they would rape and beat you, and if that didn't work, they would kill you.

Minji thought that she could call Jin whenever she wanted. She recited his uncle's phone number to herself whenever she needed comfort. She didn't want to contact him yet, though. No, she would pay off her debt and then call him. She would lie to him.

The girls who had been here for six months said that they were almost done. Most girls didn't stay here for longer than a year, and before Minji arrived two girls had recently finished paying off their debt. They had been given the choice to continue working, and this time they'd be paid, or to leave. They left. Minji had heard that the girls who left often worked at garment factories or restaurants, and some of them even married their customers. Some girls did come back, but this wouldn't be Minji.

She had a plan. She just had to last six or seven months, and then she'd be free.

The next night at work, Minji knew one of the customers was trouble. When he entered the lobby he stared at the girls without any embarrassment or uneasiness. He had obviously done this many times before. Mrs. Shim recognized him and said in English, We have some new girls.

I see, the man said. He was an older white man with a grey mustache and tinted eyeglasses. His black sweater hugged his skinny body, and Minji noticed his shiny black shoes that glistened under the lights. He gazed directly at her, and she quickly stared down at her feet. He said to Mrs. Shim, Her.

Mrs. Shim called her name, and she stood up. The man slipped a wad of cash across the counter, then walked to the stairwell ahead of her. Mrs. Shim waved her hand. Minji felt her steps getting heavier. She hated this part, the walk up, because it was when her mind was still active and she worried about what was coming. She counted the steps, trying to shut down her thoughts.

The man found an open room and walked in. He had barely looked at her. He moved to the massage table and sat on it. He crossed his legs at his ankles and watched her walk in. When she closed the door he said, Take off your clothes.

I have to give you a massage, she said.

Forget that part, he replied. Take off your clothes.

She stood there for a moment, and then pulled off her blouse. She wasn't wearing a bra, and felt the chill. She unbuttoned the back of her skirt and let it fall to the floor. She left on her underwear. She recited Jin's telephone number in her head, over and over.

He said, Take that off too.

She pulled down her underwear and stepped out of it. She shivered.

He said, Turn around and bend over.

She did. She heard him walk to her, and when he ran his hands over her body, she shivered again. She recited the telephone number backwards and forward.

Then he pushed her to the roll-out mattress on the floor. He said, On your hands and knees.

She did this. She sped through the phone number again and again, but found that she knew it too well. It no longer distracted her. She tried adding the numbers up.

She heard him reaching for the massage oils, and squirting it into his hand. When he pushed his fingers inside her she tensed up. He said, Don't move.

But then he moved his fingers higher, and pressed into her anus. She tried to move away and said, No.

He grabbed her neck with his oily hands and said, You do what I want you to do.

Not that, she said.

I paid for you.

No—

He backhanded her in the head, and she collapsed to the ground, letting out a cry of pain. He moved on top of her and grabbed her throat, squeezing. He said, You do as I say. Understand? I am a regular customer here, and I know what I am allowed to do.

He squeezed, and she couldn't breathe.

Understand? he asked again.

She nodded her head, feeling her eyes bulge.

He loosened his grip, and she sucked in air. She lowered her head and held her throat. She heard him unzipping his pants. His fingers pushed into her anus.

She began crying silently and shaking her head. She whispered, No, please.

He laughed and said, Good, good. Keep doing that.

9

Jake sighed when he heard Yunjin's voice on the phone. He suspected this was going to be about money, but he hid his annoyance and said, How are you?

Your brother is getting himself into deeper trouble, she said.

I know. I warned him about it.

Who is this Mr. Oh? she asked.

Jake hesitated. Is there something the matter?

Yunjin replied, Our rent is late again, and we have nothing left.

Jake sat back in his office chair and stared up at the ceiling. He had made the mistake of giving Yunjin his cell phone number. At first she had been shy about calling him, but now she seemed to call every other week. He said, You need to talk to Sam.

I did, she said. He will not do anything! We will end up on the street!

I don't know what you want me to do. I already lent him too much money.

Tell him to pay the rent. He will listen to you.

Yunjin, he said gently. I shouldn't get involved.

What about David? she asked. What will we do if we

get put on the street?

Jake could imagine this getting worse, and having to bring them to his house in Montclair. He said, How much do you owe?

Last month and this month. Twenty-eight hundred dollars.

Maybe you should find a less expensive apartment.

I don't know how.

Jake said, My brother will be angry if he knew you went to me.

I don't care. He's drinking more.

How often?

Every night.

Jake rubbed his head, but stopped himself. He wondered if this habit was making him lose his hair faster. He said, I'll be at the Shilla tonight. I'll drop by your apartment with a check—

No. I will go to the restaurant. I don't want Sam to know.

What will you tell him about the rent?

He won't ask.

They hung up, and Jake wrote out a check, looking up the property manager's name in his records. This was the second time he had paid their rent, and he wasn't going to let this happen again. Tonight he'd tell Yunjin this was the last time; she should find a cheaper apartment.

He felt sorry for her because he knew Sam only married her so she would take care of David, and he treated her like a maid. Yunjin was good to David, and Sam should appreciate her more.

Jake wondered if maybe he should send for a bride from Korea; it would be easy enough. But he wasn't sure about being attached. He was in no hurry. Eventually he would find someone, but she had to be perfect. Like Sunny. Of course he couldn't help having an ideal like her in mind.

When someone like that came along, he would know it.

But this reminder of Sunny depressed him. He closed the door to his office, hearing Tim clicking the keyboard of his laptop, and sat down heavily in his chair. He propped his feet onto the desk and pulled out a cigarette. He twirled it in his fingers, remembering how Sunny used to scold him for smoking. She told him that her father had died from lung cancer, and he had smoked all his adult life.

Sunny used to lower her voice and lean forward when she was being serious; it was as if she were sharing a secret, and it made everyone also lean in and listen closely. When she told Jake about her father, he was thrilled to be learning something so personal, something that Sam had never told him, that her father had been a sailor and had seen the world. Her father had started smoking because everyone on the cargo ships smoked.

She told Jake about her father's dragon tattoo on his arm, also a souvenir from one of his travels. Jake remembered that night she talked about her father: she and David had come to the Shilla for dinner because Sam was stuck at a construction job in South San Francisco. Sunny said, The dragon tail and body was faded from the sun, but the head was always under his sleeve. I used to poke the body and make the dragon dance.

She leaned in closer. She said, He smoked two packs a day for many years. I know you don't smoke that much, but it's still dangerous.

He quit for her. He put on weight, he found himself craving a cigarette after every meal, but he wanted to show Sunny he had the willpower. She noticed that he had stopped and gave him a small gift, a wooden dragon that her father had bought in Taiwan, one of the legs broken off and the fins worn smooth from her fingers. She told him it was one of many gifts her father had brought home, and she wanted Jake to have it as a reward for quitting smoking.

She waited anxiously for his reaction, her eyes wide and expectant, and he told her that no one had ever given him something so important and meaningful. She clapped her hands together and said, Good!

Her cheeks flushed, as they always did when she was happy or excited, and she smiled broadly, then covered her mouth. He wanted to tell her not to cover her crooked tooth; he liked it. But he didn't say anything. He just thanked her.

He never said anything, and he wished he had. He wanted to say how much he liked her small hands, her small wrists. He liked how she wore scarves to hide her neck which she thought was too skinny. She continued to wear scarves through her chemotherapy, but the scarves migrated to her bald head. Her hands withered, her wrists shrunk.

When Sunny got sick he moved the dragon from his bookshelf to his nightstand where he could see it as soon as he woke up and right before he fell asleep. He memorized which fins had the veneer rubbed off and tried to handle it in the same way, wondering if the similar hand positions were like holding hands over time. The sicker she grew, the more the dragon became a talisman, and if he had been a praying man, he would have asked it for help, for hope.

When she died, he put the dragon back on his book-shelf because its proximity was too painful. With each month that passed—he changed the calendar on the wall next to his bookshelf—he'd see the dragon and his memories of Sunny seemed to become as familiar and worn as the dragon fins. He knew the Sunny of his memories were eclipsing the real Sunny, but what did it matter? Sunny was gone. All he had were his memories.

David accompanied Yunjin to the Shilla that night to visit his uncle, and they sat him down in a corner table, put a bowl of bibimbap in front of him, and talked quietly at the next table. David listened to them while he ate, pretending to read the comics of an old newspaper. The restaurant had two rooms, one for larger groups with barbecue grills at the table, and this smaller one filled with couples sharing plates of bulgogi and pajun.

He understood more Korean than either Yunjin or Uncle Jake believed, so often he would be privy to conversations they thought were private. Tonight, for example, he heard his uncle warn Yunjin that this was the last time he'd pay the rent. Yunjin said, Do you think I like this? Do you think I want this? I don't know what else to do.

You have to take over the finances, he said. Sunny did that.

I don't know how.

Learn.

She lowered her voice, but David heard her say, I don't know how much longer I can live like this.

Jake shook his head. Don't talk like that.

Maybe I should get a job, she said. Can I work here?

Jake hesitated. You should discuss it with Sam.

What about your new club in the city?

You should talk to Sam.

But if he agrees?

What about David?

He is old enough to take care of himself.

David almost looked up at this, but kept staring at the newspaper. He suddenly felt more adult.

Jake said, Saja is fully staffed, but maybe you can help in the kitchen.

Already? You haven't even opened yet.

I have a partner who takes care of staffing.

A partner? Who?

That is not important. First clear it with Sam, then you can talk to Tim, who will be managing the kitchen staff at Saja.

Yunjin read the check he had just handed her, and

folded it. She slipped it into her pocket. David watched her from the corner of his eye. She said to Jake, Thank you.

Jake asked if she wanted anything to eat. She shook her head, but called over to David, and said, You want more bibimbap?

David said he was fine.

Jake said to him, Come join us here.

David brought his bowl to their table, and sat down. Jake asked him what he was doing this summer.

Nothing, David said.

When I was your age I was already working at a toy factory. I swept the floors and ran errands.

What kind of toys?

Dolls and plastic animals, he said, smiling. The owners of the factory knew my parents. They offered my brother the job, but he didn't want it. I jumped at it. I saved enough to buy my own bicycle, and I used the bicycle to deliver packages. Soon I had other kids working for me.

What did my father do? David asked.

Jake smiled wryly. He said, Not much. He played a lot of baseball. He skipped school to play baseball with other kids. Once my father found out and used a bamboo cane on him.

Yunjin said, He did that a lot?

Cane us?

No, Sam didn't attend school?

Jake nodded his head. That's why he did so badly. He just didn't care.

To David, Jake said, You have to do well in school if you want to get anywhere in life. You understand that?

He said he did.

With that, Jake stood up and told them to eat as much as they wanted. He had more work to take care of. Yunjin thanked him, and sat with David while he finished his bibimbap. She said, Your father did not know how lucky he was.

Why?

My mother keep moving around, so I never get to stay at school. I study on my own. I wish I had school. If I had good school, I never skip.

Did you go to college?

She stared at him. She said, I never finish high school.

Why not?

My uncle and aunt say I don't need. I just work for them.

What kind of work?

Everything. Like maid.

She looked at his empty bowl and said they should go.

They walked home in the warm evening and stopped in front of Lake Merritt, the string of lights surrounding the edges reflecting off the water. A cool breeze rippled the surface. Yunjin said, I like here because it remind me of lake back home.

David saw the sadness in her posture, a heaviness in her shoulders. He asked her what was wrong and she said, Sometimes I miss Korea.

I thought you didn't like it, he replied.

She turned to him and gave him a small shrug of her shoulders. Home is home, she said.

10

Sam showed up at Club Saja again the next night and joined Im and Koman at their regular booth upstairs. They were eating dukbokee, stabbing the spicy rice cakes with their chopsticks while sloshing down OB beer. They were talking about thirteen of Cho Il Hwan's men—the crime boss of the Chungchong province—who cut off their pinkie fingers in protest of the Japanese Prime Minister visiting the Yasakuni shrine. The shrine commemorated Japanese soldiers, many of them convicted of war crimes against Korea. The thirteen men covered themselves in Korean flags, cut off their pinkies and were about to present them to the Japanese embassy when they were stopped by police.

Did Cho cut his off too? Im asked Koman.

No. It was just his men. Cho cut his off years ago to protest something else.

Why copy the Yakuza? That's to atone for mistakes.

Koman shook his head. No, Ahn Jung Geun did it during the Japanese occupation when he swore to assassinate Japanese leaders.

Im said, But the Yakuza have been doing it for much longer. It's from the samurai, isn't it? Cutting the pinkie weakens the grip on the sword.

Koman said, It's from the Bakuto, before the Yakuza. Gamblers cut off their fingers for a bad debt.

Im snorted. Koreans should come up with their own thing.

Koman said, It's about honor. It's a gesture.

Im laughed. Honor? You know what I do if someone had a bad debt with me? I wouldn't ask them to cut off a finger. I'd put a gun in the back of their head.

Koman asked Sam, What do you think?

Sam wasn't sure if he was asking about bad debts or danji, finger cutting. He said, Honor is a luxury when you're just trying to survive.

Im rolled his eyes. Sounds like a fortune cookie. Are you starting a new career?

Sam held back his annoyance. He was about to tell Im to go steal some batteries, but Koman told Sam to have a seat.

Koman said, Mr. Oh was glad you got Hyung to change his mind.

Im pointed to Sam. He had a little trouble breaking a finger, though.

Sam nodded his head. It's true. I wasn't sure how.

Im said, You just go against the joint.

Koman said to Sam, Tonight you'll pick up the receipts at Yang's and move that and the receipts from here to our banker.

Sam hoped that they were done hurting people.

Im glanced behind Sam and said, Ah. Here's the pajun.

Sam turned. The waitress who looked like Sunny was approaching with a tray of the potato pancakes, and she met his eyes.

Im said, Watch out. She might drop it on you.

Koman smiled.

The waitress bowed to them and said, Your pajun.

She put it in the center of the table, the small black apron over her skirt brushing against Sam's sleeve. He kept still. She backed up and asked if there was anything else they wanted. Koman nodded to Sam, who said, A soju.

Im said, More beers.

Sam asked her what her name was.

She paused, then said, Unha.

Koman said, She is new.

Im added, And she spills things.

Unha's face reddened and Sam said, She didn't spill anything here.

Just wait, Im said.

Unha bowed again, this time some of her hair falling out of her barrett. As she walked quickly down the hall she pushed her hair behind her ear. Sam watched her disappear down the stairwell, and he said to Im, Why are you so rude?

Im's face hardened. What did you say to me?

Sam stood up and said, I need to go to the bathroom.

Im was about to reply, but Koman cleared his throat and told them both to get ready to leave for Yang's. He said, And stop bickering like two old women.

Sam went downstairs and saw Unha loading a tray of drinks at the bar. He approached her and said, Im is very rude.

Unha said, I don't care.

My name is Sungmo, he said, bowing quickly. Most people call me Sam.

Her forehead was perspiring, and he resisted the impulse to offer her his handkerchief. Instead he asked her how she liked the work here.

It's busy and tiring, but I am adjusting, she said. She pushed the same lock of hair behind her ear.

Where are you from?

Taeshin.

There is a university there.

87

Yes! You know it?

My brother was thinking about going there, but he decided to study here.

How long have you been here?

Over ten years.

Oh! You are an American now.

I'll never be an American, he said. In English he added, Because I still have accent.

She replied in English, It is not that bad.

You speak English, he said in Korean.

A little. That's why they hired me here.

How long have been in the U.S.?

Two weeks.

That's all? Everything must be so confusing, he said.

She thought about this, and Sam was surprised that she was considering his comment so carefully. She finally said, I have been working too much to be confused.

Have you seen any tourist sights? The Golden Gate bridge?

She smiled wistfully and wiped her forehead. I have seen cable cars, she said.

Sam remembered when he and Sunny first arrived here and visited all the main tourist attractions, including the Golden Gate bridge, Mount Tamalpais, and Alcatraz.

She asked, What should I see?

What do you like? Alcatraz is interesting.

What is it?

A prison. An old prison.

She blinked. Why would I want to see a prison?

Sam chuckled. Do you like mountains?

I like nature, she said.

Muir woods is nearby. Big trees. You would like that.

I wouldn't know how to visit.

Sam didn't think, barely even heard himself say, I can show you.

You? she asked. She focused on him more intently. Really?

Do you have days off?

Wednesday.

Sam said, I can show you then. It will be quiet on the weekday. I haven't been there since… He stopped himself, not wanting to mention his late wife.

Since?

Since I first moved here.

She glanced to the tables and said, I have to get back to work.

Sam followed her gaze and saw two men at the other end of the club waving her down. He said, Wednesday, then?

I would like that, she said. She smiled and hurried off.

Sam watched her for a moment, then headed to the bathroom. He saw Choon staring at him, and nodded to him. Choon nodded back with no expression on his face.

When Sam and Im walked into Yang Acupuncture and Massage, Sam asked who Yang was.

Im replied, No one. Made up name.

They do acupuncture here?

Not anymore, Im said. The dirty brick building had frosted windows in front with a small sign and an arrow pointing toward the alley. Im led Sam through a side entrance, the heavy metal door groaning. From inside there was a beep. They appeared in a lobby, and a middle-aged woman behind a high counter jumped out of her seat and bowed low, revealing a bald spot. Sam saw a dozen young women sitting around the lobby in uncomfortable chairs and an old overstuffed sofa. There was a TV attached to the upper wall that was playing a soap opera.

The women recognized Im. They straightened up, tensed. Im asked the woman about competition from a massage parlor a few blocks away. The woman said business was good, and she had the latest earnings for him.

Im said to Sam, You want a free one?

Sam hesitated.

Im said, Pick a girl.

Sam moved closer to him and whispered, Do you mean a free massage?

Im laughed. If you want a massage that is fine, but I am getting more than that. He scanned the room and pointed to a young girl in a black papery dress and a red hairband. The girl stood up and glanced at the older woman, who waved her hand with a flick of her wrist. The girl walked to the side stairwell, and Im followed her.

The older woman asked Sam which girl he would like.

He had never been with a prostitute before, and was worried about diseases. He asked if he could just have a massage.

You can have whatever you want, the woman said. Choose a girl.

All the girls were watching him now, and he felt embarrassed to have to choose. The only one who wasn't looking at him was a pale young girl who seemed to be intent on tugging at her finger. He pointed to her and the older woman called her name.

Minji looked up. She stood slowly, her body unfurling into a lanky teen's sullen stance, her shoulders hunched. She paused, and her boss waved her hand to her. Minji kept her gaze to the ground, and walked into the stairwell. Sam followed. He could hear the slow, heavy trudge in her steps.

At the second floor she led him to a room toward the end of the hallway. He heard Im's voice through the doorway, his deadened monotone ordering the girl around. Sam felt queasy. What would Sunny say if she could see him now?

In the small massage room, Minji told him to take off his clothes and lie on the massage table. Sam said, I just want a massage.

Minji seemed puzzled. Her hair was greasy, a few small pimples on her forehead.

He repeated himself and added, No sex.

You just want a massage? she asked, her voice tentative.

Yes, he said.

She suddenly seemed more nervous, her eyes frightened, and asked, What kind of massage?

I don't know, he said. A relaxing massage.

He took off all his clothes except for his underwear and lay on his stomach. He heard her squirt massage oil into her hands and she began rubbing his back, the smell of cherry surrounding him. Her hands and the oil were cold. His back tightened. He had not been touched like this for a long time. She stopped and asked if he was okay.

I am fine, he said. He tried to relax.

After a few minutes she found a rhythm to digging her fingers into the muscles in his back. He slowly sank deeper against the table. Her hands weren't very strong, but the repetitive kneading eased some of the tension in his shoulders. Minji asked if this was all right.

It is very good, he said. My shoulders feel—

There was a yell in the next room, and a woman's fearful screech burst out into the hall. Sam heard Im yell, Stop!

Sam quickly jumped off the table and wrapped the sheet around his waist. He opened the door and saw the girl Im had chosen on the floor of the hall, naked. Im walked out of his room, his shirt off and his pants half-buttoned. He reached down with a long, lean arm and his hands clamped on the girl's arm. She looked around fearfully.

Sam asked, What happened?

Im's eyes were blank. He replied, Nothing. Go back inside.

Sam saw the girl's terrified expression, her mouth

opening but only a choked cry coming out. Sam said, You are hurting her.

Im sighed and let go of the girl. He said to Sam, You are beginning to annoy me. Go wait in the car.

Now?

Now. Get your clothes on and go.

Sam said, But I am not finished with my massage.

You are now.

Im grabbed the girl by the arm and pulled her up. The girl whimpered. Her lower lip was becoming puffy and her nose continued to drip blood.

Sam said, You hurt her.

Im closed his eyes for a moment, taking a deep breath. He said, If you do not shut up you will no longer work for us. He gave Sam a cold look, then pulled the girl into the room, slamming the door.

Sam went back into his room to dress.

Minji said, Help me.

Sam pulled on his clothes and said, What?

Help me.

With what?

She began to cry quietly, covering her mouth. She wiped her eyes and moved closer to him. Help me get out of here.

Sam stepped back, stumbling over his shoes. He said, I…I do not know what I can do.

Tell the police, she whispered. Tell someone.

I am sorry, he said. I cannot.

Please—

He hurried out of the room and down the stairs.

Unha's night started out slow, but then it seemed that the more tired she became, the more customers came in, most of them young Korean men and women, college-aged, some older, but all of whom unconcerned that it was two in the morning. She felt like she still hadn't caught up with her sleep, and it didn't help that she shared a small apartment with four others, two of whom liked to go to clubs with different men, coming home drunk and waking everyone up.

One of these girls, Ginny, was nice and friendly most of the time, but last night she had argued with a girl named Soonhee and had slapped her in the face. The others quickly stopped the fight and Ginny went to sleep almost immediately, but Unha had been too awake and startled to fall asleep again. She worried that Ginny would wake up and attack someone else.

This evening though, Ginny seemed fine. She saw Unha watching her and smiled. She waved her fingers, long fingernails painted red, and made a smoking motion to tell her she was going to take a break outside. Ginny had the small, skinny body of a teenager, but was in her twenties. Her skin was smooth and rosy, and sometimes she wore too much makeup, but tonight she had on only a pale red lipstick.

Ginny walked up to her and said, I'm going to take a break. You okay?

I'm okay.

You look tired.

Unha was about to say that she had been woken up in the middle of the night by Ginny's fight, but instead just said, I am not used to this schedule.

It gets easier. I've been here now for over a year, and it's no problem.

Have you paid back your debt?

Yes. A while ago. Now I'm making money. And saving.

You can leave?

Whenever I want, but Hyunma says I'm one of her best waitresses. I need a smoke. I'll be back. I'm supposed to work the booths upstairs. Can you cover? Table twenty-eight needs drinks.

Unha was already busy with her tables, but said she'd cover it.

Ginny went out into the back alley, and Unha hurried to the bar to get table twenty-eight's drinks. Lee slid a tray to her and motioned his head upstairs.

Unha carried the tray toward the stairwell, but Choon blocked her way with his girth. She told him that she was handling Ginny's tables and needed to get these drinks upstairs. He gave her a small smile, his chubby cheeks creased by his eyes, and he said, You are very pretty.

Startled by this, she didn't know how to respond.

Choon said, Maybe you have a drink with me later.

She recovered. She shook her head. Thank you, but I am very tired.

He took another step toward her, and she moved back. He said, You don't have to be afraid of me.

I have to serve table twenty-eight, she said.

He moved aside. As she walked by him he leaned toward her and said, Maybe another night.

She said, I don't think so.

By the time she returned to the apartment it was four in the morning, and she was so tired that her vision blurred. Streetlamps had fuzzy auras and car headlights arced and trailed along the streets. Her fingertips ached. Her lower back trembled with pain. She walked slowly up to her floor, and when she let herself in two of the girls were deep asleep while Ginny and Soonhee were still fully dressed, whispering in the kitchen. They looked up at her. Ginny asked, What took you so long?

Unha was surprised to see the two girls friendly again. She said, Hyunma wanted me to help clean the dishes.

Soonhee said, All the new girls have to do that. She wore a wrist full of bracelets that jangled whenever she talked. She had wide eyes, making her seem startled.

Ginny said, Choon was asking about you.

Unha sighed.

Soonhee giggled. He's so fat he can hardly walk.

Ginny said, Watch out for him.

What should I do? Unha asked.

Ignore him, Ginny said. Or go out with one of Oh's top men.

Soonhee said, Ginny did that.

Ginny shrugged her shoulders. Yung bought me a nice diamond necklace.

Before he dumped you, Soonhee said.

Unha said she needed to get to bed. Ginny said, We're going out. Want to join us?

I'm too tired.

I have pills.

Unha shook her head. I just want to sleep.

Soonhee said, I saw you talking to that guy. Who is he? Is he new?

Sam, she said. I don't know if he's new, but he's nice.

Ginny said, He doesn't look rich.

Unha found this conversation too confusing to follow, and was about to say goodnight when she remembered to call home. She asked them how she could do this.

Why? Ginny asked.

To let my mother know I'm okay.

Soonhee told Unha to use a phone card and call from a payphone. You can buy one at the grocery down the street.

Unha thanked her and trudged to her mattress. She heard the other girls sleeping deeply, some snoring. Ginny and Soonhee continued whispering. How were they so awake? Unha curled up and wondered if this would get any easier. Sleep. That was all she wanted. She didn't even care about eating. Unha thought about Sam, and right before she sank into her pillow and drifted off she imagined walking with him in a forest.

11

David heard singing and sat up in his bed. The voice was melodic and quiet, the words unrecognizable. He realized it was Yunjin. He climbed out of bed and walked out into the darkened hallway, following the soft voice and the glow from the kitchen.

When he looked around the refrigerator he saw Yunjin sitting at the kitchen table, making mandu, filling the dumplings with a meat paste, and sealing the edges with egg yolk. Rows of flour-dusted mandu covered a tray. She wore a pale blue nightgown and her hair was pushed back with a white headband that glowed against her black hair. Streaks of cold cream were smeared on her forehead, and glistened under the kitchen lights. She asked, Why are you up? It's late.

I heard you singing, he said.

I'm sorry. Did I wake you up?

Why are you making mandu? Dad can get it for free.

Your father hasn't been bringing home food, she said.

Where is he?

She shrugged her shoulders. She said, You should go to bed.

He sat down at the table and watched her pinch the edges of the dumplings. He asked her why she used the egg yolk.

It's like glue, she said.

He smiled at the description, imagining using Elmer's glue on mandu.

You help me, she said. Wash your hands first.

He did this at the kitchen sink, standing on his toes to reach over the basin, and he returned to the table. She showed him how to dab a ball of meat into the center of the dough, smear egg yolk along the edges, and pinch the edges closed. When the dough stuck to his fingers, she told him to use more flour.

He asked, What were you singing?

She asked with surprise, You don't know the song?

No.

She hummed it again and said, You never heard it?

No.

She said, It's *Arirang*. Famous song.

What it is about?

Crossing a mountain. How come you don't know Korea's most famous song?

No one told me.

Your mother?

He shook his head. He asked, What are the words?

In Korean?

In English.

She said, Arirang is the name of a mountain pass. So the song means, Arirang, I am crossing Arirang pass. The man who abandoned me will not walk ten *li* before his feet hurt.

He laughed, and asked, What's a *li*?

Chinese distance. I don't know how far. It is a sad song.

That's the whole song?

She thought for a moment, then said, The other verse is: Many stars in the sky, many sorrows in my heart. But look over there at Baekdusan mountain, where flowers bloom even in winter.

How did you learn it?

Yunjin said, My mother sang to me.

They were quiet for a while as he made more mandu. He asked, Why did your mother kill herself?

Yunjin stopped making her mandu. She said, Why you want to know?

I don't know.

She finished the mandu, and shook her head. The refrigerator clicked on and whirred.

What's the matter? he asked.

She said quietly, My mother kill herself because she was very sad.

Why?

Yunjin stared at him and said, You don't need to know.

I want to.

You are very young.

He said, No I'm not.

She smiled. After a moment she said, My mother had no one. She felt very alone. She think the only way to stop feeling bad is to die.

He said, Oh.

You tell me about your mother, she said.

This caught him off-guard. He asked, What do you want to know?

Tell me something you remember.

Anything?

She nodded her head.

He thought about this, and said, She collected things.

Like what?

Her father used to bring home things from traveling. He started giving her small statues of animals. She used to have a shelf full of small animals.

Any kind of animal?

Mostly elephants and turtles.

Why elephants and turtles?

He said, Elephants because they are smart. Turtles because they know how to protect themselves. Both live long.

What happened to the animals?

I think my father got rid of them, he said.

Yunjin made a clucking sound. She told him to wash his hands again, and she put away the finished mandu. As she cleaned off the kitchen table she was quiet, and he lingered. He said, Your mother had parents, though. Right?

She nodded her head. She said, In my town they have small minds. My mother leave for bigger town, but get pregnant with me. When she come back they all hate her. When she give birth to me and they all see that I am half black. Even worse for her. They treat her bad. Her father, my grandfather, beat her, and tell her to go away forever. Her mother say she ashamed of her. So my mother bring me to another town and try to work as cleaning person, but everyone hate her. She has no money and no friend. So she kill herself.

Then you went to the orphanage and your uncle and aunt's, he said.

Yes, she said. You go to bed now.

He asked, Do you miss her?

Yunjin stared at him, and then said quietly, Yes.

Yunjin's nights were lonely, but she didn't mind the solitude. She had trouble sleeping, and often would wake up to find Sam in bed next to her, snoring, the whiff of alcohol settling around them. She would then get up and drift around the apartment, watching TV, reading, listening to the classical music station, cooking, or sometimes going to sleep on the sofa. She was used to an intermittent sleep schedule because of her aunt, who woke up dozens of times throughout the night and demanded help to get to the bathroom.

Yunjin's aunt suffered from some kind of gastrointestinal illness that restricted what she could eat—mostly rice and bean sprouts—and over the almost ten years that Yunjin lived with them, her aunt grew thinner and more bitter, directing her frustration at her husband and her niece, whom she viewed as no more than a servant.

They lived in a small two-bedroom apartment in Shinchon, not too far from Yonsei University where Yunjin's uncle worked in one of the medical labs as a researcher. Yunjin spent her days in the apartment, cooking and cleaning. Her aunt was learning English, and Yunjin would secretly listen to the same tapes and read the same books whenever her aunt was napping. Yunjin wanted to sit in on some of the classes at Yonsei, but her aunt wouldn't allow it.

So this life in the United States wasn't bad compared to Seoul. She preferred the quiet, free from her aunt harping about the way she vacuumed the carpet or the way she made the pat chuk, a red bean and rice porridge. Her aunt hadn't wanted to send Yunjin to the States, but her uncle said it was time, that she couldn't live at their place forever. Yunjin liked her uncle who had a soft-spoken patience that amazed her in the face of her aunt's constant nagging. He was also very thin, probably because he tended to eat whatever Yunjin prepared for his wife, and wore thick eyeglasses that magnified his eyes, giving him a frightened look.

Yunjin's aunt was shriveled and gnarled, with hollowed-out cheeks and a whining rasp that Yunjin could still hear in her mind, her aunt calling her name from the bedroom, Yuuunjiiiin. Even now, across the world and a year later, Yunjin cringed at the memory of her aunt's voice.

She heard Sam come through the front door. The refrigerator opened, glass clinking, and then there was the pop and hiss of a beer bottle. She lay still, wondering if he was coming to bed. But after a few moments she heard him mumbling to himself and she relaxed. He'd be out there for a while.

They had had sex only once, and that was shortly after

she had arrived. It had been quick and painful; she had been awakened in the middle of the night, and she had hardly known what was happening before it was over. She had bled. She had been sore. But it hadn't been repeated, and she wasn't sure why. She also wasn't sure how she felt about it. Didn't he want another child with her? Was it because he thought she was ugly? At the same time she didn't want to have sex with him. She found him physically repellent, and he always smelled of alcohol.

She heard him say, What can I do? I can't do anything about it.

She fantasized that she would get a job with Jake and be free of Sam. Maybe she would take care of David, because his father couldn't. It would be a nice family, her and David and maybe Jake. She could see that happening. She could envision a different and better life, and comforted herself with the possibilities.

The last thing Jake wanted was any more responsibility, especially if it was his brother's. No, Jake knew what he wanted and how to get it. He wanted never to worry about money like his parents had, he wanted control over his own life and future, and he wanted to be respected.

Tonight, for example, all the waitresses made sure to bow to him and ask permission to leave. He thought of the times he had seen his parents act subservient to their bosses at the factory; once they had practically begged to have time off when both of them were sick with the flu and they could barely walk, let alone work the assembly line. Jake had driven them to the factory because neither of them were in any condition to drive through downtown Seoul traffic, and he had watched them almost kneel in front of the floor manager, who gave his mother the day off but not his father. He saw his father's expression, a mixture of pain at the thought of a day of stamping metal sheets, but also relief that his wife would rest.

They were still working there, in their mid-fifties, even with the money Jake sent them, because they had no retirement savings. The factory had a pension for them, but an accounting scandal with the parent company wrecked the fund, which lost more than two-thirds of its value. The workers were helpless. They were stupid for trusting the company. Jake vowed never to be exposed like that.

He was slowly building his own businesses—he owned the Shilla, had commercial real estate in Oakland, and now, with the Seoul Silver, he was building his flagship restaurant. Mr. Oh was a silent investor in the Silver, but Jake was the full owner on paper. Once the Silver got established he could use it as collateral for another restaurant, one that he hoped to open in Berkeley.

Mr. Oh owned forty-nine percent of the Seoul Silver, and was a necessary investor. Oh supplied the alcohol, the food, and would soon supply the labor. Jake would have gone through Oh anyway, because this gave Jake access to Oh's network of restaurant and club contacts. It was a calculated risk to work with a gangster, but Oh had enough legitimate businesses to make this worthwhile.

One of Jake's waitresses, Nunhee, lingered in the dining room while he checked the receipts. He looked up, and asked if she wanted anything.

She ducked her head shyly, and said, I wanted to make sure you didn't need anything else.

Jake was about to dismiss her, but paused because she seemed unusually nervous. She had trouble meeting his gaze, and she kept shifting back and forth on her feet. She had changed out of the black T-shirt and apron uniform, and wore jeans and a suede jacket that was a size too large for her. She had folded up the cuffs, and the shoulders hung too low.

Jake rarely saw his waitresses out of uniform; they looked more vulnerable in street clothes. Nunhee seemed younger.

Need anything? he asked. I think everything is fine here.

She nodded quickly. She paused, then said, I heard there's a new soju bar on Shattuck.

Is there? I didn't know that. He sat up. What kind of food are they serving?

I don't know, she said. I haven't been there yet.

Jake asked, Where on Shattuck?

Fifty-third? Right under the freeway.

Terrible location, he thought. He said, Interesting.

He waited, and when she didn't say anything else, he thanked her. Have a good night, he said.

She hesitated, then left the restaurant.

He was thinking about the possible competition when it struck him that maybe Nunhee was waiting for him to ask her to go to the soju bar. He rubbed his head and thought about the few times they had talked recently—she had seemed unusually attentive to him. In fact, this was the second time she had lingered after work.

It would be a disaster to date one of his waitresses. Resentment from others. Worrying about giving special treatment. And what would he get out of it? Companionship? Sex? He wasn't interested in either. He wondered if something was wrong with him. Shouldn't he want sex?

He was oddly uninterested in pleasures of the body, including food or drink. He ate when he needed to, and usually chose the simplest, quickest meal. He never understood Sam's drinking. Why would anyone want to get sloppy drunk?

For Jake the true pleasures came from control over himself, over others, the purity of willpower, the highs of guiding his own future. Relationships required the yielding of some control, and he didn't like this. His last girlfriend, actually a friend of Sunny's, had lasted only a few months; he suspected she was just looking for a husband with good financial prospects. This would have been fine if she had something to offer him, but she hadn't. She was suspiciously subservient. He never felt like she was being herself. And when Sunny got sick he couldn't imagine dating anyone. It seemed wrong.

After finishing the receipts at The Shilla, Jake locked up and drove to his house in Montclair, a hillside neighborhood in north Oakland. He had bought the house a few years ago, and recently had it reappraised; already it was one of the best investments he had ever made, appreciating over thirty percent a year. He was thinking of expanding the deck out back and adding a hot tub, but he'd wait until the club was finished.

He did have the storeroom in the basement converted into a sauna last year, and his nightly routine included turning on his heater as soon as he came home, so that by the time he was ready for the sauna the rocks were hot. Tonight, he read his mail in the sauna—bills and business magazines—and then lay on the wooden bench and breathed deeply. The hot, dry air filled his lungs. He felt the germs inside him dying. His heart beat faster, the pulsing in his temples soothing him. He liked to stay in here until he sweated through the towel.

He tried not to worry about his brother working with Mr. Oh.

Part of Jake's agreement with Mr. Oh was that no one would know about Oh's financial involvement. Oh was funneling cash through the Seoul Silver and Jake could lose everything if the IRS found out. He couldn't trust Sam to keep this quiet; he could imagine his brother wanting a cut of this.

No, he would let Sam handle his own affairs. He knew there was a difference between working *with* Mr. Oh and working *for* Mr. Oh, and Jake would never do the latter. It was too dangerous. Jake knew about Mr. Oh's legitimate businesses, but almost nothing about the illegal businesses. He didn't want to know.

12

It was a cool, foggy morning in Marin, and Sam worried that Muir Woods would be too chilly. Unha wasn't wearing the right kind of clothing—she had on shiny, pointed shoes and a dress that would probably get caught on branches and shrubs—so when he saw the low fog in the hills he revised his plan to hike along the main Redwood Canyon trail. He realized that the only clothes Unha would have would be for the club. He didn't want to say anything to make her self-conscious. The Redwood loop would be fine. He and Sunny used to walk that route often. He remembered the way she had folded up the cuffs of her baggy jeans, and walked with a bounce, her arms swinging broadly as if she were marching.

When he and Unha drove onto Highway 1 through Mill Valley, Unha peered up at the trees. Sam stared at the houses here, wondering what it would be like to own one of them. He could hardly imagine being that rich.

Unha told Sam that she missed forests like these. She said, I think I prefer this to the city.

Sam agreed with her, and explained to her that where

he lived in the East Bay there were parks and places to hike. He said, I live across the street from a large lake. Sometimes I walk around it in the mornings.

She asked, A lake?

A very big lake. One of the biggest in the Bay Area.

They pulled into the parking area by the Visitor Center. There weren't many other cars in the dirt lot, parking stalls marked by long, gnarled logs. He paid the entrance fee and walked with Unha into the first section of the woods, the wooden planks lining part of the path already snagging her small-heeled shoes. He checked the map and told her that they could walk up to the second bridge to see Bohemian Grove.

Unha stared up at the canopy of leaves. She whispered how nice and quiet it was here, and asked him if he came here often.

I used to come often in the summer.

With your late wife, she said.

This startled him. He said, How did you know?

Some people at the club told me.

Yes, he said, wondering what else she knew. She died almost two years ago.

How did she die?

Cancer, he said.

They fell quiet as they continued walking. He wondered if she knew about Yunjin, and then felt guilty about being here. He told himself that this wasn't a date, that he was just showing Unha some sights. She didn't have anyone here to help her. He was being a friend.

He looked up at the trees. The sun was breaking through the fog, diffuse light filtering down in narrow shafts, angled columns of white light. Unha followed his gaze.

It's so quiet, she said.

Do you know why we don't hear any birds?

No, why?

Because there aren't any insects here to feed on, he said. There aren't many flowers down here because of the shade, and the tree bark has something in it that insects don't like. No insects means no birds.

Unha asked, How do you know that?

They have tours here. Do you want to go on one?

She shook her head. She said, I just want to look around with you.

As they walked down the path together, heading for a huge Redwood stump with a placard next to it, Sam saw her wobble on her shoe. He stepped closer to her and took her arm. She smiled at him, and held onto him. For the first time in many, many months, Sam was happy.

How could he not compare Unha with Sunny? It was more than a physical similarity that made him remember small details of his late wife; it was their personalities. Like Sunny, Unha was curious about everything. She stopped and read all the placards, asking Sam to translate the difficult words, and she then repeated them, committing them to memory. She said with delight, Every tree really needs hundreds of gallons of water a day!

Her enthusiasm was surprising, and Sam found himself looking at everything through her eyes, and appreciating it all over again. He watched her lean over the railing to peer at the fish in Redwood Creek. She pointed to them, and read the placard. She said in English, Anadromous?

Sam repeated it.

She read the placard slowly, nodding. Then in Korean she said, That means they can go in salt water and fresh water. Anadromous. Anadromous.

She turned to him happily and said, Anadromous.

He thought, She is beautiful.

Then he remembered that he had to pick up some groceries later for Yunjin. He stifled the thought.

With Yunjin, Sam felt more pity than anything else. He was very grateful for her taking care of David, but he was not attracted to her. Not physically, not emotionally, not anything. He tried to have sex with her once, more out of obligation than any desire, but felt the fear in every part of her body, and he found that he had trouble staying hard. He never tried again, and she didn't seem to care, which was fine with him.

Later, she told him she wasn't pregnant, and he was relieved. They couldn't afford another child. He also worried what that child would look like.

Now, as he and Unha sat on a bench across from a cluster of ferns that glowed green in the sunlight, he tried not to feel bad for Yunjin. He should never have married her. He had been scared and overwhelmed, and his brother had relayed their mother's advice of finding a new wife in Korea. At the time it had sounded ideal; he was neglecting David, often leaving him alone for entire afternoons and evenings. Sunny used to take care of all the finances and household details, and Sam didn't even know how much money they had in their checking account until the insurance ran out.

Realizing that she knew nothing about his situation, he said, I have to tell you something.

She said pleasantly, Yes?

I have a son.

She blinked. A son?

Yes. David. His Korean name is Kwan Gi. He is eleven.

You are taking care of him by yourself?

No. I brought someone over from Korea.

A relative?

He said, A wife.

You are…married, she said. You remarried after your first wife died.

I did.

109

She turned to look at the ferns. Oh, she said.

It was a marriage of necessity, he said. She wanted to come to the U.S. I needed help with David.

Do you love her?

No. I don't even know her.

How long have you been married?

Seven months.

And you don't know her?

He shook his head. We do not get along, he said.

They fell quiet. Sam said, Once she gets her green card, then I will divorce her. As soon as he said this, he realized it was true.

She sat still for a while, then stared up at the trees. She said, Does she know this?

She is unhappy, Sam said. She feels trapped. He recalled a recent argument when she said she felt like she was a prisoner. He had taunted her, telling her to leave whenever she wanted to, but he knew she couldn't. He regretted being so mean. He sighed to himself, not sure how their relationship had deteriorated so badly.

To his surprise, Unha reached over and patted his arm. She said, Let's enjoy this nature.

He nodded his head and they walked to a Redwood tree at the end of the path, the monstrous trunk rising up into the canopy of leaves. It was so quiet that Sam heard Unha breathing. He felt a peacefulness that had eluded him ever since Sunny died, and for the first time since he could remember, he let himself relax.

PART III

TO MOURN FOR MINJI

13

Sam accompanied Im on his rounds, checking on two garment factories in South San Francisco and Daly City. The glow from the Muir Woods trip hadn't dimmed, and he wanted to try another outing with Unha as soon as he could. It was almost like his trips with Sunny, and those gave him something to look forward to all week. He thought again about Sunny marching down the path and it made him smile. He remembered that she used to wake him up early on the weekend mornings with her call to attention, saluting him at the bed. He wondered where she got this military sensibility from. Her father was a merchant sailor, not a naval sailor. Sam used to groan when she woke him up, since he liked sleeping in. But she stood at attention, saying, Time to get up!

Now he often struggled to get out of bed after ten. Today he met Im at noon and as they made the rounds, Sam was slowly piecing together Mr. Oh's businesses. If Mr. Oh was at the top of the pyramid, then his sister and Koman shared the next level, with Hyunma running Club Saja and the massage parlor, and Koman overseeing the various liquor distributors, importers and two garment factories.

Each factory was simply an open floor of a large warehouse building with fifty sewing machine stations, and women hunched over them, running fabric from a box by their feet. They threw the finished pieces into another box. Sam walked with Im through the first of these factories, and was struck by the solemnity—no one talked as the overlapping whirring and staccato hum of the old machines filled the air. Sam's nose itched, the smell of chemicals and fabric filling the room. He asked Im what they did with the clothing.

Im said, Big stores want the clothes fast.

What about importing it cheaply?

Im shook his head, and explained that computerized inventory let the stores know instantly what they needed to stock. They didn't have to waste storage space. But this meant they needed to get the inventory quickly.

Sam said, And importing clothes from Asia takes too long?

They still import, but the fashion clothes come from local companies who can get them into the stores fast, Im said.

They are all illegal? Sam asked, nodding to the women.

Im shook his head. Not all, many.

The floor manager, a young Korean man with shiny, chubby cheeks, hurried over and bowed to Im, then to Sam. He told Im that they needed more women.

Im asked how many.

Four, the man said.

What happened to them?

Two got sick. One never showed up. One is refusing to work.

Im straightened. Refusing?

114

The man said, She is in the office with my wife.

Why is she refusing?

The man said, We docked her pay for being late.

Is she legal?

The man nodded his head.

Im said, Fire her. We will replace her.

The man hesitated, then said, She threatened to go to the police.

Im's face became stony. He said, We will talk to her. Im motioned for Sam to follow.

They walked down the factory floor, their shoes clicking on the bare cement floor. Some of the women glanced up at them as they passsed. Sam saw that many of these women were very young, maybe even in their teens. They were pale and sickly, their hair tied back in ponytails or concealed under scarves. They squinted, trying to focus in the poor lighting. The whirring and humming of the machines swelled around him. He was getting dizzy from the chemical smell.

They entered the back office that had just a desk with a computer, a few chairs, and a filing cabinet. Sam saw the wife, an older woman, scolding the young woman in a quiet, harsh voice. The wife turned and bowed quickly, but before she could say anything Im told her to leave them alone. The wife studied Sam, then hurried out.

Im said to Sam, Close the door.

Sam did.

The young woman sat in the chair with her arms folded. She had a high pale forehead and long, thin black hair. A brief glint of fear passed across her smooth face, but then she raised her chin defiantly. She said in Korean, Either I get my full pay or I am telling the police.

Im asked, What is your name?

Joo-ma.

Sam saw that she couldn't be more than twenty years old. Her fingernails were painted with sparkles. He glanced at

Im, who had on a dull, heavy-lidded expression, and Sam's stomach tightened.

Joo-ma, Im said quietly. You are going to get back to work, and you will accept the cut in pay. You will not go to the police.

She curled her lip and says with scorn, Who are you?

Im studied her. He reached down and grabbed her small pocketbook.

She said, Hey—

Im slapped her across the face, and she cried out in pain, holding her cheek. He threw the pocketbook to Sam and said, Check for identification.

Sam stared at the girl. He thought, Not again.

Im said, Now.

The girl yelled, You can't do that to me!

Im crouched down and punched the girl in the stomach. She cried out and curled up in the chair. Im then grabbed the back of her neck and leaned into her. He said, Shut up.

Sam opened the pocketbook and pulled out a small purse. Inside he found a driver's license and a bunch of old BART tickets. He gave the license to Im, who read it as he yanked her upright.

Joo-ma's voice shook as she said, You can't do this. She held her stomach.

Im said, You will go back to work and shut up. If you do not, I will find your family and kill them.

Joo-ma stared at him.

Im reached down to his shoe and pulled up his pant leg cuff, revealing a knife holster strapped over his dress sock. He pulled out a slim throwing knife.

Joo-ma let out a small cry.

Im said, Is this address current?

Her gaze never left the knife. She whispered, What?

Is this where you live?

She nodded her head, hypnotized.

116

Do you parents live here?

She nodded her head again.

You will be a good girl, Im said. You do not want to hurt your parents.

She shook her head.

Im moved toward her, grabbed her arm, and brought the knife to her ear. Her body shook violently and her voice rose a pitch as she said, Wait! Wait!

Im said, I do not want to hurt you too much, because I want you to get back to work. But I don't think you need an ear to work. Will you work?

I will, I will, she said quickly.

But I should visit your parents.

No—

You do not want me to?

I will work. I will not go to the police. Please.

Im said, I will come back in a few days. If I am told that you are not being good…

The girl began to cry.

Sam felt a wave of hatred toward him.

Im waited a moment, smiling, then slowly reholstered his knife and rolled down his pant cuff carefully. He brushed the creases and turned to Sam. He said, Hit her in the face hard.

Sam asked, What?

She rebelled, Im said. The other girls saw. We have to show them that this cannot be tolerated. Punch her in the face to bruise her.

No, Joo-ma said, still crying. I will be good.

Im stared at Sam, waiting.

But she is just a child, Sam said.

Im tilted his head. He asked, Shall I tell Koman you are no longer interested in working with us?

No, Sam said.

You hit her or I will, Im said. And if I hit her I will

break her neck. Do it now. We have to go.

Im moved toward the door.

Sam walked up to Joo-ma. She shook her head quickly, her eyes wide and frightened.

Sam said, I am sorry.

He raised his fist, and she closed her eyes and hugged herself. Sam also closed his eyes.

Over the next few days Unha didn't see Sam, and worried that he was avoiding her. She went over the trip to the forest in her head many times, hoping she hadn't offended him somehow. Maybe she was too disapproving over his wife. She hadn't really said anything, but maybe he sensed it. But the visit to the woods had been the highlight of her week; all she had to do was close her eyes and she could picture the way the sunlight filtered down through the tall treetops. She could smell the earthy ferns.

When she realized that Sam was her only friend here, she tried to make friends with Soonhee, asking her if she'd seen most of the tourist sights in the Bay Area. Soonhee jangled her bracelets and looked curiously at her. She asked, Sights?

Like the Golden Gate Bridge, Unha said, and remembered that Minji had wanted to see this as well.

Soonhee smiled indulgently and said, No, I really don't think so.

Why not?

It costs money. I am trying to save.

Unha said, The tips?

The tips and also the allowance. Do you think I'm going to work here forever? She glanced over Unha's shoulder and said, Choon is watching you again.

Unha nodded her head, but didn't look. She realized she should be saving her money too, but before she could ask her more about this, Soonhee went to tend to another table.

Unha tried to ignore Choon. Ever since she turned him down he had become a silent, annoying presence, constantly watching her throughout the night. He didn't talk to her; he just watched.

Throughout the night she sensed his gaze on her and she grew more rattled. She lost her concentration and forgot some drink orders, then almost dropped a tray of appetizers. Finally she walked up to Choon and asked, What are you doing?

What do you mean? He stared at her with a blank, stupid expression. She thought he looked like a dumb ox.

Why are you staring at me?

I am not.

Stop it.

He smirked. You think you are so good? You are just a whore.

Unha stepped back. What?

You are a bitch. Go suck on someone's dick, you whore.

She said, Um chang se gi. Your mother is a whore.

Choon took a step forward, and she spit toward the ground but hit his pants. He cursed and stepped back. She walked quickly to the bar, and picked up her latest drink orders, her face aflame and her head pounding. She refused to turn around to check where he was. Instead she talked to Lee, the bartender, until she calmed down.

Then, later that night, while still wary of Choon and exhausted from a surge in customers—a birthday party with a bunch of young men getting drunk and loud—she took a break in the coat room, sitting on a stool and gulping down a soda. A young man with a buzz cut and an acne-covered face stumbled in through the swinging doors. The music swelled, then cut off as the doors closed. He squinted at her, and said in English, You're Unha?

119

She stood up. Yes?

He swayed back and forth. Yeah, he said. You are hot. No doubt.

She blinked, confused, and said in Korean, What?

He moved closer to her, cornering her, and she held up her soda can. He looked at it, puzzled. No thanks, he said.

What do you want? she asked in Korean.

He said in English, That dude said you'd blow me for twenty.

What? She had no idea what he was saying. You are drunk—

No, man. Twenty sounds cool. Here. He reached into his back pocket and pulled out his wallet. He held up a twenty-dollar bill. Okay? Here.

She didn't take it. No. I don't know what you are talking about—

You want to go to my car? It's outside in the parking lot. He shrugged his shoulders and said, Here's cool.

What are you talking about? she asked, loudly.

He began to unbutton his jeans, and she backed up into the wall, yelling, Wait! What are you doing? In Korean, she said, Leave me alone, you stupid boy!

He paused. What?

She said, Go away.

He replied in English, But… but the dude said—

I don't know what you think, but I don't do that. Go away. Now, or I will scream.

He backed up, holding up his hands. The twenty-dollar bill fluttered in his fingers. Hey, hey. Take it easy. I think I got some wrong info, that's all. I'm sorry, man. Totally sorry.

She shrieked, Go away!

He staggered back, tripping over his feet, his eyes frightened. He mumbled again that he was sorry and ran out of the coat room.

Unha stood there, breathing hard. After regaining her

composure she walked out of the room and saw Choon in the doorway by the stairwell, his arms folded, a large smirk on his face. She realized he had done this to her and ran over to him, her vision blurry from tears. He laughed and pointed at her, and she reached down as she passed a table, grabbing a bottle of beer, and the customer said in Korean, I am not finished with that... and she took two quick steps forward and hurled the bottle at Choon, who looked startled as the bottle spun, beer spiraling out, and he ducked as the bottle crashed into the wall behind him, beer exploding in white foam. He glanced at the bottle on the ground, then turned toward Unha, breathing heavily. He moved toward her.

Unha stood there frozen, then turned and raced to the front entrance. The customers at the nearby tables stared as she brushed by them.

Hyunma appeared from the kitchen, seeing her running, and she yelled at her to stop. She then barked Choon's name, and he stopped. Hyunma crooked her finger, motioning them to follow her back into the kitchen. Choon obeyed immediately. Unha hesitated, and only when Choon disappeared into the kitchen did she follow.

When she entered the kitchen Choon was already lying, telling Hyunma that Unha was being rude to customers and starting a fight with him.

That is not true, she said. He told a customer I was a prostitute!

Look at the beer, Choon said. She made a mess.

Enough! Hyunma cut the air with her hand. To Choon she said, Go back to your station. No more distractions.

Choon grumbled but left the kitchen.

Hyunma said to Unha, One more mistake and you will not work here anymore.

But I did not do—

I do not care, Hyunma said coldly. Do you under-

121

stand? I can replace you very easily.

Unha was stunned. This wasn't the same friendly, talkative woman whom Unha had first met.

Hyunma's expression was hard, her mouth set tightly. She said in a low voice, Go back to work.

Unha nodded her head and left the kitchen.

14

David found Yunjin standing in front of a mirror, practicing her English. She said to her reflection, I would like a glass of water, please.

He asked her what she was doing and she said that she noticed Americans were less expressive in their language, that they spoke blandly, while Koreans tended to emphasize words and phrases with more mouth and eyebrow movements. Listening to Korean, she could hear the intonations in almost a song-like way, but Americans spoke evenly, calmly.

She stared at herself, then looked at him. I used to hate mirrors.

Why?

I did not like to look at myself.

She told him that everyone had called her ugly and whenever she saw her reflection she was surprised to see a dark, strange face. Her hair was curly, so she had used Vaseline to straighten it, but after a few hours her hair would begin to curl again, and become greasy and dirty.

She asked him what he was doing, and he said, I am going out.

To do what?

Explore.

Explore?

Look around.

It's dangerous for you to be alone.

He frowned.

She said, You show me sometime.

Why?

I want to see more.

He told her that today he was going to visit a tae kwon do studio in Berkeley.

How you get there? she asked.

BART.

You take the subway by yourself?

He shrugged. Sure.

You show me how.

Do you have money?

She asked, Where you get your money?

Sometimes I sneak on, but sometimes I use Uncle Jake's birthday money.

You save money? You are very good. Better than your father. I come with you?

He thought about it, and shrugged his shoulders. Sure.

They walked to the 19th Street BART station in downtown Oakland, the closest station to their apartment, and he showed her how to buy a ticket. They then went down to the platform and he pointed to the map, telling her which trains they needed to take to go to Berkeley.

He could see how nervous she was by the way she kept glancing at a homeless man sitting on the ground against the wall. A few black teens stood by the escalators, and stared blankly at the ads on the wall across the tracks. David wondered if she was like his father, prejudiced against blacks, even though she was half black. He had heard his father talk about how he was once mugged by a black man, and how you always had to watch out for them. His uncle was less biased, because many of his customers were black and Hispanic, and he got to know some of them, but David's father worked with other Koreans while doing carpentry, and rarely interacted with anyone else.

While they waited for the train, Yunjin asked if he was looking forward to school in the fall. He wasn't, and when she asked why, he didn't want to explain how his only friend in his grade, Chris Brannon, had moved to Los Angeles last year, and he didn't really connect with anyone else. It didn't help that teachers tended to like him, and he was often labeled the teacher's pet within the first few weeks of the new school year. He kept to himself, did his work, and went home as soon as he could. He even avoided taking the bus, which he was supposed to take because of the distance, and walked whenever he could.

He told her he hated school.

She said, I didn't go to school in one place for too long, and when I stay with my aunt and uncle I stop. You should take advantage.

The train entered the tunnel and he told her to step back. She did. Warm, stale air blew over them as the train blew its horn and approached. Inside the cars were empty, and when the train stopped and the doors opened, Yunjin turned to him, waiting for his instructions. He suddenly felt older.

Kim's Martial Arts sat in a large former car dealership off Shattuck, where huge windows exposed the open, padded floor. Rows of young men and women with their bright white uniforms punched and kicked the air in unison, their yells startling David with their volume. One of the young Korean men wearing a black belt saw David and Yunjin, and left the line, trotting over to them.

The man asked if he could help them, and when Yunjin replied in English that she and David were just looking, the man asked in Korean, Would you like to meet Master Park? He is in the back office.

Yunjin waited for David to answer. He had been intending just to watch from outside, so this made him nervous. He said in English, I don't know.

Come, the man said. He likes meeting other Koreans.

The man beckoned for them to follow and Yunjin nodded to him and went along. David didn't want to be left alone here, so he hurried after them.

The back room was another open area with weights and three large punching bags tethered to the floor and ceiling. A desk with a computer sat in the corner, and leaning back in an office chair was a man in a black sweatsuit, his black hair shiny and wavy, his feet propped up on the desk. He saw them, sat up, and said into the phone in Korean, I have to go. We will talk later.

He hung up and bowed to them. Welcome, he said to Yunjin. To David he said, Are you interested in joining our dojang?

David was about to say no, but Yunjin replied, We are thinking about it. She stared at the man, who introduced himself as Mr. Kim. Yunjin told him her name and David's, and David bowed.

Mr. Kim paused, and said he could give them a tour.

Yunjin said, How about you give David a few free lessons? Then we can decide.

Mr. Kim said to David, Have you studied before?

He shook his head.

To Yunjin he said, We don't usually do this, but maybe I can make an exception. He smiled warmly at her.

Yunjin smiled back at him. David almost never saw her smile. She then caught him staring, and said to Mr. Kim, That would be very good. When can he get started?

We have a children's class tomorrow, he said. How does that sound?

They looked at David. He nodded dumbly.

On the way home he thanked Yunjin for getting him free lessons, but found himself apprehensive. He asked her what if Mr. Kim realized he wasn't going to sign up for real? What if he did badly at the lessons? Was he supposed to have a uniform? How would they pay for it?

Stop, Yunjin said. Just go and see how it is. Wear what you wear when you practice by yourself.

He bit his lip.

You worry too much, she said. You just got three free lessons! Enjoy it.

She seemed energized, her voice more confident. She patted his head and said, Maybe I go with you. I can explore more.

Don't take tae kwon do lessons with me, David said, raising his voice at the thought of her trying to do kicks next to him.

No, no. I drop you off and pick you up.

I don't need it. I can do it myself.

Maybe I want to.

He didn't reply, thinking about what he should wear tomorrow.

Yunjin and David were surprised to find Sam home that afternoon. He was arguing with his brother on the phone and studied them as he said, I told you I will try, but I have to go with Im later today.

Yunjin and David heard Jake's sharp voice from where they stood. Sam's forehead was sweating, and he wiped it with the back of his hand. He glared at them, and David went to his room while Yunjin moved toward the kitchen.

Sam continued arguing, telling his brother that he could not help with the carpentry at the Seoul Silver because of his work with Mr. Oh. He apologized, then yelled, I am doing the best I can! He slammed the phone down.

He began arguing with Yunjin, telling her that there was never any food in the apartment, and she retorted that she never had money to buy food and he didn't bring any home from the restaurant.

David sat down with his Kung Fu book, and studied it.

When he got off the phone with his brother, Jake calmed himself. Sam was ungrateful and selfish. After all Jake had done for him, Sam would refuse? Incredible. Jake sat in his office, trying to think of solutions. He called Tim on his cell and told him to work with the contractor to get a new carpenter. Tim said, He's going to ask to up the budget—

Do what you can. We can go up another few thousand, but that's it.

Tim agreed, and hung up.

Jake had to fire the carpenter who had been building the booths. Tim had discovered that the carpenter had lied to the contractor, padding the bill for the materials and then using cheap pine that barely held together because the carpenter hadn't followed the design specs. The contractor was going to charge Jake the overages, but Jake said it was the contractor's fault. Either way, Jake got rid of the carpenter and the booths still needed to be finished.

His brother could do a decent job, and Jake needed him. It would take Tim at least a week to find and interview a good carpenter. They could no longer rely on the contractor. Maybe Jake should get rid of him too.

He had told Mr. Oh that the club would open in less

than three weeks, and the ads already had gone out to the local Korean newspapers. Opening day couldn't be changed, and a club with no booths would be a disaster.

Jake called Mr. Oh to tell him what was happening. Mr. Oh was quiet for a moment, then said, Do you want me to talk to the carpenter?

No, he has to go. He is incompetent. But my brother is good, and I was wondering if you can spare him for a couple days.

He works with Im now.

I know.

Mr. Oh said, There's no one else? Your brother is coming along all right with us.

Just for two days, at most three. This is urgent.

I will talk to Im, Mr. Oh said.

Thank you.

Jake then walked into the main dining area and checked the unfinished booths again. He ran his fingers along the uneven sawed edges of the back, the misaligned joints, and the mangled nail heads. Most of this could be covered by the upholstery, but it was still terrible work. Sam would never have done this. If he was lazy about most things, he was precise and attentive with his carpentry. He had built furniture in Korea, and was beginning to do more of that before Sunny got sick; he had actually sold a small table and a child's highchair. And some of the work Sam had done at the Shilla and here was good. Early on Sam had renovated the office in the Shilla, and Jake had watched his brother spend hours on the built-in shelving.

His brother could've made a career of it if he had cared enough. He was missing that drive to better himself. He had some of it when he and Sunny first arrived here, but now there was nothing.

He could understand what happened to Sam; he had been broken. But a year had gone by and Sam still hadn't begun to recover. In fact, by working with Mr. Oh, Sam was probably making things worse for himself.

Jake had done the best he could for his brother. At some point he would have to stop.

15

Sam waited for Unha's shift to be finished, catching glimpses of her throughout the club, though he knew not to act friendly with her in front of the others. They hadn't had a chance to talk since visiting Muir woods a few days ago. He couldn't help staring at her in the large mirrors, her hair pushed back with a headband, her brisk, almost gymnastic movements around the tables and customers. She was good at her job. He could tell. He met her as she was leaving the club, her steps now heavy and slow. She saw him, stopped, and said, It is so late. You are here?

I was with Im, but I was waiting for you, he said. He noticed small bags under her eyes, her cheeks sagging, and he added, I can drive you home.

Thank you. It has been a bad night.

Why?

She told him about dealing with Choon, and Sam tensed. He said, I should talk to him.

No, I do not want to get into any more trouble.

Sam kept quiet, but now saw Choon as an enemy. He would size him up better tomorrow. He led Unha to his car, and as he drove her the few blocks to her apartment, he tried not to think about the girl at the garment factory. He had never hit a girl like that before, and it disgusted him. He had given her a black eye, and he had found that his hands were shaking afterwards.

Unha said, I really enjoyed the trip to the woods.

I did too. We should do it again soon.

This is my apartment building, she said, pointing. But let's ride around a little.

Sam slowed the car, then noticed that farther down the street a few of the other waitresses were approaching. He wondered if she didn't want to be seen with him. He sped up and turned onto a side street.

He said, Do you get along with the other waitresses?

Yes, she said. We are friendly, but we are not friends.

Why not?

She shook her head. I don't know, she said. I think we are just different.

Sam stopped the car at a red light and said, Can you have lunch with me tomorrow? When do you start work?

Early tomorrow. Ten.

How about breakfast?

I don't think I will have time.

Sam waited. When she didn't say anything else he cleared his throat and said, I know I am married—

Maybe my next day off we can go somewhere else, she said. Maybe the mountains? What did you say it was?

Mount Tamalpais. Yes. It's beautiful there. It is also near the woods we went to.

I would like that. It will remind me of the mountains near Taeshin.

Wear hiking shoes. Do you have something comfortable?

She shook her head.

Sam had donated all of Sunny's clothes, but he said, What size are you? I will get you a pair.

Oh, no. You don't have to—

I want to.

But...why? Why are you so nice to me?

He paused. Don't you know?

Even in this pale light he saw her blush. She stammered, Thank you. I should get some sleep.

He drove around the block and pulled up to her building. He said, I hope to see you tomorrow.

She nodded her head without looking at him and climbed out of the car. She shut the door quietly, and Sam watched her walk to the front entrance. She turned around and waved. The light above her shadowed her face, but he thought he saw her smile. He waited until she was inside before driving away, and felt in his chest a lightness that made him laugh to himself.

Unha stood in the foyer and watched Sam's car drive away. The clock on the wall ticked loudly. As she walked up to the apartment, she wondered if she would ever find a husband and have a family. Sam wasn't a real possibility—he already had a family. No, he would be her friend, that was all. Tonight, though, when he asked if he could have lunch with her, she had felt lonely. She had thought, What about your wife?

She used her key to open the apartment door, but found it unlocked. Inside Ginny and Hineh were arguing quietly while the others were asleep on their mattresses. Ginny asked Unha what took her so long to get back, and Unha said that Sam gave her a ride.

Ginny smiled slyly. A ride? We walked and got here faster.

We talked a little, Unha said.

Talked, Ginny said. Liar.

Unha frowned and went to her mattress without replying. Why did she feel so much older than them?

She washed up and stared at herself in the mirror. She was losing weight, her cheeks sunken, her chin more pointed. She pulled up her shirt and saw for the first time her lower ribs pressing against the skin. There was plenty of food at the club, but she was always too stressed and too tired to eat. Today, all she had was a bowl of rice and a few mandu. Her mother would say she looked like a war orphan.

Her mother. Unha still hadn't called her, even though she had bought a phone card. She just was always too tired by the time she got home, and in the mornings she was rushing to get ready for work. If she didn't call soon, she would keep putting it off.

She found the card and asked Ginny what time it was in Korea.

Hineh said, Late afternoon, I think.

Unha imagined her grandmother and mother beginning to prepare for dinner, and she had a pang of homesickness. She followed the directions on the calling card and dialed the long series of numbers, and then her home telephone number. Even pressing these buttons made her feel strange. She didn't know what she would say. It took a few seconds for the connection to go through, and then Unha heard the phone ringing. Once, twice… It kept going on, and with each ring she felt more and more nervous. Her stomach tightened.

Then, finally, her mother's faint, echoing voice came on and said, Yeobuseyo?

Hearing her mother's voice scared her for some reason. It was so faint, so far. Without thinking, Unha hung up.

Ginny said, What happened?

No one home, Unha said. Her hands were sweating. She stared at the phone. She listened to Ginny tell Hineh about how the man she was dating planned to take her to one of the most expensive restaurants in the city, and how one day he was going to propose to her.

Unha thought, What could I have told her? She was a waitress. She worked six days a week, ten hours or more a day, and owed thousands of dollars. Why couldn't she talk to her mother? Maybe because she knew she couldn't lie to her. Maybe because the minute she started talking she would burst into tears. No, maybe she should write a letter. A postcard. Maybe she'd call later when she had better news.

Unha curled up on her mattress and felt more alone than ever. She thought of Minji and wondered if they would've been friends if they hadn't been separated.

Minji crawled across the floor, her knees burning on the carpet, her palms rubbed raw, while the man towered over her, shirtless, his hands on his waist, his wrinkled, flabby stomach hanging over his belt. He spoke in Korean with a strange accent. He said, Crawl to me.

She was naked, shivering, and raised her head, but he said sharply, Do not look at me.

She bowed her head. She heard him approaching and she tightened her stomach as she saw his shoe rise up and swing toward her ribs. She cried out when he connected, the breath knocked out of her, and she fell over and curled up on her side, gasping for air. She squeezed her eyes closed. She tried to disconnect herself from everything and a dullness crept into her body. She inhaled slowly, ignoring the pain, imagining that the air that filled her lungs was sleeping gas. She felt her senses shutting down. She no longer felt her burning knees or her scraped palms or her aching ribs. She imagined herself in another place, a familiar place. She once worked at a candy store at the Lotte Mall. She had worn a white and red blouse and skirt with a white cap, and she would weigh out loose candies into a paper bag. She had enjoyed herself there.

The man said, Keep crawling to me.

She did, but tried to keep her eyes closed. The sound of her knees on the carpet filled her ears. The man breathed loudly through his mouth. She heard him kneeling in front of her and unzipping his pants. He said, Suck me.

She opened her eyes, flinching at the sight of his erect, angry red penis, and moved toward the massage table to get the cherry oil. He said, No. Without that.

She hesitated and he smacked her in the head. He said, Suck me.

She tried to stifle a cry, but couldn't. He said, Good. He grabbed the back of her head and pulled her toward him. She instinctively pulled back, but he hit her again and she let herself be pulled to him. She closed her eyes and smelled the musky, sour sweat coming from his groin, and when she put him in her mouth she tasted something sour and sharp, and she gagged.

He yelled at her to suck him, but she kept coughing and tried to pull away. He hit her again, much harder this time, sending her to the floor. She lay there on her side, flattening herself against the carpet, covering her face. The man stood up and walked around her. She was breathing heavily. She thought of a big wedding celebration dinner, the pyehbeksang, that her friend had when she married. It was supposed to be a formal dinner, but all her nieces and nephews were running around and yelling, ignoring their parents. It was chaos, but Minji had enjoyed it. She knew she would never get married. She would never call Jin. She would never see him again. She began crying.

The man startled her by pushing her onto her stomach, lying on top of her, straddling her, then entering her from behind. She stifled a cry of pain, and pressed her forehead into the carpet. He thrust into her harder, and grabbed her hair, yanking her head up and hurting her neck. He said, You bitch.

He pulled her hair harder and thrust faster. She couldn't breathe with her neck stretched back, and she tried to arch her back to ease the pressure, and he said, Yes. That is good.

She gasped for air. She managed to get a deep breath. He continued pumping inside her.

She remembered the plane ride out of Seoul and remembered looking down at the Han River as they left Korea. She had been so excited, so happy to be on a plane for the first time in her life.

The man reached forward with his other hand and grabbed her throat, squeezing. He kept pulling her hair back and thrusting into her. She couldn't breathe at all now, and she struggled, trying to yell for him to stop, but he only tightened his grip and pulled harder. Yes, yes, he said.

She thrashed her body, trying to turn away, but he had her locked against him, and she felt her eyes pulsing, her chest burning. Something cracked in her throat, and her body convulsed, and she felt everything shimmering, sparkling, the light above becoming a crystal, rainbow colors falling around her, and she heard him yelling with pleasure, and he yanked on her hair hard, too hard, and something else cracked, and her vision darkened, with the sparkling lights fading quickly, the sounds around her dimming, and all the pain suddenly went away as she felt herself spiraling to the ground.

16

Sam told Im that he had nothing to do with this.

Im replied angrily, We are helping your brother? Don't insult me. I don't know how your brother is connected with Mr. Oh, but I am not a fucking carpenter.

Sam said, I am.

What the fuck am I going to do?

I don't know, Sam said. He was about to say that Im could hold the nails while Sam hammered, but he stopped himself.

Im pressed the accelerator and the car lurched forward. He muttered something that Sam didn't hear.

Sam and Im had arrived at Saja that afternoon, and Koman had given them their orders: go to the Seoul Silver and help Jake with the renovations. After some confusion Sam told them that he was a carpenter and had been working for his brother before Mr. Oh. Im said, No wonder Mr. Oh let your debt slide. Your brother must have vouched for you. Lucky.

This dug at Sam, but he kept quiet, and now, as they drove over to the Silver, Sam said, Look, you can go. There's not much for you to do.

And have your brother tell Mr. Oh that I am lazy? No.

Sam glanced at him, surprised. He wondered again about his brother's relationship with Mr. Oh, and intended to press Jake on that. Jake had always been secretive and cagey, his need to control everything around him extending to the control of information. Even Jake's decision to study in the U.S. had been a secret until all the details were worked out, and Jake just announced it one night at dinner.

Im pulled up in front of the Silver, and motioned to his suit. He asked, Should I change?

Depends on what my brother needs, Sam said. But there are extra coveralls in there.

Im grunted and climbed out of the car. Sam walked with him through the front entrance, and they saw Jake on his cell phone. Sam gave him a look, a what-is-going-on look, and Jake gave him a half shrug. He continued talking into the phone, saying, The meeting is tomorrow at two o'clock, but pointed Sam toward the unfinished booths in the other part of the club.

Im looked around, and said, It's big.

Sam said, I guess we need to work on the booths. Let me check them out first.

Im said, I need a smoke. He walked back outside.

Sam inspected the framing, and almost laughed at how bad the workmanship was. The two main supports of the benches were misaligned, so a sudden weight would buckle them. He turned to his brother, who was hanging up his phone. Sam shook his head, Who the hell did this?

The contractor found him, Jake said.

You should fire not just the carpenter but the contractor. This is a hazard. This thing will fall apart and a customer will sue you.

Can you fix it?

No. I have to take it apart and redo it. Look. All that's holding this platform is two nails. If a fat man sat on this...

Fuck!

Sam said, How did you get Mr. Oh to send us? Are you working with him?

How long will it take to redo?

Sam studied his brother. Cagey as usual. He said, All the booths are like this? Even the ones that are finished?

I don't know. I think so.

Two weeks, Sam said.

I don't have two weeks.

I can probably call in another person, Sam said.

What about Im?

Sam shook his head. You need someone who knows what he's doing.

With help, how long?

A week?

Jake rubbed his temples. Goddamn it.

How are you working with Mr. Oh?

Jake looked up at him. He said, You don't need to know that.

Sam smiled. You won't tell your own brother?

Im stepped back inside and said to Sam, Koman just called. We have to go.

What? Jake said. You haven't started here yet.

Im said, This is an emergency.

But what about—

Orders from Koman, Im said. To Sam he said, Come on. Now.

Sam said to his brother, who seemed panicked, I'll be back later. Tonight. Okay?

Jake said, I need your help.

Tonight, Sam said.

You owe me.

This stopped Sam. His brother had never said that before. Sam said, I will be here tonight. I can also call some people I've worked with before.

Im said, Come on!

Sam saw the anger in his brother's eyes. Before Sam could say anything else Jake turned and walked into the kitchen.

They were driving to Yang's Acupuncture and Massage, and Sam asked Im what their job was.

Im said, They had some trouble.

What kind of trouble?

One of the girls.

Sam asked, What do we do?

Im didn't reply.

They drove into Chinatown, and Im pulled up in front of Yang's. He kept the engine idling and looked around. Then he drove into a side alley. He put on the hazard lights and popped the trunk. He said to Sam, Stay here until I get you.

Im climbed out and walked through the side entrance of Yang's. The clicking of the hazard lights distracted him. Sam stared out onto the street, where, in the bright morning sun, everything was dirtier than he remembered. Old newspapers and plastic grocery bags drifted in the gutter when a car sped by. He peered through the windshield at the side entrance of Yang's, wondering what was going on.

Sam felt guilty for leaving his brother with no help. He wasn't sure if he could call anyone for carpentry help because he didn't have any phone numbers. He'd have to contact Pak, the contractor he worked with, but he wasn't sure where he was right now. The housing slowdown had forced Pak out of the area. Yes, Sam owed his brother a lot. That was obvious. Tonight, Sam vowed to himself. Tonight he would go to the Silver and help out. Without Jake's money who knows how much worse things would have been for Sunny. At least she had died peacefully. She had been on morphine, the nurse checking the dosages every few minutes. Sunny had drifted off to sleep, the pain easing away. She had died without saying goodbye.

He felt the heaviness of this memory. If he believed in God and Heaven, then perhaps he wouldn't still feel so depressed about her. He would believe she was in Heaven, not rotting in the ground. He had come to accept the randomness of life and death, but he didn't like it. He thought, We are just insects.

Im peered out of the side door and waved him in.

Sam pulled himself slowly out of the car. He was tired. He craved a drink. He wanted to see Unha. He wanted to help his brother. He had too many things to worry about.

He walked through the side entrance and found Im with the older woman who seemed to run this place. The lobby area was empty, the TV off. Im motioned for Sam to follow him upstairs.

What is going on—

Im shushed him.

It was strangely quiet here. Sam peered down at the stairwell. The woman was watching them anxiously. At the top of the stairs Im said to Sam, I need you to be calm.

This rattled Sam. Why?

Last night one of the girls was killed.

How?

We are not sure, but she might have been choked to death.

Sam said, Was it Minji?

Im backed up, his eyes wide. How did you know?

It was Minji?

How did you know? Im said, his voice harsher.

She asked me for help, he said.

142

When?

When we were here and she gave me a massage.

Im studied him. What did you say?

How could I help her? I don't even know her.

Im asked, Did she say she was in trouble?

No. She just wanted to get out of here.

Im nodded his head thoughtfully, and said, Come on.

He led Sam down the hall and into a room. On the floor was a body wrapped in dark green garbage bags with blue masking tape. Sam's stomach tightened. The figure was in a fetal position, and he could make out the head and the arms curled up at the chest. He smelled something bad, then realized it was shit from the body.

He wrinkled his nose.

Im said, They release their bowels.

Sam turned away. He tried not to picture her pleading for help. He tried to clear his thoughts.

Im said, We will carry her to the trunk. We have to move fast.

And then what? Sam asked.

And then we get rid of it, Im said.

Sam stared at Minji's body. He heard her plea for help in his head. He thought, I could've stopped this. He said, She was too young.

Im ignored him and picked up her legs. He said, You get her head.

Sam hesitated. Are you going to tell the police about this?

Are you joking? Come on. Hurry.

Sam looked down at her and thought, Please forgive me.

Come on!

Sam bent over, holding his breath, and lifted her up delicately.

•

Unha began her shift with the wariness of a skittish deer. She watched Choon in the mirrors and from the corner of her eye, and when she saw him talking to Lee, she suspected they were plotting something. She felt her cheeks heat up. She made sure she knew where Hyunma was at all times, so she could run to her if needed. As the club slowly filled up and Unha grew busier, she felt comforted by the crowd; she could concentrate on her work.

She was becoming more efficient, taking orders from a few tables at a time, inputting them all into the computer without even thinking about the keystrokes, and then gliding to the kitchen and the bar. She learned that being friendly with the customers earned her bigger tips. One older man gave her a twenty-dollar bill even though he had only ordered a few drinks for himself and his wife. She was careful with the younger men, though. When they had a few drinks they tried to ask her out or even touch her. She couldn't depend on Choon to stop them, so she had to be friendly enough for a good tip, but not encourage any conversation.

She was good at this job, and thought that she could continue working at a club like this after her debt was paid. She didn't like not knowing exactly how much she owed and how long she would need to pay it off, but Ginny said she had paid hers off in a year.

But Unha wondered if Ginny had actually tried to leave yet.

A group of young men and women entered the club, and Hyunma led them upstairs. She beckoned Hineh and Unha to follow. Unha made sure she was close to Hineh as they passed Choon, who stared at her without any expression.

Upstairs, she and Hineh took the drink and anjoo orders, and hurried back downstairs. As they filled the orders and checked on their regular tables, Unha noticed Choon talking to Hyunma and motioning in her direction. Hyunma didn't look toward her though, and just nodded her head.

Ginny came over to Unha and said, Hineh needs to take a break. I'll take over her tables upstairs. Did you check on them?

Unha said she was going to in a moment.

See if Hineh's table needs anything, okay?

Unha saw Choon walking over to Lee, and said, I'll go right now. She hurried around the tables and toward the stairwell, glad to avoid Choon. Upstairs, she found Hineh's table wanting another bottle of soju, and her table needed some of the empty dishes cleared. She quickly bussed the table, leaving the dishes on the bus cart for later, and returned downstairs to input the soju order.

Lee motioned her over to the bar and said, The Jinro Gold is in the stockroom. Can it wait a few minutes?

They are very impatient, she said.

He asked her, Can you grab two bottles? They are on the shelves. Jinro Gold.

She checked her tables, which seemed fine, and nodded to Lee. She walked into the kitchen where the heat coated her face and made her sweat. The storeroom was next to the walk-in freezer, and she pressed her palm on the metal freezer door, cooling herself. She walked into the storeroom, where boxes of liquor lay stacked up to her shoulders. She searched the shelves until she found the Jinro, and then grabbed two of the Golds. She turned around and saw Choon standing in the doorway. He said, Who will help you now, you stupid whore?

17

David finally realized after seeing Yunjin talk with Mr. Kim again that they were flirting with each other. There was a moment after David had finished with his first lesson, when his thigh muscles were burning in pain, and his T-shirt was clammy and cold, that Yunjin was standing next to Mr. Kim, talking, and David saw her laugh and shyly cover her mouth. He had never seen her do this before, and he wondered why she was acting so strangely. Then Mr. Kim faced her, standing less than a foot away, his voice quiet, and although David couldn't hear what they were saying, Mr. Kim was standing too close for this to be anything but an intimate conversation. David was startled. He took a closer look at Mr. Kim, whose neatly-trimmed beard hid his expression. He was shorter and more compact than his father. He used his hands when he talked.

Yunjin glanced over at David, and asked Mr. Kim something. He turned and studied David, and replied. Yunjin beckoned.

Teacher Kim said you did good, Yunjin told David.

Very good for a first time, Mr. Kim said. He asked David if he had done tae kwon do before.

He shook his head.

But he studies books. I see him practicing from books, Yunjin said.

Mr. Kim asked David what book, and when David told him it was an introduction to Kung Fu, Mr. Kim smiled. He said to Yunjin, He should join this dojang. He has a lot of potential.

We still have two free lessons, don't we?

Yes.

I do not know if we can afford regular lessons, Yunjin said.

Sometimes we have scholarships or work-study. We can talk about that after the third lesson.

Yunjin said to David, Would that be good?

He nodded.

After they left and went on BART, he asked Yunjin what Mr. Kim had meant by work-study. She explained that he would be like an apprentice, working for them for free lessons. He tried not to show his excitement, but Yunjin looked at his expression and laughed. She said, We will see.

Yunjin had been sure Mr. Kim was being so nice to her because he wanted the business, but his mention of a scholarship had changed her mind. She wondered if he actually liked her.

She spent the rest of the day fantasizing about him, imagining that he would want to lure her away from her marriage. She could work at the dojang. But what about David?

The thought of leaving David, even in a fantasy, made her uneasy. She didn't think Sam could raise him alone, and she had grown attached to the boy over the past few months. Sometimes she worried that Sam would abandon her and take David away. Once, when they were fighting, he told her he wanted to send her back to Korea, that if she was so unhappy here, he could very easily contact her aunt and uncle.

This shut her up. She would never return to them. She would rather live on the street.

All she had to do was close her eyes and she could picture her aunt lying in her bed, her face red from the heat she liked to keep on in the room, her hair greasy and sticking up in back, and Yunjin could hear her grating, scratchy voice demanding that Yunjin hurry up with lunch, or complaining that Yunjin was ungrateful for all that they had done for her.

It took a year away from them for Yunjin to realize how miserable she truly had been. She couldn't believe that when she had first learned of her arranged marriage and proposed trip to the U.S. she had been afraid and hadn't wanted to go.

She heard David leaving the apartment. She was about to ask where he was going, but then decided to let him be. Both he and Sam were secretive, and she wondered if it had to do with his dead mother. Her ghost was everywhere. Even though Sam had gotten rid of her things and Yunjin couldn't find a picture of her, the memory of her felt imprinted on everything here—the sofa, the carpet, the walls. The brown sofa had once been striped, and Yunjin knew Sunny had sewn the new fabric on herself because Sam had mentioned it during one of his drunken ramblings. She listened intently whenever Sam started talking to himself. It was the only time she learned anything about him.

A few months ago she had heard him say that he wanted to be dead.

She was in the bedroom, but the door was open and his voice drifted down the hall. The TV was on low. She sat up in bed and heard him mumble, then say clearly, I wish I were dead.

She waited for more, but he stopped. Her first

thought was what she would do if he committed suicide. Then she wondered if she was supposed to take care of David. Then she realized that she didn't care if Sam died, and this shocked her.

Sam dug a grave in the sandy dirt with a new shovel Im had bought. They had driven down Highway 1, along the ocean, past Pacifica, along the shoreline and onto a dirt road leading into a wooded area with gnarled trees and thick brush. It was dusk, the highway quiet, the crashing waves the only sounds drifting from the beach. Minji's body was still in Im's trunk. Sam had heard it shifting and sliding with every turn; he still couldn't quite believe that he was doing this.

He widened the hole as the dirt kept collapsing around the sides. He heard Im struggling with the body. The wind kicked up sand, blowing it into Sam's eyes. He squinted, tears forming, and stopped digging. Im began ripping out the lining of his trunk, throwing the pieces of fabric onto the ground next to Minji's body. Another gust of wind blew sand over the garbage bags, making a sheeting sound. Im asked why he had stopped digging.

Sam continued deepening the grave. They hadn't spoken since they had left the hardware store, and Sam was glad for this. He realized that this kind of thing wasn't that unusual for Im, since he seemed to know exactly what to do and where to go, and Sam understood something about himself as they drove to get rid of Minji—he could not do this kind of work. He saw Minji's pleading face whenever he closed his eyes, and he knew it would be worse after tonight.

Im grabbed Minji's torso and dragged her across the sand to the hole. One of the plastic bags slid off her body, exposing her head. Sam stared. Her eyes and mouth were open, but sand covered half of it, falling into one eye and crusting at her mouth. Even in this dim light he could see the bruises on her neck. He thought, I am sorry.

Help me, Im said, dragging her into the hole.

It's not deep enough yet, Sam said.

It's fine.

Sam reached down for Minji's legs. They pulled her into the middle of the hole, and Im threw the pieces of his trunk liner over her face. Im grabbed the shovel and pushed the dirt over her. Sam watched, fighting his nausea. For a moment he thought he saw her leg move, and he straightened, his heart beating quicker. But it was just the sand shifting the plastic bag. When Im finished piling the sand over her, Sam asked what they were going to do now.

Cover our tire tracks, get rid of the shovel, and go back to the club, Im said.

And my brother's club?

Too late. Tomorrow.

And her? Sam asked, nodding to the lump of sand.

What about her?

That's all? We just leave her here.

What else do you want to do?

Sam shook his head. Was it this easy to dispose of a human life? Then he thought of Sunny, and how she was buried at the Mountain View cemetery in Piedmont, and except for the more ceremonial nature of her funeral, it wasn't much different. Both were in the ground. Both were soon forgotten. Sam hadn't visited her grave since her birthday last year.

Come on, Im said, handing Sam the shovel. I will drive the car to the road. Cover the tire tracks. We will have to get rid of our shoes later.

Sam took the shovel. He watched Im drive the car down the dirt road and then wait at the fork that led to the highway. As Sam threw sand along the tire tracks, he glanced back at Minji's grave and wondered if anyone but him would mourn for her.

•

Unha, trapped in the storeroom by Choon, kept calm and asked him what he thought he was doing by blocking the doorway.

He said, You think you are so high class? You think you are better than me?

The club was noisy, music pounding and echoing into the kitchen. She wasn't sure if anyone would hear her if she screamed.

She stared at him, thinking quickly of what she could do. She said, Please let me out. I have work to do.

He stepped into the storeroom and closed the door behind him.

She tensed.

He said, Stupid whore.

She said calmly, What if I tell all the other girls that you can't have sex?

He looked confused. What?

What if I tell them that you cannot have an erection?

He said, What are you talking about?

If you do not leave me alone, I will tell everyone that you are impotent.

I will show you that I am not.

And that your penis is tiny.

He didn't know how to reply to this, and sputtered, I can crush you with my hand—

All the girls will laugh at you. What will you do? Show everyone your penis? You will leave me alone or you will be the biggest joke here.

He moved toward her, lumbering on his squeaking shoes, and Unha sidestepped him and backed away. She asked, Why can you not be nice? If you want to date a woman you have to be nice, not a stupid ox.

His face reddened. He said, I am going to kill you—

With your tiny limp penis? She laughed at him. She found that the more she taunted him, the more in control she felt. She said, You are pathetic. You are stupid security guard who has to try to scare women into sex. Did you ever have a girlfriend? Or do you always have to force women or pay women? Pathetic.

You bitch, he said in a low voice. He moved toward her, his arms spread out, his body crouched forward. She feinted left, then right, and he tracked her.

She yelled, Hyunma! Hyunma! Someone help me!

Shut up!

He lunged for her and she evaded him, but the floor was slippery, and she almost lost her balance. He then moved surprisingly fast as she stumbled, and he grabbed her arm, yanking her so hard that her vision blurred. She tried to kick him, but he threw her back into the shelves, the back of her head slamming into the wood and stunning her. He grabbed her arm and pulled her toward a table. She tried to free herself, but his grip was too strong. He clutched at her breast and twisted his grip, saying, You want to see my penis now?

She screamed in pain.

She saw a platter of silverware on the table. She felt his hand reaching underneath her skirt. She grabbed a fork, reared up and stabbed him in the neck.

He stiffened, his eyes widening. He let out a startled, Shit!

She left the fork in him. He backed away and touched his neck. Blood spurted from the wound. He grunted, checking the blood on his fingers with shock.

The door opened, and Hyunma stood there, taking this in. Choon wheezed, his bulky arms reaching up and trying to grab the fork, his body staggering back. He yanked it out and more blood bubbled out. He quickly pressed his hand over the wound, and yelled to Hyunma, I have to go to the hospital!

He tried to rape me! Unha yelled to Hyunma. I had to stop him!

152

Hyunma, who looked even tinier when she stood next to Choon, said to him, Go tell Lee to take you to the hospital.

I am going to kill her, he said.

Hyunma said, Go! Now!

Choon stomped out of the storeroom.

Unha said, He cornered me—

Come with me, Hyunma said. She turned abruptly and walked out into the kitchen. Unha followed. The cooks and a few of the waitresses stared. Hyunma pointed to a chair next to the back exit. Wait here.

For what? Unha asked.

You are finished here.

But he tried to—

Hyunma's tiny hand darted up and slapped Unha's cheek. Shut up, Hyunma said. You sit here and stay here until I tell you to move. Do you understand?

Unha sat down, stunned, her heart beating quickly. She touched her stinging cheek. She heard a commotion outside the kitchen, people yelling. Someone shouted, Call an ambulance! He passed out! Bring him outside!

He's too heavy!

He's bleeding!

Unha then realized what she had done. She placed her palms on her knees, trying to steady her hands, and heard Hyunma say, It was the new girl.

Hyunma pushed through the kitchen doors and approached. She said, Take off your uniform. You are done here.

I don't have a change of clothes, she said.

Hyunma didn't reply, but just stared at her.

Where will I go? Unha asked.

Do you know how many girls want this job? You made a very big mistake.

Where will I go?

Soon you will beg to have Choon fuck you.

153

Unha's voice caught in her throat. Where will I go?

Hyunma shook her head. Keep the uniform, she said. It does not matter.

Hyunma walked out of the kitchen.

Where will I go? Unha called to her.

Unha sat quietly, wondering if she should run away. Where could she go? What could she do? How could she live? She remained frozen in the chair, a dizzying cloud of thoughts confusing her. She couldn't decide what to do, and so did nothing. One of the cooks began frying noodles, the sizzling filling the kitchen.

After a half an hour, when the ambulance had gone, Hyunma reappeared in the kitchen with Lee and another man, someone Unha hadn't seen before. His face was weathered, the skin along his cheeks rough and pocked, his upper lip scarred. He said to Hyunma in a nasal voice, Yes. She is good.

He had on a long black leather coat. His hair was greased back and shiny. He said quietly to Unha, Come with me.

Where am I going?

He turned to Hyunma, who said to Unha, Another club.

What kind of club? Unha asked.

The man said to Hyunma, You were right. She will be trouble.

I told you.

Unha asked Lee, What is happening?

Lee shook his head. I am sorry, he said. Goodbye.

The pitying look in his eye frightened Unha, and she stood up. I don't want to go, she said.

Hyunma turned around and ordered the cooks out of the kitchen. They scurried out. Unha looked around frantically for help.

The man pulled out a small roll of duct tape. He said,

154

Just calm down.

She tried to make a run for it, heading for the back exit, but Lee grabbed her arm, and then Hyunma held her shoulders. She struggled as the man moved up behind her and pressed a strip of tape over her mouth. She tried to twist her head away, but the man gripped her head tightly. She tried to kick him from behind but he swung his arm around her neck while Lee grabbed her wrists and twisted them behind her back. Hyunma took the tape and wrapped her wrists. She thrashed and the man said, Her ankles.

As Hyunma reached down Unha kicked her in the temple, and Hyunma cried out in pain. The man behind her cursed and threw her to the floor. Unha hit her head, dazed, while Lee quickly taped up her ankles.

They stood up. She was dizzy, her vision blurring. Hyunma rubbed her temple and said, Take her out back.

She looked down at Unha. I knew you were trouble as soon as I saw you, she said, and she kicked her in the chest, the point of her shoe stabbing into her. Unha moaned into the tape; she tried to roll away, but Hyunma stepped on her hip.

Stop, the man said. Do not damage the merchandise.

Lee and the man picked her up. Lee said quietly, Do not fight. You will only make it worse for yourself.

Unha breathed heavily through her nose.

The man said, I need something to cover her eyes.

He stared down at her with a calm, cool expression that terrified her.

PART IV

DREAMS OF THE OCEAN

18

Sam drove to his brother's club instead of going home and found Jake working in the back office. Jake looked him up and down and said, What happened to you?

Sam then noticed the tear in his pants, the dirt and mud streaks, and said, Nothing.

You are filthy. Wash up, will you? Don't track mud in here.

Sam nodded and went to the bathroom. He thought, I just buried someone.

The bathroom renovations were almost finished, new blue tiles still dull with grout oozing from the edges, bright overhead lights that hurt his eyes, and Sam studied his face in the polished mirrors, his reflection so detailed that he noticed for the first time wrinkles in the corner of his left eye. Why just the left eye? He wondered if he squinted with just this eye. As he washed up, and cleaned his pants with a damp paper towel, he found that his hands were still shaking. He stopped. He took a deep breath. Minji was dead. He couldn't believe it was that easy to make someone disappear.

He walked back through the main dining area and stopped at the booths. Instead of helping his brother he had been burying a girl who was murdered. What was wrong with him? He bent down and saw that the edges of the backboard should be sanded down before the upholstery was added because the burrs could tear the fabric.

Jake appeared from the back office and said, I am going to have to delay the opening.

Because of this? Sam asked.

This and other things, Jake said. It happens.

Sam rolled up his sleeves. I can work on this now. You can help.

Jake said, It's late. Shouldn't you get home to your family?

Sam repeated, My family. He focused on the booths and searched for sandpaper. He said, You can sand down the backboard edges. I can reattach the base. Where are the tools?

Jake took off his sports coat and rolled up his sleeves.

They worked quietly for a while, and Sam realized how much he missed the calming effect of carpentry. He could think about other things or he could focus on the task, but either way, when he worked with his hands he fell into a familiar, soothed mindset. He remembered when he used to make small projects when he was apprenticing in Seoul, small chairs, bureaus, even a large joinery picture frame. He would work on these by himself and on construction jobs with his employer. Both were satisfying in their own way. He liked seeing a house being built from the foundation up. His nails in the framing helped keep it standing. The smaller projects were more detailed and difficult, and he liked giving them away as gifts. He had made Sunny a jewelry box with a tiger maple top, but he donated it to Goodwill after she died.

He asked his brother, Do you still have that rocking chair I made?

Jake said, It's at my house. In the living room. Don't you remember?

Right. I forgot.

Why don't you do that anymore?

Sam said, I haven't made anything since Sunny got sick.

I know, Jake said. Why not get back into it?

Sam shrugged his shoulders. He didn't know what to tell his brother. He didn't feel like doing anything, especially making furniture. What was the point?

Jake said, I heard from Mom.

Sam stopped pulling out a nail. How are they?

Good. They want us to come out there. They want to see David.

Sam said, Maybe.

They still can't believe they haven't met their grandson yet.

Sam continued pulling out nails. He thought, Why can't everyone leave me alone?

What's it like working with Im? Jake asked.

Sam said, He's a little crazy.

You haven't had to do anything illegal, have you?

No, Sam said quickly. To change the subject he asked, Why can't you tell me how you work with Mr. Oh?

Jake was quiet for a moment. He stopped sanding the backboard and said, He is a silent partner for this club. He supplies all my alcohol. It's a business relationship.

That's why he told me and Im to come here.

Yes.

Do you know he has a brothel and other illegal—

I don't know and I don't want to know.

Sam laughed to himself. He said, A turtle who pulls his head into his shell has to come out eventually.

Jake said, I don't know where you get those dumb sayings. Then he put the sandpaper down. He said, I'm not the one who has been hiding out the past year.

What do you mean?

You are the one who has been in a shell.

Sam said, I am doing the best I can.

No, you are not. It looks like you have given up.

I did not come here for a lecture, Sam said, his voice hardening. Do you want help with this or not?

Go home to your family, Jake said. You can work on this tomorrow.

Sam stood up. His knees cracked. Why do you do that? he asked.

Do what?

Keep pushing me. Keep telling me what I do wrong. Keep telling me what to do.

Jake stood up. You're the one who accused me of being in a shell.

You know that Mr. Oh prostitutes young girls. He has sweat shops and uses violence on everyone. He is a gangster, and you are partners with him?

You work for him.

I had no choice! Sam exploded.

You could've chosen not to borrow money from him. I told you—

Fuck you, Sam said. I am going home. He walked toward the front entrance.

Jake said, I'll tell Mr. Oh you don't have to come back. You can do whatever you do with Im. Good luck.

Sam stopped, but then continued out the door. He wanted to work on the booths, but now couldn't tell his brother that. He headed toward his car, wondering which bar might be open.

David woke up when his father returned home at dawn, and crashed into the television set, knocking it off its stand. The glass cracked with a concussive pop. Yunjin ran out of the bedroom and yelled that he had ruined the TV, and he was nothing but a drunken fool. David's father was unusually quiet. David climbed out of bed and watched them from the hallway. A wispy cloud of dust sprinkled around the TV. His father stood swaying and staring down at it.

Yunjin said, I am so sick of you.

He smiled, and said, Has anyone ever told you how ugly you are?

Yunjin sucked in air. She said, You are mean and small. I hate you.

He nodded thoughtfully. I should never have brought you over here.

Yunjin said, When it's time and I get my green card, I will divorce you.

He said, Good.

I feel sorry for you and your son.

Leave me alone, he said. He walked around the broken TV and sat on the sofa heavily. Yunjin saw David in the hallway. She couldn't meet his gaze. She walked by him without saying anything, and David stared at his father, who leaned his head back and groaned.

Yunjin closed her door quietly, and David continued to stand there, wondering if he should go back to bed. The sun was rising outside. He heard Yunjin crying. He decided to get dressed and go out. It was a new day and he had plenty of exploring to do.

19

The rhythmic thumps of the car driving fast on a freeway were the only sounds Unha could recognize. The blindfold was so tight around her head and eyes that her scalp throbbed, and she felt the knot digging into the back of her head. Her arms, still tied behind her back, had fallen asleep. The tape around her mouth was loosening with her saliva, but she still breathed heavily through her nose. She had to go to the bathroom.

She was lying on her side in the back seat. The man driving the car hadn't spoken. She tried not to think about where she was going. But she knew. How could she not? He had said, Do not damage the merchandise. She had heard him clearly.

She would have to escape. She wasn't sure how or where or when, but she would not become a prisoner. She knew that Sam would help her. But she didn't know how to contact him. She realized she didn't even know his last name.

The man's cell phone rang, and he answered it with a

curt hello.

He was quiet, then said, One hour. No. Just a little. All right. One hour.

After a while he asked, Are you okay?

She was not sure if he was on the phone.

He repeated, You, in the back. Are you okay?

She grunted through the tape.

He said, Wait.

She heard him lean in his seat. The car swerved a little, and he cursed. Then, after a moment, she felt his hand grope her face, and then his fingers found the edges of the duct tape. He tore it off, and she winced in pain.

He said, Are you okay?

Drool spilled down her chin. She cleared her throat and said, My arms are numb.

Roll onto your stomach.

She tried to, but she was too curled up. She couldn't move her legs out of the way. She said, I can't move.

He sighed. He asked, If I untie your arms will you do something stupid?

No, she said.

I will not take off your blindfold. You must not take it off yourself.

All right, she said.

She felt the car slowing and then turning. She heard gravel pinging the car, the rushing of other cars around them louder now. Her heart beat faster when she heard him unbuckling his seat belt and climbing toward her. She felt him reaching over her and tugging at the tape around her wrists. He said, Too tight. I need a knife.

He climbed back to the front. He rustled something, and then climbed back toward her. He said, Do not move.

She remained still as he sawed away at the tape, and she felt her limbs loosening. When he cut through the tape her arms were so numb that she couldn't move them.

He asked, Better?

I cannot feel anything.

They fell asleep, he said, and pulled her up, yanking her feet out and pushing her into an upright position.

Then, slowly, the stinging began to creep into her arms, and she groaned in pain. The skin felt as if it were being peeled off. She said, It hurts.

I will leave your hands free, but you better not do anything. Do not take off the blindfold.

Why?

We do not want you to know where you are.

Why?

No more questions. Do not move from that position. I can see you in the rear-view mirror. Do you understand?

I understand, she said, wiping her face of the saliva.

He returned to his seat and started the engine. As they accelerated and pulled back onto the freeway, Unha opened and closed her fists, trying to get the circulation going. The pain in her arms was excruciating, but she continued flexing her muscles; she needed her arms to be functional before trying to escape.

He asked, What is your name?

Unha, she said.

How long have you been in the U.S.?

A month. Where am I going?

He said, To a new job.

What kind of job?

He didn't reply.

Sitting up in the car felt more solid, more secure. Her ankles were still taped together, but there was more leeway now, the tape stretching. She slowly pushed her ankles farther apart, up and down, working the tape.

She asked, Can I use a bathroom?

No, he said.

I do not know if I can wait much longer.

No.

She said, Then I will stain the seats.

He sighed and said, If I see a place I will pull over.

The feeling in her arms had returned. She knew he would have to cut the tape around her ankles to let her walk to a bathroom, so she stopped loosening it. She didn't hear as many other cars around them, and she wondered if they had turned off an exit.

After a while she felt the car coming to a stop. The man said, I will free your legs, but I will leave your blindfold on.

How will I see?

I will tell you where to go.

She didn't argue. She heard him climb out, open the passenger door, and lean over her. He cut her ankles free, and grabbed her arm. Come out, he said.

She pulled herself painfully from the car, her legs wobbly. Immediately she felt brush and small bushes around her legs. A jolt of fear passed through her, suddenly afraid that he was going to kill her and leave her body in the woods. She listened for other cars, but the sounds of a freeway seemed far off.

She prepared herself to run. Her back broke out into a sweat. The man tightened his grip around her arm and said, Do it here.

Where?

Right here.

With you here?

I am not leaving you alone.

The pain in her bladder was too much. She lifted up her skirt and pulled down her underwear, then squatted. She felt leaves brush against her skin. As she relieved herself, the man loosened his grip and stepped back. When she finished, she said, Can I wipe myself?

He replied, I don't have anything.

She pulled up her underwear. The man said, Wait. She paused.

He said, Move here.

He pulled her a few feet away. She stumbled.

Lie down, he said.

What?

Lie down, he said, and tried to push her onto her back.

What are you doing? she asked, her voice rising.

Get down there. He forced her off her feet, her body landing on dirt and grass, and he let go of her arm. She heard him unbuckling his belt.

She pulled off her blindfold and was startled to find it dark. Trees to the left. Thick brush to the right. He towered over her, but stopped unzipping himself. She jumped up.

He said, Hey!

She saw him quickly fixing his pants, but she turned and ran toward the brush.

20

Sam drove to Club Saja, barely able to see straight from his hangover; his vision pulsed in sync with his heartbeat. He shivered, his skin covered in goose bumps. He wanted to throw up again, but tightened his gut and swallowed the bile back down. He didn't even remember how he had gotten home last night, but he had apparently driven, since his car was parked crookedly on the street.

At the club he searched for Unha, but she wasn't there. He asked one of the waitresses if she would be coming later, but the waitress said she didn't know. He went upstairs and found Im drinking coffee in one of the booths. He asked what they were doing today.

Your brother doesn't need us, so we have another job.

What is it?

Im sipped his coffee, then said, You are going to give a man one more chance to pay Mr. Oh back.

How much does he owe?

Im said, Fifteen thousand.

Less than I owe, Sam thought. He asked, What if he does not have it?

Im grinned. He said, Then you will kill him.

What?

Im stood up. Let's go.

What?

But Im walked past him and down the stairs.

Sam rubbed his forehead, the nausea building. He took a few deep breaths and followed Im. On the main dining floor Sam saw Choon talking to Hyunma. Choon had a large white bandage criss-crossing the side of his neck. Sam stopped.

Choon said, What are you staring at?

Your neck.

What about it?

What happened?

None of your fucking business, Choon replied, and turned back to Hyunma.

Im called to Sam, Let's go.

Sam rode with Im through the Caldecott Tunnel, heading toward Walnut Creek. They hadn't spoken much since leaving the city. Sam was furiously thinking of ways to get out of this job. No longer was he simply in Mr. Oh's debt—he knew too much of the business. He could be a liability if he left them.

Had Jake known about this? How much did his brother really know about Oh's businesses?

They emerged from the tunnel, and Im said, Give him a chance to point to another person for the money. A family member or a friend.

Why does he owe? What was the money for?

Gambling debt.

Sam stared at the shiny malls in the distance. He said, I do not know if I can kill anyone.

170

Im said, Koman spoke to Mr. Oh. If you have to do it, half your debt will be erased.

Half, Sam said.

Half. What is that? Over ten thousand.

But I don't know.

You buried the girl with me. What's the difference?

I didn't kill the girl.

You helped cover it up.

Sam inhaled slowly, trying to calm his stomach. Im drove erratically, cutting in and out of the lanes, and this was making Sam more nauseous.

Did you see Choon's neck? Im laughed.

What happened?

They had some trouble last night.

What kind of trouble?

A waitress did that to him, Im said. Choon is a shithead, letting some girl stab him with... with a fork! Im laughed loudly.

Sam kept still. Which waitress?

I don't know.

Was it the new one?

I don't know. Choon probably deserved it. I wish I could've seen it.

But what did he—

Never mind that, Im said. Focus on this job. Remember to make sure we can't get the money from someone else.

How will we know?

Jung is weak, Im said. We will know.

Mr. Oh wants him dead over fifteen thousand?

Im said, Jung is a loud mouth. He talks too much and Mr. Oh wants to make an example of him.

Sam thought again of his own debt and kept quiet.

The sun was glaringly bright in Walnut Creek, reflecting off the sleek building complexes lining the streets. Large shopping centers and mirrored office towers crowded the skyline. Sam found it claustrophobic. He thought about Muir Woods and then about Unha. He worried that she was the one who had gotten in trouble. He focused on the job and tried to steel himself for what was to come. He hoped he wouldn't have to do anything, that Jung would have the money.

Im headed into a neighborhood with winding streets and large, almost identical homes with crisp green lawns. Sam asked, Jung lives here?

Nice, isn't it? This stupid fuck pretends he is rich.

Im peered out at the houses, checking the addresses, and then said, There it is.

Sam saw the pastel orange and white house with overgrown shrubs and weeds sprouting up in the sidewalk cracks. Im parked in front and looked up and down the street. He said to Sam, Go get him. Tell him we want to talk while driving.

Sam climbed out and walked to the front door. He rang the doorbell. After a moment a young girl appeared. Sam, surprised, asked in Korean, Shouldn't you be in school?

I'm on vacation, she said in English.

Is your father home?

She left the door open and walked back through the house, calling out, Dad!

Sam peered in, seeing overstuffed white sofas and a wide-screen TV.

Jung waddled in wearing a blue and white sweat suit. Balding and overweight, he peered at Sam suspiciously and said, What do you want?

Sam pointed to the car. Im wants to talk to you.

Jung's face paled. He stepped forward and lowered his voice, You came to my house?

Come, Sam said. Time to talk.

Wait, let me just—

Sam grabbed his fleshy arm and pulled him out the

172

door. Now, he said.

Jung was barefoot, and walked stiffly across the pavement. He exaggerated the pain of walking without shoes, leaping up and saying, The sidewalk is hot.

Im motioned to Sam to put Jung in the front seat. Sam opened the door for Jung, who climbed in and said to Im, I was going to call you.

Yes, of course, Im said.

Sam shoved Jung's seat forward to get into the back seat, and Im drove off.

Wait, Jung said. Where are we going?

Just driving, Im said. It might look strange for us to talk in front of your house.

My daughter is home alone, Jung said. I cannot stay out long.

Im said, Where is the money?

I am working on a deal that will—

You are a liar, Im said. People saw you at the card club a few nights ago. You are borrowing more money from someone else and losing it. This will stop.

Jung was quiet. He said to Im, I can get the money—

You have had more than enough chances, Im said. Mr. Oh feels that you are not taking him seriously.

I am! I am! His voice rose into a whine.

Sam saw that Im was waiting for him to chime in. Sam grabbed the seatbelt strap next to Jung, pulled out some slack, then looped it around Jung's neck and yanked hard, choking him. Sam asked, Do you have any friends or relatives we can get the money from?

Jung gasped, and clawed at the seat belt.

Sam tightened his grip, pushing his knee against the back of the seat in order to get more leverage. Im smiled.

Jung choked and cried out, I already borrowed money… Please…

Im sighed. He said, We heard about you boasting at

the club, telling people that you're not afraid of Mr. Oh. That was very stupid, Jung. Very stupid.

I was drunk! I was...

Jung gagged and tried to suck in air. The smell of his sweat became stronger, more sour, and Sam realized he was smelling fear.

Im said to Sam, Let him talk.

Sam loosened his grip.

Jung said, I can get the money by next week.

Im shook his head. You keep saying that. Tell us who your relatives are, and we will ask them for the money.

I can't, Jung said. And they don't have any more. I borrowed everything I could.

Im nodded his head slowly. He continued driving, but headed for the freeway. He glanced at Sam, and said to Jung, Then that is very bad news for you.

What do you mean?

When neither Im nor Sam answered him, Jung lurched forward, grabbing the door handle, but Sam tightened the belt around his neck, choking him. Jung gasped, Wait please! I have a family!

Yes, Im said. You should've thought of them when you were gambling away Mr. Oh's money.

Jung sobbed, I have a daughter, a young daughter.

Im continued driving.

21

David went to the tae kwon do school without Yunjin, and even though Mr. Kim wasn't there, he told the instructor, a tall pale white man named Roger, that he was going to do their work-study program. Roger said there weren't any beginner classes this morning, but he could watch and help clean the floors after the class. Roger said, You're the first work-study we've had in a while. You must have made an impression on Sungsengnim Kim.

David was surprised to hear him use the Korean form of "teacher." He saw David's expression and said in Korean, Yes, I speak a little Korean. Do you?

David replied in English, Not really.

Well, he said in English, have a seat over there. This is the advanced class coming in now.

David settled into a cushioned chair and watched the class file in, some already swinging their arms and stretching their legs as they lined up. Most of the students were young white and black men, though he did see a couple of women in the back. There were two teens, but everyone else seemed to be older, all brown or black belts. Roger stood in the front of the room and told them to get in formation.

As the practice began with waist and leg stretches in unison, David saw the difference between the other practices and this one—all the motions here, even the stretches, were smoother, and their uniforms snapped loudly and crisply with every movement. When they began kicking and punching, the hall echoed with their yells, and even their bare feet on the floors shuffled softly as one.

David kept wanting to stand up and try the kicks they were doing, but didn't want to attract any attention.

Mr. Kim arrived as the practice was finishing and he saw David on the bench. He asked him if his mother was here and David said no. Mr. Kim said, The beginner lesson isn't until this afternoon. Didn't you see the schedule?

I came to help clean, David said.

Mr. Kim studied him. If you're here to clean, then why are you sitting on the bench?

David jumped up. He realized he had forgotten to bow, so he did.

Mr. Kim said, First, no street clothes in here. Let's find you a uniform.

I can't buy one, David said.

Who said anything about buying? Mr. Kim asked. You will earn everything. Come. Follow me.

While David was trying on children-sized tae kwon do uniforms, Yunjin was at home counting how much cash she had hidden away over the past few months. She had managed to save almost two hundred dollars, the bulk of that her own money she had brought from Korea, but knew it was nothing if she were to be left alone. She needed a job. She had to prepare for a life without Sam, and she knew where to begin: Jake.

She thought about Mr. Kim, who was handsome and kind and, when compared to Sam, was beyond ideal. David's next lesson was this afternoon. Suddenly she wondered if David had already left for Berkeley without her. She stood up, alarmed. She wasn't sure how to get there on her own. Maybe he had done that on purpose, not wanting her with him.

Her hands began sweating at the thought of navigating the subway by herself. But she had to go to the dojang because she had to see Mr. Kim. She checked the time. She would give David another hour or so to come home. She knew he wouldn't miss his free lesson, so if he didn't show up, then she would know he had gone without her.

She hid her money in the envelope with her immigration papers and stuffed these in the back of her bureau. Then she realized she needed a few dollars for the BART ticket and took the money back out and grabbed a ten-dollar bill. She hesitated. Did she want to use this up for something as frivolous as seeing a man?

Yes, she did.

She hid the envelope and called Jake's cell phone, but she got his voice message. She said, I need to talk to you about getting a job. I will call you again later.

She hung up.

Now she had to wait for David. She took out a pen and began trying to remember the way to the subway station and the Berkeley stop. Yunjin closed her eyes and tried to envision the streets, worried about getting lost.

Unha was in fact lost, fighting the exhaustion, the utter cold, and shivering from the night of running and hiding in this wooded expanse. She might have been running in circles, and was grateful for the morning sun beginning to light up the sky. She thought she heard a freeway, but she wasn't sure. She had cuts all over her face and arms from the whipping branches; her clothes were torn. Her tight shoes had deadened her chafed, blistered toes.

The man was nearby. She heard him cursing quietly to himself, searching for her. When she had first run, all she could hear was her own panicked breathing, her head pounding, the sound of branches snapping by her ears, and she had stumbled and crashed through shrubs and down a ravine in total darkness. Slowly her eyes had adjusted. She had clawed her way up the ravine and took off again with the light of the moon guiding her.

She didn't hear the man for a while, but then saw his flashlight. This sent her off again, and for the past couple of hours she kept running and hiding, then taking off when she saw his light. She thought she could outlast him. She thought she would eventually run across a road, a car, anything, but she kept stumbling through more brush.

Now, as the sky turned orange and purple, she got a better view of the woods. Steep brown hills with pockets of trees spread as far as she could see. Thick, thorny bushes surrounded her. She was in a shallow valley, and needed to get to higher ground. Then she would know where to run.

She smelled something metallic, then wiped her nose. Blood. Her nose was bleeding. When had this happened? She tilted her head back and squeezed her nose.

Then she heard him approaching. She froze. He was not going to give up. She heard him crashing through bushes and cursing. She held her breath. Her nose continued to drip. Her heart was beating so loudly she had trouble hearing anything else. She tried to calm herself, tried to think clearly, but all she could do was tell herself not to breathe so loudly.

The man climbed out of the ravine and then stopped. He was only a dozen feet away. He became quiet, and she knew he was listening for her. Her lungs burned, her eyes watered, but she slowly inhaled and held her breath.

The man stepped forward, crunching dead leaves.

She curled up in a ball, her cheek pressing against her knee. The man walked slowly down into a clearing, his steps fading. Should she stay here or should she try to run? She had to get up to the hill and find out where she was, then she could run.

She slowly exhaled, and the pulsing in her head dizzied her. She worried the man would circle back. She waited another few seconds, listening. Then, slowly, she unfurled herself and started to rise. A branch beneath her cracked.

There you are, the man said, jumping out from behind thick bushes. He had tricked her, pretending to walk away.

She let out a startled yell and ran. She twisted her ankle on a rock, and almost fell, but recovered and lunged away. The man came after her, only a few yards away, and now that it was light she couldn't hide. She tried to cut through prickly bushes, and the thorns tore her shirt and scratched her arms. She glanced back and saw the man hesitating, then pushing through. She wheezed, her lungs hurting, and blood sprayed from her nose.

She tripped again, and the man leapt forward, coming up to her. He grabbed her arm, and she screamed. She kicked his leg, twisting in his grip, but he was too strong. He reached down and slapped her hard.

Stunned, she stopped kicking. Then he grabbed her throat and she struggled, gasping for her breath. He said, Stupid bitch.

He grabbed her hair and twisted, saying, I should fuck you right here.

His arm brushed her mouth and she bared her teeth and bit him, clamping her jaw so tightly that a muscle in her neck twinged with pain. He yelled and hit her head with his other fist and let go of her throat. She kept her teeth in his arm and jerked back, tearing the flesh. He grunted and pulled

179

at her lips, trying to free himself. He yelled, Stop! He slammed his fist into her forehead, but she didn't let go.

He tried to push into her, forcing her down, and she kicked his knee. He cursed, and as he stumbled he pulled his arm free, leaving a piece of his skin in her teeth. She spit it out and tried to roll away, but he jumped on top of her and slammed her head into the dirt. She tried to claw his face, but he was too heavy and too strong, forcing her arms back. He was breathing hard, and said in her ear, You will pay for that.

He forced his bloody forearm into her throat and pushed hard, choking her. She kicked and thrashed, but he only leaned more of his weight into her throat. She felt her eyes bulging, veins in her temples pounding. She stopped kicking, and he said, I will kill you if I have to.

She lay still.

He said, Are you going to be good?

She tried to nod her head, but couldn't. He released some of the pressure off her neck. She sucked in air.

He slowly climbed off her, and examined his bloody arm. She saw that his face was scratched up, his clothes also torn. He looked down at himself and said, Fuck. He moved toward her and punched her in the head, and she blacked out.

22

Jake met with Mr. Oh at a hotel bar in the Embarcadero. Mr. Oh was about to fly to Seoul on a business trip, and had only a few minutes to speak with Jake before his driver took him to the airport. When Jake entered the lobby of the Golden View, a small luxury hotel with dark green plush sofas, shiny mahogany furniture and brass lamps, he saw Mr. Oh with a young woman at a small table. The woman was typing on a lap top. They both noticed Jake, and Mr. Oh stood up, telling the woman to keep working. He walked to Jake, and they bowed and shook hands.

Mr. Oh's expression was distracted, and he kept glancing back at the woman. He explained, My new assistant. She is checking some brokerage trades before I leave.

Jake followed Mr. Oh into the bar, and they sat down. Jake said, Thank you for meeting me.

I assume this is about the Seoul Silver.

It is. I have to delay the opening.

For how long?

Three weeks.

What about all the publicity?

I know, Jake said. It is unfortunate.

Mr. Oh frowned, the skin around his mouth wrinkling. He said, I understand delays are sometimes unavoidable, but this could set a bad tone.

Bad tone?

Delays trigger more delays.

No, Jake said. The club will be ready in three weeks.

Mr. Oh leaned back. He said, I would like you to take care of another cash package.

Jake stiffened. I thought I was done with that.

Given the delay in the club, I think this is appropriate. And you can use the cash to pay the labor.

Jake was quiet. He had already laundered over one hundred thousand of Mr. Oh's cash, and had stomach problems from the stress. He said, How much?

Fifty.

Jake felt his insides tightening. He said, That's much more than I've ever—

Once the club is up and running, we'll work out a more regular, smaller amount.

Jake thought, This is punishment. He said, You have it here?

No. I will send Koman with it.

The usual arrangement?

Of course, Mr. Oh said. He looked up. The woman was standing at the bar entrance. He said, I have to take care of this. Expect a call from Koman.

Jake stood up with Mr. Oh, and they bowed. He watched Mr. Oh hurry to the woman and say, Are the orders complete? The woman escorted Mr. Oh back to the lobby table. Jake sat back down and rubbed his stomach. His cell phone rang. He checked the screen—it was Sam's home phone, and Jake suspected it was Yunjin. He turned it off.

•

Jake first met Mr. Oh when he was opening the Shilla, and two men appeared one night asking for the owner. Jake knew who they were before they introduced themselves. Other restaurant owners had warned him about Mr. Oh. When the men said they wanted to supply Jake all his alcohol and food, Jake said that would be fine, and he wanted to talk about help with his labor and his expansion plans. The men, unused to such compliance, were taken aback. They groped for a response, and Jake said, If you are not empowered to help me, then perhaps you can introduce me to someone who can.

With this, Jake met Koman, and began a tentative working relationship that grew when Jake tipped Mr. Oh off on a land development in downtown Oakland. Both Mr. Oh and Jake bought up the nearby vacant warehouses, and when the lofts and condominiums were built, the commercial land jumped fifty percent in value.

Then Koman asked Jake to use his restaurant to help launder twenty thousand in cash. It was very simple: Jake began registering more cash payments at the restaurant, and then would pay Mr. Oh's distributors higher fees. Jake would offset the increased income with the increased expenses, so he didn't lose anything, and Mr. Oh would have a legitimate, taxable source for his money. Soon after, there was another twenty thousand. It required months of funneling the money into the restaurant while being overcharged for the liquor and supplies, but eventually the accounting worked out.

But Jake wasn't paid a cut, and he always worried about the IRS noticing the steady increase in cash transactions. It was true that his work for Mr. Oh resulted in his partnership in the Seoul Silver, which of course would continue the laundering, but now Jake had collateral for a larger loan for more restaurants and businesses outside of Mr. Oh's reach.

He was learning from Mr. Oh, who was patient and

methodical. It could take months, even years to clean so much cash, but Mr. Oh was in no hurry. Jake wondered how many other restaurants and nail salons and groceries Mr. Oh used for similar purposes.

Jake didn't want to know where all the cash was coming from, but already suspected what Sam had told him—the massage parlors, the illegal workers, the prostitution. All these were rumors that Jake had heard about for years.

Well, it was too late now. Jake was enmeshed in Mr. Oh's businesses, and the influx of fifty grand meant more double accounting, more work for Jake. But he had to be patient and methodical like Mr. Oh. He had to continue working for Mr. Oh, and slowly build his own businesses, and then, once he had his own empire, he could untangle himself from Mr. Oh's. And Jake was young. Mr. Oh was old. Mr. Oh would not live that much longer. Jake had time as his ally.

This comforted him as he drove back to the Seoul Silver. He tried not to think about how he was probably as indebted to Mr. Oh as his brother was. He told himself that he was in control whereas Sam was not.

Sam didn't want to ask in front of Jung where Im was driving, so he kept the seat belt tight around Jung's throat while they headed somewhere outside of Orinda, a smaller town west of Walnut Creek. They continued through a regional park and down a long, winding road through a residential neighborhood and onto a dirt road. Im seemed to know where he was going, and soon Sam saw how isolated this area was.

Im was quiet. Jung cried, pleaded a few more times, then began asking where they were going. Im told him to shut up. Sam didn't think he could kill him. He began thinking of ways to get out of this. Then he wondered if this was some kind of test, and what would happen if he failed.

Jung said, I made a mistake. I'm sorry. Please.

Im continued driving on the dirt road, the pebbles crunching under the tires. He looked around and then slowed. He said to Sam, You see anyone around?

Sam said he didn't. All he saw were trees and hills covered with dry, brown brush.

Im stopped the car. A cloud of dust billowed past them. He said to Sam, Bring him out.

Jung breathed quickly. He said, Wait. Wait.

Sam pushed Jung's seat forward, making him grunt. Climbing out of the car, Sam felt the heat hit his face. He pulled Jung out, and Jung yelped when his bare feet landed in prickly weeds.

Im walked around the car and pulled out his gun from his shoulder holster.

Jung whimpered, shook his head back and forth, and said, I'll do anything. Anything you ask.

Im checked the chamber of his gun, then gripped the muzzle and held out the gun to Sam.

Jung said, Oh my God.

Sam stared at the gun. He took it, and was surprised to find it so heavy.

Im forced Jung onto his knees. Jung said, My daughter. No one can take care of her.

Sam said, What about your wife?

My wife left me.

Sam asked him, She left your daughter, too?

Yes. She said she could not live with me, and I would not let her take my daughter.

Sam asked, Who is watching her right now?

No one! he cried. I have been trying to tell you! She is alone at home!

Im smacked him in the face and said, Shut up.

Sam watched Jung crumple to the ground, crying. He curled up, covering his face, and kept saying, She'll be all alone.

Im nodded to Sam. He said, Do it.

Sam looked down at Jung.

Im waited.

After a moment Jung raised his head, staring at the gun, and then shook his head slowly at Sam. Please, he whispered. Please don't.

Sam asked Im, What about the police?

Im said, He will just disappear. None of his friends would dare talk to the police.

Sam aimed the gun at Jung's forehead. Jung kept his eyes open, and said again, Please.

Sam turned to Im and said, I can't.

Im said, Yes, you can, and you will.

Sam lowered the gun and shook his head. I am sorry.

I am telling you that you have to, Im said.

Sam held the gun to Im and said, No.

Thank you, Jung said. Thank you very much.

Sam kicked him in the stomach and said, Not for you, for your daughter. You are pathetic.

You are making a mistake, Im said, and took the gun. He crouched down and pressed the muzzle against Jung's temple. He said, Do you think we are joking with you?

No! No! I can get you the money! I can sell my car! I can sell my plasma TV!

We have given you too many chances. And you continue to gamble—

I will stop! I will!

Im said quietly, You are so pathetic. He turned to Sam. What do you think?

He replied, What kind of car does he have?

Jung said, Acura Integra. I can get more than ten thousand for it.

Im said, Why didn't you sell it before?

I need to drive.

Im said to Sam, I think Mr. Oh was more concerned

by this fuckhead's bragging and loud talking, acting like he isn't afraid of Mr. Oh. It is bad for business.

I was drunk! I was stupid!

Sam said, How about you hurt him very badly so he and everyone will know?

Im said, You do it.

Me?

Im said to Jung, On Friday you will come to Club Saja with all the money you owe. If not, I will visit you alone, without my softhearted colleague here. If I hear you've been to the card clubs, to any bar or any place where you are spending money…

You won't.

Im said to Sam, You better make it good.

Im holstered his gun and walked to the car. He climbed in, turned on the engine, and waited.

Sam focused on Jung. He took a deep breath and kicked him in the face hard, shattering his nose. Jung screamed in pain. Sam kicked him a few more times, making sure he broke the skin and Jung bled. Then he reached down and grabbed Jung's arm, twisting it back and up. He yanked it against the shoulder socket and felt it break. Jung screamed again. Sam dropped his arm and it lay twisted at an awkward angle, Jung writhing and crying. Sam gave him another kick in the face, which knocked out a tooth. He then walked back to the car, checking his shoes for blood.

When he climbed in he said, I think everyone will know he was taught a lesson.

Im said, This was a test. And you failed.

Im shifted into gear and slammed his foot on the accelerator, the wheels spinning in the dirt. They jolted forward and sped off.

23

At Kim's Martial Arts David swept the floor after the advanced class finished, using a long, heavy, push broom that had fine brown bristles and black tape crisscrossing the handle. He piled the dust, dirt and bits of paper and fabric into long lines by the wall, then used the small hand broom and dustpan to collect this. He was wearing his new uniform that fit almost perfectly, and he kept looking at himself in the large mirrors, amazed that Mr. Kim had given this to him. He wanted to wear it all the time.

Mr. Kim checked on him while he was sweeping, and he studied him for a moment, then headed for his back office where David heard him talking to Roger about leading the kickboxing class at noon. Then David saw Yunjin standing outside the front window, peering in. She shaded her eyes and leaned against the glass. He was annoyed that she had followed him here. This was his place, not hers. But she saw him, pointed to his uniform, and hurried to the front entrance. There was something childlike in her enthusiasm that David, as a child, recognized and found odd. He wanted to tell her to leave, but couldn't. She walked in and said, You have a new uniform!

They gave it to me for work-study, he said. How did you get here?

Subway, but I almost got lost. I remember to take the red line.

Richmond line, David said. Yes.

I like your uniform, she said, her gaze moving away.

David knew she wanted to see Mr. Kim, so he said, He's in back.

Who?

Mr. Kim.

She turned a shade darker, and looked toward the doorway.

Then, as if they had summoned him, Mr. Kim appeared. He saw Yunjin, and approached. They bowed and greeted each other, and Yunjin thanked him in Korean for letting David come here. As they talked David drifted away with the broom, hearing Yunjin ask him polite questions about how long he had had this studio.

David saw Roger carrying a bag of shin pads, and he motioned for David to bring in more from the back room. He did this, and Roger explained that this was for the kick-boxing class. He told David to bring in the gloves, masks and torso padding. When they piled everything in, he told David that he could watch, and once it was over he should return everything to the back room. He said, Then, after that, I'll be teaching the beginner class. You ready for it?

I'm ready, David said.

He mussed David's hair and gave him a playful kick in the rear.

By the time the beginner class was finished, David had soaked his uniform with sweat, and he was exhausted. Mr.

Kim and Yunjin had been talking the entire time. Even Roger noticed them, glancing in their direction a few times during the lesson, and David couldn't imagine what they were talking about.

David became distracted a few times, and Roger barked at him to stay awake. The other kids laughed and David was angry at Yunjin for being there.

He changed into his clothes and balled up his uniform, which was now damp and cold. Roger told him that he could go home then; he had worked hard that day. Roger said, Tomorrow I'll start teaching you the first white belt form, Chon-hi Hyung. Okay?

What time should I come?

Early afternoon. Air that out, he said, pointing to David's uniform. Or else it'll smell.

Okay.

He bowed, and David quickly returned the gesture.

Yunjin saw him waiting by the door, so she said something to Mr. Kim, who nodded. They bowed and he disappeared into the back office. Yunjin asked David if he was ready to go.

As soon as they left the studio David asked her what she was talking to Mr. Kim about.

Many things, she said.

Like what?

He knows Chuncheon and the area I grew up. His father was a soldier and he also live near U.S. Army bases.

David was jealous that she was getting to know him so well, and he said, I want to come here by myself.

Why?

This is my…job now, he said. I don't want you here.

She was quiet. He couldn't look at her because he knew he had hurt her feelings. After walking for a block she said, I don't have anything else.

He turned to her. Her eyes were watery. She said,

190

David, you are my only friend.

This stopped him.

She shook her head. I like this. Please let me come with you.

He was startled by the power he had. She was waiting for him to respond, and he said, Never mind. It's okay.

She smiled. Good, she said.

They continued walking, but he was shaken by this responsibility. He thought, I am too young for this.

The sidewalks of downtown Berkeley were crowded with students, shoppers and homeless men and women panhandling and clustered by the BART escalators. Despite the warm afternoon weather, a few of the homeless wore heavy winter coats. Although there were homeless men and women in David's neighborhood in Oakland, some of whom had begun to recognize him, there always seemed to be more here in Berkeley. A street musician with a guitar sang a folk song to passersby. Yunjin and he stopped for a moment and listened, then walked down into the BART station.

He asked Yunjin what else she and Mr. Kim talked about.

She said, He tell me he is tired of tae kwon do. He practice it ever since he was a child. His father teaches it. He wants to give most of his teaching to his top students and do more business. He want to open more studio and focus on all kinds of martial arts, not just tae kwon do.

There was something in her voice—admiration? The beginnings of a crush? David didn't quite understand it, but knew enough to be wary.

She said, Maybe tomorrow I will ask him for a job.

He kept quiet. He wanted to say, Find your own place, but he didn't want to hurt her feelings again. They waited on the platform for their train. He already felt his legs beginning to ache. He didn't want to return home, but didn't know where else to go. He said to Yunjin, Do you want to see the university?

Yes, she said quickly.

He realized that she didn't want to go home either. They walked back up to the street and headed to the U.C. Berkeley campus.

When Sam returned to Club Saja, he searched for Unha, and still couldn't find her. He asked one of the waitresses if Unha had taken the day off, but the waitress didn't know.

Did she come in today?

The waitress looked uncertain, then said, I don't know.

Who stabbed Choon? Was it Unha?

I don't know, she said, and hurried away.

Sam saw Choon at the bar with Lee. He approached. They stopped talking.

Sam asked, Have you seen Unha?

Who? Lee said.

The new girl.

Choon and Lee glanced at each other. Lee shrugged his shoulders. Choon stared at Sam with heavy-lidded eyes.

Sam said to Choon, Was it Unha who stabbed you with a fork?

Choon said, Mind your own fucking business.

Sam asked Lee, Have you seen her? Unha?

Lee shook his head.

Sam studied them. They were lying to him, and the only reason why was because Unha had been the one. He knew she had had trouble with Choon before, and said to him, What did you do to her?

Choon turned away and said to Lee, Who the fuck is this guy?

Sam was about to reply when Im appeared in the stairwell and motioned for him to come up. Sam followed. In one of the booths sat Koman. Sam approached and Koman said, What happened today?

With Jung?

Koman nodded his head.

Sam said, I couldn't do it.

You missed this chance to erase half of your debt? Koman asked.

I know.

You also questioned Im's authority in front of Jung?

I didn't mean to.

Mr. Oh left me in charge while he takes care of some business overseas, Koman said. I feel that Mr. Oh has given you too much leniency. I won't.

Sam said, I understand.

I don't think you do, Koman said. You are almost finished here. One more mistake and that's it. Is that clear?

Sam was suddenly tired of everyone here. He said, Yes.

Koman motioned him away.

Sam brushed by Im and walked down to the main floor and left the club. He kept thinking about Unha. The image of Minji in the dirt kept flashing before him, and he tried to keep himself calm by telling himself not to think the worst. She could have just taken the day off.

He drove quickly to her apartment building, double parked his car, and buzzed the front intercom. After a moment a young woman's voice came on and asked in English, Who is it?

He replied in Korean, Is Unha there?

There was a long pause, and the woman said, There is no Unha here.

Sam took a deep breath. He checked the apartment number. This was where he had picked her up last time. He said, She lives here. Unha. She works at Club Saja.

The woman said, There is no Unha here.

I know she lives—

193

There was a click.

Hello? He buzzed it again.

What? the voice said sharply.

He said, This is Sam. I work for Koman. You have probably seen me at the club. Tell me where Unha went.

I told you I don't know anything!

Click.

Sam cursed. He stepped back and looked up at the windows, although he wasn't sure which was Unha's. Then he saw a woman walking down the street, a smaller Korean woman wearing a black leather jacket and high heels. He recognized her from the club. She was heading toward him, so he stood in the doorway and waited.

She saw him and smiled. Yes? she asked.

I have seen you talking with Unha at the club.

The woman's smile dropped.

Sam said, What is your name?

Ginny, she said. You are Sam.

Yes, he said, surprised. I am trying to find Unha.

Ginny studied him. She said, Unha left.

Where?

She went away, Ginny said.

Where?

I don't know.

Sam said quietly, Something happened, right? Was she the one who stabbed Choon? Did they take her away?

Ginny stepped back. She said, I cannot talk about—

Why?

She seemed confused. Sam wanted to press his advantage. He said softly, I know you are friends. I just want to help her. Where did she go?

She whispered, They took her away.

Where?

I don't know.

Who took her? Hyunma?

194

No. I didn't see, but someone else came for her.

Who came for her? Where did she go?

I don't know! Ginny cried, and then said, She didn't know how to behave. She shouldn't have caused trouble.

Sam grabbed her arm. What happened to her?

Sometimes Hyunma will…sell a girl. Someone else will pay the debt.

Who?

Ginny shook her head.

How can I find her? Who will know?

I don't know, she said, pulling her arm from his grip.

Sam thought of Minji, and said, I thought you were Unha's friend.

She said, Leave me alone.

How can I find her? Help me.

Ask Choon.

He won't tell me, Sam said.

Soonhee saw some of it, Ginny said.

Where is Soonhee? Which one is she?

Ginny said, She will be working at the club later. She is the one with the silver bracelets.

Sam didn't remember her, but would return to the club tonight. He said, Do you think Unha is all right?

Ginny stared at him sadly. She shook her head. She whispered, They carried her away.

24

Unha couldn't move. Even the slightest shift in her position on the floor sent deep waves of pain throughout her body. She could barely see out of her bruised, puffy eyes, and the entire left side of her mouth was swollen. She had heard someone angrily scold the man who had brought her here that he shouldn't have hit her face, because now no one will want to fuck her, but the man replied that she was going to be difficult. She wouldn't do anything anyway.

Unha's head slowly cleared. She wasn't sure where she was. An apartment. A living room. She heard the voices of two men in the other room, watching TV. She looked down at her naked body and was shocked to see cuts, bruises and rug burns on her legs and arms. A stinging on her lower back made her suck in her breath quickly. She shivered and searched for a blanket or her clothes, but there was nothing. A mattress lay in the corner.

She had a sharp steady pain bubbling in her gut. She wanted to throw up. She curled into a ball, cradling her midsection, and then felt the sharp pain in between her legs. She noticed the blood smeared on her inner thighs. She let out a low, unsteady moan.

She heard one of the men in the other room say, This lighter is out of fuel.

The TV was playing a comedy. She heard the audience laughing. One of the men kept flicking the lighter and inhaling. Unha became more disoriented, the loud voices of the TV and the laughter infiltrating her head, and she drifted in and out of consciousness. She thought about killing herself somehow, by cutting her wrists with a sharp object, by jumping from the window, but all this took too much energy. She wanted to sleep.

She thought about her ex-fiancé, Woo Chul. If he hadn't broken their engagement, she would still be in Taeshin and they would be having their wedding and they would honeymoon at Chejudo and Woo Chul would be promoted at his uncle's farm machinery shop, and maybe by now Unha would be pregnant and they would be starting a family. Damn him. He had caused this. He had done this to her.

She cried quietly, which exhausted her. She fell asleep and dreamed of the beaches of Chejudo. The sound of the waves became the sound of television static when she woke up again and found herself shivering.

She pulled herself up, and stifled a cry, the pain in her stomach shocking her. She touched her cheek, the bruise tender. She couldn't stop shivering. She stood up slowly and limped across the room and peered into the bedroom, where the two men were sitting against a bed, a sheet of tin foil and a blackened glass tube lying on the floor in front of them. The TV static flickered over them. She immediately thought of running, but had no clothes. She wasn't sure what they did with them. She checked the bathroom and found her blouse, her skirt and her torn underwear balled up on the floor. When she saw the underwear she remembered hearing a

197

heavy, fast breathing in her ear, a grunt, and the crunching of leaves under her, sharp rocks cutting into her lower back. She knew she had been raped; she whimpered. She held onto the sink and steadied herself. Her heart beat rapidly in her ears as she put her clothes on and tried to clean the cuts on her feet with water and toilet paper. Her toes were swelling up and discolored. She focused on her feet and shut everything else out. She needed her feet healed to run.

But she heard someone outside walking up the steps. Panicking, she hurried back to the living room and lay down on the floor. The door opened and a man's voice said, Check on her.

Unha opened her eyes and saw two young women and a man approaching. The women leaned over her and one of them asked in a soft voice, Are you all right?

Unha shook her head.

The woman said, Bobby, she's all beaten up.

Bobby walked quickly to her, and peered down. He was a small, wiry man, his eyes darting up and down her body. Goddammit, he said in English.

He turned and yelled in Korean, Where are you two idiots?

He walked into the bedroom and said, What is this?

There was a crash, and the sound of glass shattering. Bobby yelled, Is this what I pay you for? Getting high and passing out? You stupid shitheads!

The two men came scrambling out of the bedroom. Bobby said, Who hit her face?

It wasn't us, one of them said. It was Ying. She tried to get away and he beat her up. We told him you'd be angry.

Fuck. It will take a couple weeks for that to heal. Fuck Ying.

What do you want us to do?

These two will watch her for now. You two get the fuck out of here.

One of the women said, She doesn't look too good. Do what you can. I'll be back later tonight.

She needs to have these cuts cleaned, the woman said. These are already getting infected.

I'll get a wash cloth, the other woman said.

Unha hoped that these women would be kind to her. She let them guide her to the mattress on the floor, and let them wash her feet, the cuts stinging. She smelled the strong, cheap perfume. She almost started crying again, but managed to suppress everything into a small, unsteady moan. One of the women said softly, It will be all right. Don't worry. You can rest now.

The other one whispered, This one isn't going to last long.

Sam's vision blurred, streaks of light spinning everywhere. He had lost count of how many shots of soju he had finished, and Lee kept pouring him free refills. He sat at the bar, staring out over the tables, the music loud and drilling, and he watched the waitresses walk briskly back and forth from the kitchen, holding the trays of appetizers balanced on one hand by their shoulder. He had seen Soonhee, the one with the jangling silver bracelets, but he hadn't been able to catch her alone. Hyunma was hovering. Choon was watching him. Lee was getting him drunk.

He felt the pressure of passing time, that every minute he wasted here at the club, the more danger Unha was in and the closer to Minji's fate she might come. He tried to stand up, but was too dizzy. He sat back down and saw Lee smile at him.

Sam said, No more soju.

Lee nodded. You better not be working tonight.

I'm not, he said. Then he saw Soonhee walking toward the emergency exit, probably taking a break. He steadied himself, took a deep breath, and stood up. He grabbed the bar for support.

When he walked out into the back alley he saw Soon-hee leaning against the brick wall, one foot propped up behind her. She was lighting a cigarette. Under the bare bulb her forehead was shiny, her hair plastered against her sweaty skin. She took a deep drag from the cigarette, shook out the match, jangling her bracelets, and blew out a long thread of smoke that blossomed up to the light.

Sam asked, Are you Soonhee?

She nodded her head.

Ginny said you saw what happened to Unha.

Her gaze went to the door behind him. He turned around, and saw that it was closed. He said, It is important that I find her.

Why?

She is my friend.

Soonhee wiped her forehead with the back of her hand. Her silver and jade bracelets fell up her arm. She flicked an ash to the ground, and said, You should forget about her.

Where is she?

Sold to another man.

Who?

She shook her head. I shouldn't be talking about this, she said.

Tell me, please. Who was it?

She sighed. It was a man who has come here before. He is from the south Bay. Bobby Yun. I heard he has a bunch of nail shops and bars down there.

Sam felt ill. He smelled rotting garbage. He said, Brothels?

She gave him a half-shrug.

You don't know the name of the bar?

She said, No, but a girl who used to work for him also worked here. She said one of his bars was in Mountain View, right across from the big mall.

200

What mall?

I don't know, but the bar was right next to an Indian restaurant. She said she always smelled curry.

And he owns nail salons, Sam said, trying to retain all this, but the facts seemed to dissipate into the air. He tried to focus, tried to think of more questions, but he was distracted by her bracelets, which she jangled nervously.

The door behind Sam opened. He whirled around. Choon stood there and said to Soonhee, What are you doing?

Taking my break.

Break is over.

Soonhee flicked her cigarette onto the pavement and walked back in. Choon then stepped out and said to Sam, What the fuck are you doing?

Nothing.

You are getting very nosy, he said.

Sam stared at the bandages on Choon's neck and said, Unha stabbed you with a fork.

You are fucking drunk.

A small girl like her stabbed you, a big fat man. Sam laughed.

Choon swelled up and said, Are you fucking stupid?

You couldn't handle a small girl like Unha, so you had to have her sent away, Sam said. You are the stupid one.

You better shut up and go home, Choon said, stepping forward.

Or what?

Or I'll drive your head into that brick wall.

Sam laughed again. Are you twelve years old? Is that what you used to tell kids at school? Where did Unha go?

Choon said, Right now she is probably being fucked in the ass by a bunch of different men.

Sam ran forward, trying to tackle him, but Choon stepped aside and pushed him off balance, forcing him into the door. Sam tried to protect his head and crashed forward, slamming his shoulder into the doorframe and collapsing. Choon kicked him in the ribs, which Sam hardly felt. He thought, Too much soju.

Choon said, You are a shit drunk. Go home before I really hurt you.

Sam squinted up. Choon's broad face loomed over him. Sam said, You are very fat.

Choon sighed, kicked him again, and went back into the club.

That night David's father came home and threw up all over the kitchen. David heard him retching and moaning, the sounds of the tap running in the sink mingling with the intermittent gagging. Yunjin ran down the hall and into the kitchen and he heard her yell, That is disgusting! You better clean that up!

His father moaned.

David climbed out of bed and walked quietly to the kitchen door. When he looked around the corner he saw his father slumped over the sink, his shirt wet and dripping with water. He grabbed a dish towel and wiped his face. Yunjin stood there with her hands on her hips.

David's father said, Leave me alone.

You smell like…like garbage.

Fuck you.

David crept back to his room and closed the door quietly. He curled up in his bed and tried to sleep. He drifted off for a while, but was reawakened by the sound of yelling. Yunjin was calling his father a failure, a useless drunk.

Then he heard a slap and silence. He kept still. After a moment Yunjin let out a long, low wail of pain, a cry of anguish that gripped his heart. His father yelled at her to shut up, and Yunjin yelled, You stupid idiot! You are a bully!

Yunjin screamed something else, but her voice was cut off with another slap and she cried out. But it didn't end here.

David heard them struggling, grunting, something crashing on the ground and shattering. Yunjin screamed for help and David jumped out of bed and hurried to his door.

She cried out again in pain. He ran out into the hallway, and the sounds of the struggle—heavy breathing, shuffling footsteps, muttering—frightened him. He heard Yunjin whimper, and his father said, You dare hit me, you stupid farm girl?

David peered around the corner of the hallway and saw his father, shirtless, his bare skin blotchy red; he was holding Yunjin up against the wall, one hand grabbing her arm and pushing her back. His forearms bulged. His pants were spotted with water. She tried to pull away but his father slammed her back into the wall and she hit her head. She grunted.

She tried to scratch his face with her nails, but his father slapped her with his free hand. She sobbed.

David yelled, You're hurting her!

They both turned to him, startled. They froze.

Go back to bed, his father said.

Yunjin then tried to struggle free, but his father pushed her into the wall again.

Stop, David said. Stop it!

Yunjin tried to kick his father and he slammed her back again, this time her head making a loud cracking sound against the plaster. Yunjin cried. David ran to them and tried to pull his father away. He smelled the alcohol and vomit and garbage, and he saw Yunjin's face was red where she had been hit.

His father tried to push him away, yelling, Go back to bed right now!

David didn't let go, and Yunjin struggled wildly. He grabbed his father's arm and pulled harder.

His father backhanded him, sending him staggering to the floor. The blow blurred his vision and dizzied him. He

203

sat stunned. The side of his head pounded.

His father had pushed Yunjin aside and was watching David with wide, fearful eyes.

Go back to bed, his father said quietly.

David blinked, the lights above spinning.

Go, his father whispered.

David pulled himself up slowly, and wiped away tears. Everything was blurry. Yunjin moved toward him but his father pushed her toward the living room, saying, Get away from my son.

David didn't know what to do, so he walked back to his room, his legs shaking. His father had never hit him before, and he was still dazed.

He closed his door and tried to calm himself by sitting cross-legged on his bed and breathing deeply. He heard the squeaking of the shower and then the heavy stream hitting the plastic curtain. It was a sound he rarely heard at night. Then he remembered that his mother used to take showers late at night because it helped her sleep.

This was before she got sick. His bedroom was right next to the bathroom, so the sound of the water running through the pipes hissed in the walls. He closed his eyes and imagined his mother was still alive. She would finish her long shower and hum to herself while she dried off. She would change into her soft nightgown and walk into his room to check on him. She would sit on his bed and push the hair from his face and kiss him goodnight. She would smell of soap and lotion. Her hands would be soft. Her damp hair would brush against his cheek and leave a cool trail. She would stand up slowly, whisper goodnight, and leave the room quietly, closing the door with a click. And David would dream of the ocean.

25

Jake answered his office phone and winced when he heard Yunjin's voice. He thought, Now what?

Yunjin said, I called your cell phone.

Jake replied, I've been very busy. How are you?

Sam got very drunk last night and hit us.

Jake sat up in his chair. What? What do you mean?

He hit us, she said. He hit David.

Jake said, Put him on the phone.

He already left.

Jake rubbed his eyes, not sure what he was supposed to do. Is David okay? he asked.

Yes. I cannot take any more of this. Your brother—

What do you expect me to do?

Tell him to stop drinking! Tell him to—

Yunjin, he said. I can't do that. You have to learn to deal with him.

He will listen to you!

Jake said, I will try to talk to him, but I am getting

tired of interfering in your family.

She was quiet.

He said, Do not call me every time you need help. Do you understand? You have to take care of your own problems.

But... I...

I have to go, Jake said.

He hung up and sat there, trying to figure out why this was making him so angry. He didn't want to know this about his brother, and couldn't picture Sam hitting David or Yunjin. And what could Jake say to him? Don't hit your wife and son?

Sam seemed to have inherited their father's worst traits—a temper and a love of drinking. Jake inherited their father's work ethic. In their father these traits often cancelled each other out, so that he would cut short a night of drinking because of work the next day. But Sam couldn't care less about work.

He imagined both Yunjin and David bruised and shell-shocked, and he tried to shake this image from his head. He remembered the time when they were children and Sam had watched Jake play with a toy horse with wheels. Jake had received it as a birthday gift from one of their parents' friends, and Sam walked calmly over to him and stepped on it, breaking the wheels off. Jake had stared down in bewilderment. Then, slowly, as he realized what his brother had just done, he looked up, ready to howl in outrage.

Sam said, Don't. Or I'll step on you the same way.

Jake paused, then tried to fix his horse.

As his brother walked away, he realized how mean Sam could be.

A knock on his office door startled Jake. He stood up. Koman walked in with a briefcase and laid it on the desk. Koman said, It's more than you discussed.

Jake said, How much more?

Eighty.

I can't handle that much.

Mr. Oh suggested that you find a way.

Jake stared at the slim briefcase. In there was more money than his parents had ever seen in their lives. Yet at the moment it was a burden for Jake. It made him tired. He said, This will take a long time.

We are in no hurry, and once this club is functional you can move the cash more easily.

Jake said, Mr. Oh and I agreed on fifty.

It is now eighty.

Fine, Jake said.

Koman motioned to the main dining area and said, It is looking good.

Tell me how my brother is doing.

Koman frowned. He is not good at following orders.

That is not a surprise.

Im does not like him.

That is also not a surprise.

Koman said, I thought you didn't want to know anything about his work with us.

Jake replied, I think he has been drinking more.

Koman smiled. Are you being a concerned brother?

Maybe, Jake said.

I haven't seen him. I let Im deal with him. I will ask.

Jake thanked him.

Koman began to walk out of the office, but stopped. He asked, Why don't you just pay off his debt?

I have already paid him too much.

Koman said, A bottomless well. I know the type very well. Sometimes you have to cut them off.

But he is my brother.

At some point you will have to make a choice. Really help him or let him take care of himself.

Jake said, I know.

Koman pointed to the briefcase. Just call me when

you begin cleaning it.

I will.

Koman left the club, and Jake opened the briefcase. He saw small jumbled stacks of fifty and one-hundred dollar bills, held together with dirty rubber bands. He suspected this came from the brothels, maybe even drug deals. Jake never asked. Even if it was from prostitution and drugs he had trouble connecting it to himself. All he was doing was moving money from one place to another.

He thought about Yunjin's call and pulled out his cell phone. He dialed Sam's cell number, but found that it had been disconnected. He wondered for a moment if Yunjin had been exaggerating. Sam would never have hit Sunny. Why would he hit Yunjin? And hitting David? Would he do that, even if he were drunk? Jake couldn't imagine it.

He unlocked his safe and slid the briefcase into it. Money was losing some of its meaning to him. He dealt with so much of it now that sometimes it felt unreal. Yes, he could buy many things, but he didn't want to. He stared at the tax documents, the brokerage account statements, and the extra cash in the safe. What did all this mean, really? Freedom? He didn't feel free. Security? All this extra money and his laundering of it exposed him to charges of tax fraud. He didn't feel very secure.

He closed and locked the safe. He knew he had to talk to Sam about his drinking, about Yunjin's claims. He definitely wanted to make sure David was all right. He called Yunjin back, and she answered on the first ring. He said, I can't reach Sam. His phone is disconnected.

Yes, she said. He stopped paying his bill. We are getting letters from them.

Jake sighed inwardly. He said, I will try to talk to him in person, then.

Thank you, she said.

Is David all right?

208

He is fine.

Jake tried to think of something comforting to add. He said, Sam isn't usually like this.

I am going to start looking for a job, she said. Is there something for me at your new club? A waitress?

Jake didn't want to tell her that she wasn't attractive enough, but said, Maybe kitchen help. I won't know until we are open.

I will do anything. I am going to leave Sam soon.

Jake said, What about David?

I don't know.

Jake said, Let me talk to Sam.

All right.

They hung up and Jake sat down, shaking his head. His brother was getting into more and more trouble and Jake was getting sick of it.

He stood up. It was time to get back to work.

PART V

THE SKELETON DANCE

26

Unha learned that the two women were named Heeun and Kyungja. Heeun seemed to be the elder, directing Kyungja to go to another apartment to get more clothes for Unha. While they were alone, with Unha shivering on the mattress and still stunned by how fast everything had deteriorated, Heeun gently asked where Unha was from. Unha lied, and said, Seoul. She didn't trust anyone, and in the dim light of the living room she focused on Heeun, trying to figure out what her role was. Heeun sat cross-legged on the carpet, and clasped her hands together. She wore faded jeans and a thin black sweater, and hunched over in a slouch that curved her back. She asked if Unha was hungry or thirsty.

Unha hadn't thought of that until now. She nodded quickly.

Heeun popped up onto her bare feet and walked to the kitchen. She filled a glass with water and pulled out a container from the refrigerator. Unha eyed the front door, wondering about escaping. She asked who lived here.

It's one of the places we stay at, Heeun replied. She brought over the water and leftover bibimbap.

Unha gulped down the water, and used the chopsticks to shovel the cold, hard rice and vegetables into her mouth. Everything tasted of metal, but she immediately felt more awake, her thoughts crystallizing into one theme: escape. She let out an unsteady breath, a brief memory of the man on top of her in the woods sickening her. She tightened her body and forced herself to think clearly. She needed to know more. Where was she? She asked, One of the places? You live in more than one?

Bobby keeps moving us around.

Why?

Heeun shrugged her hunched shoulders and said, To keep the neighbors from getting suspicious? I don't know.

Bobby is the boss?

Yes.

And what do you do for him?

Heeun didn't answer.

Unha asked, Were you forced?

Heeun said, Do you want more water?

Yes.

Heeun took her glass and refilled it at the kitchen tap. She said, It's better not to fight it.

Unha asked, How long have you...been here?

I have been here for five months.

And the other?

Kyungja has been here for three.

Unha drank the second glass of water and the sting in her stomach and ribs worsened; the nourishment and water reawakened her body. Ribbons of pain cut through her insides. She lay on her side, and held her midsection. She said, I am hurt.

When we go to the bar, you can have medicine. There isn't anything here.

What bar?

Bobby's bar.

I am not going anywhere. I am not becoming a prostitute.

Heeun flinched. She said, I am not a prostitute.

Do you have sex with strange men? Does Bobby make you?

Heeun said quietly, I am trying to help you. Bobby can be nice to you if you do what he says.

What if I don't?

She shook her head. Please listen to me, she said. You will make it worse for yourself.

Unha realized that Heeun was here to help Bobby, to soften Unha somehow. She asked, How long will you do this? How long will you stay with Bobby?

Until my debt is paid off.

How long will that be?

A few more months. You will only have to work about that long too.

I don't believe you.

No one works longer than a year, Heeun said.

How do you know that if you've been here for only five months?

Heeun paused.

Unha said, So what happens to you when you are done?

We get jobs. Bobby has nail salons. Sometimes they just go away. Find other work. Sometimes they go back to Korea.

The door opened and Kyungja walked in with an extra pair of jeans and a sweater. Unha tried to see what was outside, but Kyungja shut the door quickly. Kyungja was barely out of adolescence, with a gawkiness to her movements of someone not used to her body, her face still chubby with baby fat. She gave Unha the clothes and turned to Heeun for

215

instructions.

Heeun said to Kyungja, You should rest.

Heeun then said to Unha, You wash up and change in the bathroom. Then you should rest too.

I want to leave, Unha said.

Heeun glanced at Kyungja, who walked into the bedroom and closed the door. Heeun said quietly, You know you cannot. And where would you go? Bobby is giving you a chance to earn off the money you owe.

I will not become a prostitute.

Heeun sighed. She shook her head and said, I am trying to help you.

Do you really want to help me?

Yes.

Then tell me the truth.

About what?

Unha asked, How many men do you sleep with in a day?

Heeun frowned.

You said you wanted to help me.

Heeun was quiet for a while, then said, It depends on the day.

What is a day like?

We are on six-hour shifts. It depends on how busy it is, but we can have two or three men in an hour.

How many women work?

A few women at the bar, and a few women at one of the apartments.

Unha asked, How much do the men pay Bobby?

I don't know.

If you don't know, then how do you know you are paying off your debt?

She says, Bobby tells me.

And you believe him?

Yes.

Then you are stupid.

Heeun stiffened. She said, You will make it much harder on yourself.

Unha stood up slowly, her legs shaking. She winced as her stomach and ribs sent more pain through her. The soles of her feet stung, the arches swollen and painful. She limped to the bathroom, clutching the extra clothes, and said, I would rather die.

Heeun said, I used to say the same thing.

In the dim bathroom rolls of toilet paper were stacked on the floor and dirty towels hung on the rack. Unha locked the door and hurried to the small window. She pulled open the sliding frame, and saw that she was two stories up. No, the only escape was the front door. She sat on the toilet and felt the sting in her vagina. She closed her eyes and shuddered at the stronger memory of the man on top of her in the woods. She tried to tell herself that she had been beaten, not raped. But she knew. She could feel the sting between her legs. She fought the nausea rising up in her throat. She had only had sex with Woo Chul, and now… now this… She suddenly worried she might be pregnant. The thought horrified her but she told herself to focus, to get dressed and think clearly. Her knuckles cracked as she stripped off her dirty clothes and put on the jeans and sweater.

She started to wash her face, but it was too painful. She looked at herself in the mirror. She let out a small cry. She didn't even recognize herself—the left side was puffy and bruised, cuts and scrapes along her cheek and chin, and her lower lip had dried blood caked on it. She ran the hot water, and dabbed her lips clean. Water dripped onto her cuts and burned. She breathed heavily, everything hurting, even when she blinked her eyes.

A knock at the door. Heeun asked if she was all right.

I am trying to clean my wounds, she said.

She thought, I must find a way out.

When Unha walked out of the bathroom she saw Heeun sitting on the mattress. Do you feel better? Heeun asked.

Unha suppressed her anger at these two dumb girls. She told herself to keep calm. She said, What are we waiting for?

For Bobby to come here.

And then what?

And then we go to the bar and begin our shift.

I am not going, Unha said.

No, you're not. You are too beat up. But you should listen to Bobby. He will get mad.

Unha wondered if she could overpower her. But then a wave of exhaustion overcame her. She felt too weak. She couldn't even raise her arm. She had to rest, to save her strength. She would find the right time, and she had to be ready. She lay down on the mattress and stared at the front door.

27

Sam stared out at the neon signs along El Camino Real, a commercial strip in the middle of Mountain View. Most of the stores were closed and traffic was sparse. It was past midnight, and the town seemed to have shut down. There were only a few cars on the highway, the sidewalks empty. He searched for a bar along the street, across from the San Antonio mall, but couldn't find one. There were plenty of fast food restaurants, small stores, gas stations, and three Indian restaurants, but no bars. He drove up and down the strip, then slowed when he noticed a nail salon among a cluster of stores in a mini-mall. The bright red and blue signs were uniform in size and advertised pizza, a Laundromat, a real estate office, a Chinese take-out restaurant, and a sign that simply read Nails. He pulled into the parking lot.

The store was closed, but he saw a flickering light in the back. He peered through the window and saw that someone was watching TV. He knocked, and after a moment an older Korean man peered out from the room. He squinted, and shook his head. He pointed to his watch.

Sam waved him over and knocked again.

The man walked across the floor where one side of the room had small manicure tables and the other side had cushioned pedicure seats. Through the glass door the man said to Sam in Korean, What do you want?

Sam asked, Is this one of Bobby Yun's businesses?

Who are you?

I work for Mr. Oh up north. I'm looking for Bobby's bar.

The man straightened. He said, You want Kim's.

Is that the name?

He said, It's across from the shopping center.

I checked. I couldn't find it.

Behind the Indian restaurant, the man said. There is no sign. It is the door with the light over the top.

Who are you? Why are you in here? Sam asked.

I watch some of the nail salons at night, he said.

Sam thanked him and returned to his car. He drove back along El Camino Real and saw the Indian restaurant on the corner, directly across from the entrance to the mall. He parked his car in front and walked around the building, finding a few cars parked in a narrow lot. A small two-story building was attached to the back of the restaurant, with the second floor a row of apartments and the first floor a brick wall with a few translucent windows. The main door was off to the side, with a bright spotlight shining down over it. Sam approached, hearing music inside. When he tried the door handle, it was locked. He saw a button and pushed it. A doorbell went off inside. He heard movement on the other side, and then noticed the security peephole. He stepped back and let the light shine down over him.

The door unlocked and opened. A young Korean man with his head shaved, his scalp shining in the light, stepped out, looked around, and held the door open for Sam.

Sam thanked him and walked in. The smell of stale cigarette smoke hit him immediately. The dim lighting barely allowed him to see the bar to the side where a few men sat talking with women. Six empty tables filled the center floor, while a long sofa in the back had five women lounging in it. Sam glanced at the women, but didn't see Unha. When the door closed behind him a young burly man in a white dress shirt appeared from a side room and asked Sam in Korean what kind of drink he wanted.

What do you have?

Soju, Vodka, beer.

Soju, Sam said. His eyes adjusted to the darkness, and he saw a curtain separating another room in back. Everyone seemed to be moving in slow motion.

Ten dollars.

For a bottle? He turned back to the man.

A glass.

Sam said, Are you kidding?

Take a table, the man said. Choose a hostess and she will join you.

What?

The man motioned to the women on the sofa. They were watching him, and sat up when the man nodded to them. Sam asked, Are you Bobby Yun?

The man shook his head. No, why do you want to know?

I want to talk to him.

About what?

I'm looking for a woman.

The man pointed to the sofa. There are five women.

A special one, he said. Her name is Unha.

The man shrugged his shoulders. Buy some drinks, spend time with a hostess. Maybe Bobby will come by later.

Sam sat at a table. The women on the sofa were a range of ages, but all were wearing heavy make-up and short skirts. As soon as he made eye contact with a woman, a young one with a sharp nose and cat eyes, she stood up and walked over to him, her high heels making her walk with small, awkward steps. She asked in Korean, May I join you?

He nodded his head. She sat down. She motioned to the bartender.

My name is Yoonmee.

Sam, he said. She was wearing lipstick that was too red, too glaringly bright.

The bartender brought over two glasses of soju. He said, Twenty dollars.

Sam realized how they made a lot of their money. Not wanting to argue, he dug through his wallet and handed over the cash, reminding himself of how little he had left. Yoonmee handed one of the drinks to him. She asked if he was new here, and he told her yes.

He asked, Do you know Unha? She is new.

Unha? No.

She is very new.

No. Do you want to go upstairs?

What is upstairs?

She smiled, and said, Whatever you want.

She had grey teeth, and he stared. She quickly closed her red lips. He asked, What part of Korea are you from?

Seoul, she said. Let us go upstairs.

Do you know Bobby Yun?

She narrowed her eyes and asked, Are you the police?

No. I am looking for Unha, and I think she works for Yun.

I don't know Unha. The last new girl was Susy, over there. She nodded her head toward the sofa.

She might have just come, Sam said, glancing at Susy, who kept running her fingers through her long hair. Maybe yesterday or the day before.

Come from where?

Another club, he said.

She is probably resting. We don't get busy until the weekend.

Do you share apartments?

Do you want to go upstairs or not?

A small man walked in from the side door, and spoke to the bartender. Sam asked Yoonmee, Is that Yun?

She said it was, but then motioned to the bartender. He walked over. Sam was watching Yun, who wore a shiny sports jacket. He had stubble on his cheeks and a thin, scraggly mustache. He seemed jumpy. The bartender offered them another glass of soju, but Yoonmee said, He keeps asking questions.

About what?

Everything.

The bartender waved Yun over.

Sam stood up and said, I am just looking for a friend.

Yun approached and said, You have a friend right there. He pointed to Yoonmee. He asked the bartender, What is the problem?

Sam said, I am looking for another friend. Her name is Unha.

Who are you?

I knew her at Club Saja.

Yun shook his head. I do not know who you are talking about. You should go—

His cell phone rang. He turned away abruptly and answered it, and after a moment said, I will be there soon. He hung up and, jerking his head toward Sam, said to the bartender, Get him out of here.

The bartender made a move toward Sam, who backed away. I am leaving, he said. Sam headed for the door, walking past the young bald man who was watching him tensely. Sam held up his hands and walked out of the bar, and ran to his car. He drove it to the street with a view of the back parking

223

lot. He waited. Now that he knew who Yun was, he would eventually find Unha through him. He just had to be patient.

28

Jake walked into Sam and Yunjin's apartment, and saw the broken TV on the floor, a jagged hole in the glass screen. Yunjin asked if he wanted anything to drink. He said he didn't, and asked where David was.

Asleep, she said.

Sam isn't here?

No. He hasn't been home all day.

Where is he?

I don't know, but the man he works with is also looking for him.

Im? Im is looking for him?

Yes, she said. See what your brother did to me. She turned her head and pointed to a small pale bruise on her jaw.

And David?

He is okay.

Jake said, You don't know where Sam is?

He never tells me anything.

When was the last time you saw him?

I heard him here in the morning. He slept out here.

Jake sat down on the sofa. It had been a tiring day—the new carpenters had come in, and the club was getting finished quickly. He had hoped to speak to Sam to figure out what was happening to him, but now this was puzzling. He pulled out his cell phone and called Koman, asking if Sam was at Club Saja.

No, Koman said. Im is looking for him. He never showed up for work tonight.

Jake said, Could he be in trouble?

Not with us. Not yet. When you find him tell him we are going to have a talk.

I will, Jake said.

After he hung up he told Yunjin that Sam was probably drinking somewhere.

I do not want to be here when he gets back, Yunjin said.

Jake didn't reply.

Yunjin said, Can David and I stay at your house for the night?

I am sure it will be fine here.

Please, Yunjin said. For David.

Jake thought, Everyone always wants something from me.

He stood up and said, Let me check on David.

David was already awake when his uncle came into his room. He had been listening to them, and sat up as his uncle turned on the light. He said to David, You are up. How are you?

I'm okay, David said.

So I hear your father got a little wild the other night.

David nodded his head.

He didn't hurt you?

No.

Yunjin wants you two to stay at my place tonight.

Why?

Just in case your father's been drinking again.

Your house? Can I use the hot room?

The sauna? He laughed. You like it?

It's like being in the jungle.

All right. Get some clothes.

David climbed out of bed as his uncle went out into the hallway and told Yunjin that she and David could stay with him for the night. He added, But only for tonight. I'll talk to him tomorrow.

David shoved a change of clothes into his knapsack and took his Kung-Fu book. He heard Yunjin also packing a bag, and when he walked out into the living room, his uncle was waiting by the door, jotting down a note. He left it on the living room coffee table. He said, Let's go. I'm tired.

Uncle Jake's house was in the Oakland hills, where the twisting and hidden roads were as narrow as the car itself. David watched the low branches of trees smear across his back seat window. They were quiet. His uncle played classical music on the radio, and David drifted in and out of sleep until they arrived at his house. His uncle pressed a remote button and his garage door opened, floodlights blinking on all around the house.

They entered the kitchen, where bright stainless steel appliances reflected the harsh track lighting above. The last time David had been here was for his mother's memorial service, after the funeral. Everyone had brought Korean dishes, and David had made a large ball out of the tin foil covers.

Uncle Jake directed them to the loft upstairs, a guest room with a bed and a fold-out sofa. David saw the rocking chair that his father had built and given to Jake. It was small, with a wicker back, and sat poised by the unused fireplace. David moved toward it, but Yunjin told him to get to bed. She followed him up the steps, and unfolded the sofa. He crawled onto the main bed, hugging the fluffy pillow.

Yunjin tucked the sheets closer to him and said, I talk to your uncle. You sleep.

Where's my father?

I don't know.

He closed his eyes, and heard her walk quietly back down the steps.

Downstairs, his uncle said, I have to leave early in the morning.

Have you thought about giving me a job?

I told you. Once the club is running I will know if I need kitchen help.

Yunjin said, I might get a job with a tae kwon do studio.

Doing what?

The owner wants to expand the business. He needs office help.

After a moment Jake asked, How do you know this place?

David is taking lessons there.

He is? Since when?

David heard them talking about him, but he had trouble staying awake. This bed was one of the most comfortable he had even been in, and he quickly fell asleep.

That night, while David slept, Yunjin fantasized about Mr. Kim. She had spent yesterday afternoon with him while David was working and practicing at the studio, and she learned of Mr. Kim's plans to hand over most of the teaching duties to his assistants. He wanted to open more studios that concentrated on fitness, not just tae kwon do, and envisioned a small health club empire. He explained that Americans always wanted new exercise fads, and right now kickboxing and its different forms were very popular.

When he told her this, his eyes were excited, his

hands motioning quickly as he explained his plan for big studio spaces that could adapt to changing fads. She asked questions about locations and equipment, and this triggered another excited response. He leaned closer to her and she smelled his aftershave. She wondered if he was married. There were specks of grey in his neatly-trimmed beard. He had enlarged knuckles. She knew he could beat up Sam, and this pleased her.

Just before she left the studio he gave her his business card and said, Call me and let's talk more about this. Maybe you can give me good ideas.

Her fingertips tingled as she took the card and she tried not to blush. She wasn't sure if he knew she was married. But she was wearing the wedding band Sam had given her, so he must know. Maybe he just didn't care. Maybe this was common in America.

Now, while lying on the squeaking sofa bed, she fantasized about becoming Mr. Kim's wife, about helping him run his businesses, about living a normal life that didn't involve running from a drunken fool.

Jake waited until his nephew and Yunjin had settled upstairs before taking his nightly sauna. It was his quiet time and he resented having to rush through it because it was so late. He tried to calm himself by taking deep breaths and adding eucalyptus water to the rocks. He wasn't sure how he was going to talk to his brother about all of this. He had already intervened in almost every aspect of Sam's life, and now he had to talk about his beating his wife and son? No, he could begin with Sam's drinking.

Alcohol was a crutch, a sign of weakness. Wasn't it Sam himself who used to tell Jake not to be weak? Wasn't it Sam who forced Jake to do push-ups and to withstand pain whenever he got injured? Jake almost wanted to taunt his brother and ask him who was weak now? Sam may have had the physical strength, but Jake had the mental strength, and in the end, that was what mattered.

Why was he even thinking about this? Jake stood up and stretched, feeling the sweat run down his back. He was feeling better now, and poured more water over the hot rocks. A wave of minty heat blew over him. He inhaled deeply, scorching his throat.

What were his obligations to his brother, to his family? He remembered that his mother had written him an e-mail a few days ago, asking for updates and to tell her how he and his brother and her grandson were doing. He had to write her back or else she would soon send an e-mail asking if he had received the first one. She also wanted to know if he was dating anyone. Some day she and his father would be too old to take care of themselves, and then, Jake knew, he would be the one to bring them here to take care of them. Sam would never do that. He didn't have the means and he was just too irresponsible.

He thought of Koman's advice: really help Sam or let him go. How much more could Jake do for his brother? He had given him thousands and thousands of dollars, given him work, given him his time and connections and energy. He was even lending his house to Sam's wife and child. What more could Jake do? There was nothing else left.

He said aloud, his voice muted in the wooden cell, It's time to cut him off.

29

Unha had trouble understanding Bobby Yun, who was always in motion with a restlessness that kept his foot tapping and his head nodding, and he spoke quickly, running his words together. Unha needed a few seconds after each question, and then answered in what seemed like slow motion.

All I did was waitressing at Club Saja, she told him.

Pretty girl like you? he said with a leer. I don't believe it.

It was because I can speak English, she said warily, knowing this was an advantage.

Bobby perked up, his eyes blinking rapidly. His short hair was gelled back and glistened. In English he said, How good is it?

She replied in English, It is okay.

They were in the living room, Heeun and Kyungja sitting quietly on the mattress. Bobby said, Speak English to me from now on. You know you have to pay off your debt.

She replied, I will not have sex.

We will see about that, he said.

She tried to control the flush of anger. She kept her face expressionless. She noticed that his sport coat was too big for him and his shoes were scuffed.

He smiled. He had a sparse mustache that made his upper lip look dirty. He tapped his fingers on his leg and said, I am sorry that you were beaten. I do not like that.

Unha didn't reply.

He nodded his head. He said, The girls who work for me do not get hurt. They do their job and pay off their debt and then leave. Some stay on because they make good money after. You have little choice, because you owe so much. I paid off your debt of ten thousand.

I would rather die.

He said, You have some time to think about it. A couple of days for your face to heal.

I will not change my mind, she said.

Then that will be too bad for you, he said in Korean. He stood up and said to Heeun and Kyungja, You have another few hours. Rest up. Did you eat?

They shook their heads.

When the others come, I will tell them to bring dinner.

What do we do with her? Heeun asked.

Bobby asked Unha in English, You know there is nowhere for you to go. Do I have to tie you up?

No, she said.

You are illegal here, and will be arrested if you leave. Do you understand that?

I do.

He studied her. Then to the others he said, Watch her.

He said to her in English, The sooner you work, the sooner you pay your debt, and the sooner you can do what you want.

He walked quickly out of the apartment.

232

Unha noticed that Kyungja did nothing without Heeun's approval, that she kept looking up to check where Heeun was. When Heeun told Kyungja to lie down and rest, Kyungja did. When Heeun went to the bathroom, Kyungja raised her head and waited.

Unha asked Kyungja how old she was.

Seventeen, she replied.

How did you get into this country?

I pretended to be the daughter of someone.

Unha said, And you've been here a few months already.

She nodded her head.

Heeun came out of the bathroom and saw them. She said to Kyungja, Rest. Try to sleep.

Kyungja curled up on the mattress. Heeun said to Unha, You should rest too.

Unha snapped, Don't tell me what to do.

Heeun drew back. She said, The more you fight, the harder it will be.

How can you do this? Unha asked. How can you stand it?

Heeun sat down next to Unha and said, You don't think about it. You don't worry about it. It's not you.

What do you mean? Of course it's you.

She pointed to her head. You are up here. You just think of something else.

Unha thought about the man in the woods and had to keep her anger hidden. She asked calmly, Has anyone ever escaped?

No.

Ever? I don't believe that.

Where do they escape to? I heard about a raid that happened a year ago. All of them were deported.

And Bobby? Was he arrested?

233

It wasn't him. It was another group. And the women did not tell the police anything. They knew their families would be hurt if they did. I think some of the women even wanted to come back.

Unha didn't believe her, and said, How long do you have to work for him?

Not much longer. Then I will work at a nail salon. I will save up my money and open my own business.

Have you talked to the women who work at the nail salon? Why would they hire you?

Bobby runs them, she said. I need to rest. You can have the bedroom if you want.

Heeun lay on the mattress next to Kyungja, and she wrapped her arm over Kyungja's waist. Kyungja nestled her back closer to her. Unha watched them for a moment, reminded of the Ahn sisters in her hometown who as children used to sleep together like that because they only had one bed. She walked to the bedroom and closed the door. She saw the tin foil and lighter of the two men who were taking drugs here. She sat on the mattress and tried to figure out what to do. She stared at her bandaged feet. The first thing she needed were shoes. Then she wondered what size Heeun and Kyungja were. They had left their shoes by the door.

She stepped out of the bedroom and peered into the living room. Heeun was awake, and she lifted her head up from the mattress and tracked Unha as she walked into the bathroom and closed the door. She ran the water and flushed the toilet. She returned to the bedroom and waited. Eventually they would fall asleep. And when they did, she would run.

She was exhausted and would start to doze off, but then jerk awake. Her mind would not let her rest. She wondered if being dead would be better than this. No, she couldn't give up. After she lost track of time she pulled herself up slowly and checked outside. Heeun and Kyungja were sleeping, their

234

backs turned to the door. She stepped slowly across the carpet, and examined their shoes, worn-out flats with deep creases. Both would fit without the bandages, but with the bandages she had to force her feet into the larger pair. Her ribs and stomach spasmed as she bent over. She winced and sucked in her breath. She glanced over at the girls. They remained still.

Slowly, quietly, she unlocked the deadbolt, and opened the door. The hinges squeaked, and she stopped. She turned. Staring directly at her was Kyungja, her head slightly raised and peering over Heeun's sleeping body. Unha stared back. She narrowed her eyes and gave Kyungja such a venomous look, thinking, I will kill you if you speak, that Kyungja shrunk back. She burrowed her head into her arms. Unha's body tingled with pain. Her temples pounded. She waited a moment, then stepped out and closed the door behind her.

The night air was chilly. Her thin sweater wouldn't be enough. She hesitated. She was afraid. There was so much danger out there. But what else could she do? She limped carefully down the steps. This was a second-floor unit of a four-apartment building, and there were similar small buildings scattered around a swimming pool and patch of lawn. A cement sidewalk led her between the buildings to a long, covered parking lot. She heard cars beyond the lot and hurried toward the exit.

A wide, quiet street lay in front of the apartment complex, only a few cars waiting at the corner light. More apartment complexes lined the street at her right, and after the intersection on her left the street rose up on an overpass with a lane branching off onto a freeway. She wasn't sure where to go, wondering if her best option was to try to return to San Francisco and find Sam. But she wasn't sure what town she was in, if she was even still in California.

She wondered about calling the police. She definitely wanted to call Sam. She didn't know either number. In Korea the emergency number was 119 for a fire and 112 for the police. Was it the same here? She had no money to buy a calling card. She had trouble organizing her thoughts.

She walked toward the other apartment complexes, stucco and wood buildings surrounded by stone fences, thick shrubs, and short trees. She shivered. Her feet no longer hurt as much, the bandages cushioned in the shoes, but the pain in her stomach was growing the more she walked.

A few cars drove by, and she walked with her head down, her impulse to hide overwhelming the urgency to flag someone for help. She didn't know whom to trust, and suspected that every car was linked to Bobby Yun.

She heard a train whistle in the distance. She stopped walking. The whistle sounded off again. Where was that? Somewhere far, but in this same direction. She hurried. If she could find a train station, she could find a map. There would be people to ask for help. She ignored the sharp, pulsing pain in her stomach, and continued down the road.

30

Sam spent the evening following Yun to his different businesses and to different apartment complexes in Mountain View and Sunnyvale. He assumed Yun was making his rounds in the same way that Sam and Im went to the garment factories and massage parlors to collect receipts. Yun drove an old silver Porsche and sped through traffic with little regard for stop signs and stoplights. A few times Sam almost lost him, but recognized the low taillights.

Now Yun pulled into a mini mall in Santa Clara, and knocked on the front door of a nail salon. The door opened and he walked in. More lights went on inside. Sam settled back in his seat and waited.

He realized he didn't have much of a plan. If he found Unha, he'd take her. Then what? Could he bring her to his apartment with Yunjin and his son there? He couldn't afford a motel room, and his brother wouldn't help him. He thought more seriously about leaving the area, about heading to Los Angeles or New York and starting over. The only thing stopping him was his son. He didn't think he could bring him, not yet, and that meant leaving him here with Yunjin.

But hadn't he learned anything from Sunny's death, that he couldn't waste time? They had made all kinds of plans for going on vacations, for buying a house, for going back to Korea to visit family, but they kept putting it off, and then she got sick. Shortly before she died she told him she regretted that they hadn't returned to Seoul for a vacation. She wanted to see her mother one last time. Sam tried to raise the money to fly Sunny's mother over, but he barely had enough for groceries, and Sunny's mother was afraid of flying. What dug at Sam was that they had had the money to visit Korea before Sunny got sick, but were saving it for a down payment on a house.

He saw his chances for happiness fading, the longer he stayed here, indebted to Mr. Oh, to his brother, burdened by the constant memories of his late wife, by guilt for making Yunjin miserable. No, he couldn't stay here. He would just die a slow death. He had to leave. He just had to.

He sighed and closed his eyes.

He was jolted awake when Bobby Yun came out of the nail salon while yelling into his phone. From across the small parking lot Sam heard Yun say, Where the fuck did she go? Find her!

Yun jumped into his car and sped off. Sam was surprised by how fast Yun disappeared down the road, and he skidded out of the lot, trying to catch up. He saw the taillights heading for the freeway entrance, and he stepped on the accelerator. There wasn't much traffic, so Sam was able to keep tabs on Yun even as he raced into the fast lane and moved ahead.

They were driving back to Mountain View, and whatever the problem was, Yun was pushing past eighty miles per hour, leaving Sam farther and farther behind. They exited onto Middlefield Road, and Sam began to recognize the neighborhood as one of the apartment complexes they had visited earlier tonight.

Yun turned onto Shoreline Boulevard and then parked in a small lot of the Hill Vista complex. Sam slowed, then pulled over to the curb. He parked and climbed out, walking quickly toward Yun's car.

Before he could begin searching, he heard voices in Korean approaching. He crouched behind a pick-up truck and heard Yun telling someone that they should split up. Yun said, I will start at the police station and work my way back. You and Hwang also split up. Check the train and bus stations. She has no money, right?

Right, another voice said.

Keep your cell on. Don't do anything until you call me first.

They returned to their cars and Sam waited until they drove off. He tried not to assume anything; they could've been talking about another woman, but he grew hopeful. He drove down Shoreline, toward El Camino Real. He saw a Donut shop that was open 24 hours and parked.

Inside he bought a coffee and asked where the police station was. The man behind the counter, bleary-eyed, his face bloated, said it was on Villa, right before the Central Expressway. The man said to get back onto Shoreline, head north for a few blocks and turn right.

Sam found the police station easily, a huge pastel modern building with a parking lot in front, and he searched for Yun's car, but couldn't find it.

The coffee energized him. He drove down Villa and onto Castro, finding himself in a downtown area with coffee shops, restaurants and small stores. He was surprised to find a Chinese grocery, and a small Korean barbecue restaurant. The streets were empty and clean, and he drove up and down the main strip, searching for Yun's car. He saw an S.U.V. driving slowly in the other direction. The driver was Korean, and glanced at Sam's car. Sam kept his speed steady, but watched the S.U.V. in his rear-view mirror. The S.U.V. turned a corner and disappeared.

He wasn't even sure if they were looking for Unha, and he felt like he was wasting time. He drove back to the apartment complex on Middlefield, and parked in a handicapped spot, angling his mirror so that he could see any car coming in. He fidgeted. He tried not to imagine the worst. He turned the radio on and listened to a news station. A science call-in show was on, and he heard a guest speaker answer questions about a meteor shower.

There were so many things he didn't know. When he was a teen and was playing baseball with the Soyoung Club League—a private league sponsored by various factories in the Kuro-dong district—most of his teammates talked about how they wanted to be doctors or businessmen. Some even had parents who owned the sponsoring factories. But Sam hadn't cared about any of that. All he wanted to do was play baseball, and he was beginning to learn woodworking from Mr. Baek, the carpenter with whom he'd eventually apprentice.

Mr. Baek, an accomplished cellist and poet, was appalled at Sam's lack of knowledge and curiosity. Part of Sam's apprenticeship included reading books about famous Koreans, like King Sejong, who created the Korean alphabet, but Sam rarely finished the books. He just hadn't cared.

But he cared now. He knew he was moving through his life without really understanding anything. He realized this when Sunny died and he had no idea how to wrestle with the loss. He still didn't know. He wondered if it was a fault of his education. Maybe if he dug himself out of debt and made a new life for himself, he'd read more. He'd learn about everything. He'd stop drinking.

He listened to the scientist on the radio talk about the differences between a meteor shower and a meteor storm. Sam tried to pay attention, but couldn't concentrate. He sud-

240

denly remembered Sunny's "skeleton dance," something she used to do as a child when she wanted to shake off her worries. She once showed it to him, a loosening of her body and dancing with abandon. She had laughed with an unselfconscious ease, shaking her head and letting her hair fall over her face. She looked up through her hair with a silly grin and said, See? Skeleton dance.

Sam laughed to himself. Then he felt a deep, painful ache in his chest. He sank back into his seat and clicked off the radio.

31

Unha wandered into a small downtown area on Castro Street where everything was closed and dark. The streets were strangely clean, the sidewalks almost shining in the moonlight. She saw a pay phone in front of a Chinese restaurant, but was too scared to call the police, since she was here illegally, and imagined she could go to jail. She thought her best option was to go and find Sam. She wasn't sure how to do this without any money, but she had to try. At the corner she found a green metal kiosk with a map of the downtown area encased in plastic. She saw where she was, and located the train station. She was only two blocks away.

As she walked north toward the station she heard young voices, and saw three teenagers dressed in scruffy jeans and ragged leather jackets. Two were sitting on the ground, smoking. The third, a girl, was balancing on a skateboard. They turned to her, startled. She stopped, ready to run. One of them said, Jeez. What the hell happened to you?

Unha was confused. She then realized they were talking about her face. She touched her cheek, feeling the tenderness.

The girl moved toward her, peering closer. She said in a soft voice, Are you all right? Were you mugged?

Unha said in her halting English, The train station is there?

Do you need a doctor? Were you in an accident?

Unha said, I need to go to San Francisco.

The trains aren't running right now, the girl said. You were hit, weren't you? Did your husband do that?

Unha stepped back, confused. I don't know what you mean, she said.

The girl said to her friends, I think she was abused.

One of the boys asked Unha, Where do you live?

Unha then realized she didn't know the address of anyplace, not even the club. She had no money, no idea of where she was, and the concern of these three teenagers suddenly overwhelmed her. She covered her face and tried not to cry.

The other boy said, Holy shit. We should get the cops.

No, Unha said, wiping her eyes. I can't...

It's okay, the girl said. They'll know how to handle your husband.

I just...I just want to go to San Francisco.

Do you have family there?

She thought about this and said, Yes. Family.

The three teenagers studied her, and the girl asked Unha, Do you have any money?

Unha shook her head.

The girl turned to the others, and one of the boys said, Oh, man, I only have like five bucks.

The girl said, I have ten.

That's more than enough, the third boy said. But she should go to the police.

Give it up, the girl said to them, holding out her hand.

This is your good deed for the day.

But I wanted to get a burger.

This is my last five. I'm going to have to hit my parents up again.

Give it up, the girl said.

They dug into their pockets and pulled out their cash.

Unha was amazed that they were going to give her money. She tightened her stomach, close to crying, and exhaled slowly. The girl counted out fifteen dollars in cash and handed it to her. She said, The next train probably won't be until morning. But there are benches and things at the platform. You sure you don't want us to call the police?

Unha looked at the cash. I...I thank you, she said.

Just go up that street and make a right, one of the boys said.

Good for you for leaving, the girl said.

Unha was confused by their comments, but she pocketed the money, thanked them again, and hurried up the street. Even though she was cold and her ribs and stomach ached and her feet hurt with every step, she felt braver, knowing there were people who would help her.

She found the train station easily, the clean pale concrete shining under the bright lights, and she checked the timetable. The first train to San Francisco was at 4:49, two hours away. She could wait. She sat on a nearby bench, and eased off the shoes. She checked the bandages and found them crusted with dried blood. Her feet began swelling immediately, her toes pulsing. She quickly forced the shoes back on. She looked around, worried about Bobby Yun and his men. She stood up and moved to a bench hidden in the shadows.

Her plan was simple. She would work her way back to Club Saja, and hide and wait until she saw Sam again. She knew his car. She knew he worked in the late afternoon and evenings. She wouldn't tell him she was raped. No. She would tell him only that she was kidnapped and beaten. She stifled another urge to cry. The numbness was wearing off. Every time she closed her eyes she could hear the man in the woods breathing heavily against her neck as he lay on top of her. He had smelled of cigarette smoke. He had wheezed and grunted.

She shivered and tightened her body, curling up into a ball on the bench. She thought of her grandmother who had escaped North Korean soldiers as she crossed the mountains during the Korean war. She told the story many times when Unha was a child, and for the first time in her life she understood it. Her grandmother had walked hundreds of miles by herself. Her grandmother had run from men with guns. Unha pressed her lip to her knee. She pretended she was back home and her grandmother was stroking her hair.

32

David woke up to the sound of typing. The clicking of a keyboard filtered through the dark and rose up to the loft, where Yunjin snored quietly. He climbed out of bed and looked over the metal railing. Uncle Jake was sitting at the computer in the living room, the glow of the screen bathing him. David walked down the steps. Uncle Jake turned and smiled.

You should be asleep, he whispered.

What are you doing? David asked. His uncle's hair was wet, slicked back. He wore a silk robe over his pajamas, and his face was red.

E-mail, he said, motioning David over to him. Do you want to say hello to your grandmother? I'm writing her.

She has e-mail?

Just recently. My father still doesn't understand it. Come here.

David walked up next to him, and was surprised to see the e-mail was in Korean. He asked him how he did that.

It's just the font, he said. What would you like to say to Halmonee?

Tell her hello, David said. Some day I want to meet

her.

Yes, of course. She wants to meet you too. He began typing on the English keyboard and the Korean letters appeared on the screen. He then sent the message. He asked David how he was doing.

Okay.

It has gotten bad for your father since your mother died, he said.

This was the first time his uncle had mentioned his mother, and David wasn't sure how to respond.

He said, She was a wonderful woman.

David nodded his head.

Do you miss her?

David said, Yes.

You know your father is just reacting to all that. He was like that as a kid, bottling everything up until it exploded.

My dad once said that even though you are younger you were like the older one.

Did he say that? Yes, it's true. Well, no. He picked on me a lot the way older brothers do, but I guess I was the more responsible one.

He picked on you?

All the time. He said I needed to be toughened up. He used to make me do push-ups in the yard.

David smiled. What else?

Uncle Jake leaned back, the chair creaking. The computer screensaver came on, and colored lines bounced against a black background. He was quiet for a while, then said, Your father was looking out for me in his own way. Our parents were very strict, very religious. Our father used to spank us if we cursed. Your father used to protect me from that.

How?

Jake said, Once I was caught setting fire to a garbage pile, and—

What? Why?

I wanted to know if it could burn.

What happened?

The owner of the house called my parents. But your father took the blame for me. My father whipped him until he bled.

Why did he take the blame?

He said that he didn't think I could take it. That's why he wanted to toughen me up.

David said, He has said that to me, too.

Can I ask you a question?

Yes.

Does Yunjin take good care of you?

David shrugged his shoulders.

If she were to leave, would you be okay?

With just my dad?

Yes.

David said, I'd be okay.

What if something were to happen to your father? Could you be okay with Yunjin? Or with me?

What would happen to my father?

Nothing. Just asking.

David shook his head. I don't know, he said. He felt uneasy and asked where his father was.

I'm not sure, Uncle Jake said. Probably working late.

David asked if he could use the hot room.

It's really late. You should get back to bed. Maybe tomorrow.

David was disappointed, but was too tired to argue. Uncle Jake walked him back to the stairs, and watched him climb up to the loft. When David settled into bed he heard his uncle return to the computer, his chair creaking. David fell asleep to the sound of the intermittent clicking and dreamed of locusts swarming toward him, their mandibles clicking.

33

Unha stirred at the sound of a car engine revving, breaking the late-night silence. Her eyes opened, but she kept still. The air was chilly, the sky dark and starless. She glanced at the large clock standing on the corner—4:15. The train would be coming in half an hour. She began to sit up, but froze. A small Korean man was approaching, peering at her. He stepped closer. Unha recognized him. He was one of Bobby Yun's men, one of the men she'd seen taking drugs in the bedroom.

She held her breath. He stepped closer, then pulled out his cell phone.

Unha sat up, and felt every joint in her body ache with pain. The man said into his phone, I found her. The train station.

She saw that he was alone, and scrambled away.

The man yelled, Stop!

She staggered forward, almost losing her balance, swooning from a head rush, and ran for a side street, hearing him coming after her. She grimaced at the pain shooting through her feet and legs, and searched for a place to hide. Streetlamps lit the sidewalks, and storefronts had security lighting filling the side alleys, so Unha kept running away from the commercial section and down the block towards a residential area. She wanted to find somewhere dark, and saw a row of small houses down the block.

The man kept after her, but he was slow. He was panting and trying to talk into his phone. Unha cut through a side yard of a house undergoing construction, stacks of wood piled to her waist, the framing of part of the porch exposed and covered with a tarp. A dog barked nearby.

She ran through another adjoining yard, then came out on a different side street. She was completely disoriented and was propelled forward only by the sound of her pursuer, who stumbled against a low fence and cursed. Unha heard him say in Korean, Around the block. She went through a yard.

She ran along the sidewalk, passing a row of homes hidden behind fences and high shrubs, and heard a car rounding a corner up ahead. It was a small sedan, the headlights bright and shining toward her. The car skidded to a stop. She saw the driver get out, but she didn't wait to see who it was. She turned, but then the other man appeared from the yard.

Looking wildly around, she ran across the street and toward another house, heading up the driveway and around the side. She heard the men coordinating, one coming after her, the other getting back into his car and driving off. She couldn't see and had to slow down, her hands outstretched in front of her and feeling a wooden fence. Her head was pounding so hard that her vision blurred. The man chasing her moved into the yard and said, You can't go anywhere.

In the semi-darkness she saw him crouched low, his hands spread out in front of him. He walked toward her and said, Don't be stupid. Just come with us.

She leapt for the fence, grabbing the top of the

wooden slats, and yanked herself up. Her shoes slipped on vines growing along the bottom and the man ran to her, grabbing her jeans, and pulled her down. She raised her leg and thrust it back, kicking him in the knee, and he yelled in pain. She clawed back up the fence, stretching her arm over, her feet scratching at the vines. She threw her leg up and cracked the wood, and was able to shift her weight and climb over. She fell to the ground on the other side, landing heavily on a cement sidewalk, her breath knocked out of her, and she tried to pull herself up.

Someone ran toward her. She looked up. It was Bobby Yun, and he reached her in three swift steps and grabbed her hair. He slammed her head into the fence.

34

Sam snapped forward when he saw an SUV drive into the apartment parking lot and two Korean men pull a woman out of the back seat. It was dark, and Sam couldn't tell if it was Unha. He was about to climb out of his car when Yun's Porsche pulled up next to the SUV. Sam pressed up against his windshield, trying to get a better view. The woman slumped forward, limping, and the two men held her up by her arms, almost dragging her across the pavement.

Sam opened his door and stepped out. Was that her? They were walking out of his line of sight, so he moved toward the lot, and hid behind a car. She was the right height, and he thought she was thin like Unha, but he wasn't sure. One of her shoes slipped off her feet, and the two men stopped. Yun picked it up, then yanked off her other shoe. The woman tried to stop the men, but they kept moving. She looked back, and Sam's heart clenched.

It was Unha.

Her face was bruised and cut, her lips swollen and one

of her eyes puffed closed, but it was definitely Unha.

He almost called out to her, but stopped himself.

His head swirled with too many options. He wanted to go running straight at them, but knew that was dangerous. He had to be careful. What if they had guns? What if he made things worse for her?

He headed toward the main path, keeping his distance. First he'd find out where they were taking her, and how many others were there. He began thinking of what to do. Maybe he could call the police. No. He had no idea what they would do to him or Unha.

Then he wondered how else the men had hurt her.

He realized he could kill Yun.

The two men dragged Unha to the second floor of one of the smaller buildings. She tried to struggle, but they pulled her roughly up the stairs. Yun hurried after them. Sam waited until Yun followed the men and Unha into the apartment and closed the door.

He considered finding a fire alarm and setting it off. Or what if he set an actual fire at the apartment?

Then he heard a cry from the apartment, a woman's voice, and he remembered Minji. There wasn't time. He ran up the stairs and checked the doorknob. It was unlocked. He turned the handle and threw open the door.

Unha was curled up in a ball on the floor. Two of the men were sitting on a mattress. Two other girls were rubbing their eyes sleepily. Yun was standing there with a roll of duct tape in his hands, and stopped talking as he whirled around and saw Sam.

Yun said, What—

Sam ran in, heading straight for him, and before Yun could react Sam slammed his fist into Yun's face. The other men jumped up. Yun reached into his jacket, and pulled out a small revolver, but Sam quickly grabbed Yun's hand, gripping tightly, and kneed Yun in the groin. Yun cried out as

253

Sam snatched the gun away. Yun fell to the ground, holding his groin. Sam kicked him in the head and raised the gun at the other two men. They stopped.

Yun cursed and moaned. He was about to say something, but Sam kicked him in the face. Blood spurted from his nose.

Sam said to the two men, Do not move.

They looked at each other, then at Yun. They raised their hands slowly.

Unha peered at him through one eye. She asked, Sam?

Yes. Are you all right?

She said, No.

Sam said to one of the girls, You. Get their guns and give them to me. Slowly.

The girl glanced at the other one, who nodded her head. The girl stood up and moved to the men. She reached behind the skinny one and pulled out an automatic. The shorter, fatter one didn't have a gun. She handed the automatic to Sam, who shoved it into his waistband.

Yun sat up, staring coldly at Sam.

Sam kicked him again, and hurt his toe on Yun's belt. Yun sucked in his breath but kept quiet.

The skinny man said, Are you crazy. Do you know who that is?

Sam said, You two, lie on the ground. Face down. Hands spread out.

The men lay down.

Sam said to the two girls, I am taking Unha. You can come with me if you want.

They blinked, confused.

The skinny man said to them, If you leave we will find you and kill you.

Sam walked swiftly toward him and kicked him in the head. The man rolled to the side and moaned. The other man said, Just go! We will find you later.

Sam stepped toward him and crushed the man's hand with his heel. He howled in pain.

Sam said to the two girls, Get their car keys, cell phones, and wallets.

They searched the pockets of the men, and handed everything to Sam, who found a greasy paper bag in the garbage. He put everything into this and then picked up the roll of duct tape and threw it toward the girls. He said, Tape up their ankles and their wrists behind their backs.

Yun stared at him without saying anything. His eyes were calm, appraising. Blood oozed from his nose and over his mouth. Sam said, She is not property. She does not belong to you.

When I find you I will kill you, Yun said quietly.

Sam shook his head and stepped on his neck. Yun grunted. The girls finished taping up the two men and moved tentatively toward Yun. Sam said, Do it.

They pulled out strips of tape and wrapped Yun's hands behind his back, and then his ankles. They looked up to Sam, awaiting his instructions.

He asked, Do you want to come with me?

Where would we go? asked the older one.

I don't know, Sam said.

Unha pulled herself up slowly. Sam helped her and she clutched his arm. She said, You came.

I did, he said. We will go now.

You came.

He studied her with concern. She was dazed, exhausted. Her eyes were bloodshot and watery. He saw dirt embedded in the skin of her shoulder and arms.

He asked the two girls, Are you coming?

Yun stared at them without speaking. The older girl said to Sam, No, we are not going.

Then lie on the floor with them. I will tape you up

too.

They lowered themselves down, and put their arms behind their backs. Sam quickly taped their wrists and ankles. He glanced at Unha, who was leaning against the wall, watching him.

I am so tired, she said.

Sam said, Let's go. Come on.

He held out his hand, and she took it. She began shaking. He could see her trying to hold back her crying. He hurried her out of the apartment, and led her to his car.

Thank you, she said.

We still have to get away, he said. He pulled out one of the wallets from the paper bag and found it thick with twenty-dollar bills. He'd dump everything but the cash.

What are you going to do?

I'm not sure, but we should get away from here now.

Thank you, she said.

He nodded his head and held open the passenger door for her. She climbed in, wincing in pain, and covered her face with her hands. She leaned forward, and cried quietly.

PART VI

THE HOT ROOM

35

Yunjin drove with Mr. Kim to a large studio space in West Berkeley, off San Pablo Avenue. He had asked her to come along to see a possible new location, and when they drove up to the long, low building with an Antique Furniture sign partially blackened out with paint, Mr. Kim said, They just went out of business.

Down the street there were two large buildings—a boat supply store and some kind of drug company with giant metal test tubes standing at the front gate—and at the end of the block were what looked like empty warehouses. Mr. Kim said, This used to be an industrial area, but it's becoming more commercial.

Not many customers, she said, trying to sound as if she knew something about business. The wide streets had some traffic, but most of the cars were on Ashby and heading to or from the freeway.

There are more office buildings nearby, he said. During rush hour there is a lot of traffic on Seventh.

She glanced at him, still not sure why he had asked her to join him. He had said he wanted her opinion, but she couldn't understand it. What did she know about opening a business?

She pointed to the furniture store and said, How big is it inside?

I'll show you, he said. The realtor gave me a key.

He led her to the front and unlocked the door. When he walked in, he said, I don't know where the lights are, but you can still see most of it.

Yunjin looked up. The skylights were dirty, but let in enough light through the criss-crossed wooden rafters and onto the full open space below. The linoleum floor was sprinkled with sawdust. She said, A lot of space.

Mr. Kim took off his sports coat and hung it over his arm. He said, I wouldn't have to do too much to the space. Clean it up, add a layer of padding to the floor. Put in a sound system.

Punching bags?

Yes, he said. Those rafters are load bearing. Very solid.

She smelled pine oil, and asked, Why did they go out of business?

Down the road is a junk yard. They have furniture there for cheap. He said, You look different.

She had trouble meeting his gaze. She was wearing her only good outfit, her Sunday church silk blouse and dress, and said, Just in case we were meeting business people.

He smiled. You are wondering why I asked you here, he said.

Yes.

Do you think you could be my office manager?

She blinked. I have no experience, she said.

Didn't you say you took care of your aunt and uncle?

Yes.

That is what an office manager does. She takes care of

everything in the office.

Why me?

You said you were looking for a job.

But...

He said in English, And you speak English too.

A little, she said.

And we're both from Chuncheon, he said. Maybe we were even neighbors. Maybe we even talked.

She didn't tell him that while she was living in Chuncheon with her mother they rarely saw anyone. She remembered that her mother kept telling her to stay inside, away from the sun, because she didn't want Yunjin to get any darker. Even her mother thought Yunjin was ugly.

Yunjin said, I promise you I will do a good job, Mr. Kim. Thank you very much.

He stepped closer to her and said, You do not have to be so formal with me. In English he added, My friends call me John.

John?

My American name, he said. In Korean, he added, I hope we can be friends. He reached down and held her hand.

She held her breath.

He said, You don't have to be shy with me.

She didn't know how to respond, but when he leaned forward to kiss her, she drew back. She said, What are you doing?

What do you think I am doing? he asked.

I... I am married.

He blinked, and bowed slightly, backing away. I am sorry. I thought... I thought maybe...

She found herself blushing deeply, tears forming. She said, No, I am sorry. Maybe I led you to believe—

No, no. It is my fault, he said. I am very embarrassed.

They were silent. She said, I guess you don't want me to have the job anymore.

He looked up, surprised. You don't want the job?

She said, I do.

Then you will have it, he said.

But...

He let out a slow breath and said, Please accept my apologies about... I need a good office manager and I think you can do it.

Why me?

Because you are... strong.

She shook her head. No, I am not.

He looked at her and smiled. Oh, yes, you are.

Yunjin had so little experience with men that she puzzled over this for the rest of the day. Did she miss something? Did she do or say something to encourage it? It made no sense and she worried over the confusing signals. She just didn't understand men.

She knew of only a few marriages: her grandparents, who hated their daughter and granddaughter; her aunt and uncle, who only talked to each other to complain or fight; and now her own, which made no sense to her.

She had trouble believing that he was attracted to her. He didn't think she was ugly?

She thought again of her mother telling her not to get any sun. She also used to make Yunjin wash her face often, demanding she use a harsh soap that made her cheeks break out in a rash. Her mother also told her to stay away from the army base, and from any Americans. She told Yunjin, The soldiers are all killers and rapists.

As Yunjin walked home from the BART station, she wondered if she should still take the job. Wouldn't it be awkward? She would have no idea how to act. She didn't feel like she understood anything. It wasn't like her mother had instructed her in how to act. Her mother could barely take care of herself.

Yunjin remembered her mother's nervous habit of wringing her hands and of digging her nails into her wrists, clawing herself when she was upset. She had to wear long-sleeved shirts to cover the scabs, and once, when Yunjin was trying to hold her hand, she accidentally grabbed her mother's wrist. Her mother yelled in pain and scolded Yunjin, who hadn't understood what she had done wrong. Only later would she see the scabs and understand how strange her mother was.

She thought, Everyone is a puzzle. As she walked up to the apartment, she told herself to be a better mother to David. She found the front door unlocked and heard voices inside. She tensed. Sam was home. Maybe drunk. Maybe talking to himself again. She thought about leaving.

Then she heard a woman's voice.

The shock of this made her burst through the door. She found Sam kneeling on the floor in front of a woman sitting on the sofa; her face was beaten and bruised.

Yunjin stood there, taking this in, then said, Who is this?

Sam stood up slowly, his knees cracking. This is Unha.

What happened to her?

Sam inhaled slowly, and replied, She was kidnapped.

What is she doing here?

I saved her.

Yunjin didn't know what to say. The way Unha couldn't look up at Yunjin made her suspicious. She asked Sam, Is she your girlfriend?

Sam paused. He glanced at Unha.

With this, Yunjin felt something strange: relief. Everything in her head seemed to click together—this is what she needed, for Sam to find another woman.

Before he could answer she said, Let me get the first aid supplies. She looks like she needs to clean up also. Has she eaten or had anything to drink? You get her water and food. I will help her to the bathroom.

Sam seemed bewildered by her decisiveness. He stammered, then said, Where is David?

At tae kwon do.

Sam blinked. David is taking tae kwon do?

Yunjin began to help Unha up, but her legs were shaky. She sat back down. Yunjin offered her arm and said, Come. The bathroom is this way.

Sam said quietly, Thank you.

Yunjin ignored him. She thought, I am free.

36

Jake was unsure why Koman wanted a meeting, even if, as Koman had said, Mr. Oh had suggested it. Was this about the delayed opening and cleaning the cash? Jake worried as he walked into Saja and went upstairs, nodding to Choon, who had an odd smile on his face.

He heard Im talking loudly, and approached the rear booth, where he saw Koman, Im, and a stranger with a bandage across his nose, his lip puffy and his eye blackened. Koman introduced him as Bobby Yun and asked Jake to join them.

Do you want anything to drink? Koman said.

Jake glanced at the others. He was confused that they were here. He said he was fine. He sat down and waited for Koman to speak.

We have a problem, Koman said.

About my club?

Your brother, Im said. This is about your brother.

Jake closed his eyes for a moment, preparing himself.

He was glad this wasn't about his club, but maybe this was worse. He sighed and asked, Now what?

Koman explained the situation tersely, that Sam had taken a woman from Yun, and in order to avoid a misunderstanding, Koman invited Yun here. Koman said, We had to explain that Sam was not working for us in any way.

Im said, Your brother almost started a war.

Jake said to Yun, You are sure it was Sam?

Yun nodded his head.

Koman said, We need to know where he is.

Jake shook his head. I haven't seen him.

Im said to Koman, I told you he'd say that. It's his brother!

Jake stared at Im, trying to understand why he was angry. He realized that because Sam had been working with Im, all of this made Im look bad. Koman probably blamed him for not keeping a closer watch over Sam.

Jake said, I don't know what this has to do with me. I don't know anything of what my brother does. I told Mr. Oh that I don't want to know.

Koman was quiet for a moment. Then he said, Mr. Oh asked me to take care of this, and so now you are involved.

What am I supposed to do?

Find him! Im said.

Where does he live? Yun asked.

This was the first time Yun had spoken, and Jake was startled by the deep scratchiness coming from such a small man. Jake thought quickly, and said, He lives in Oakland, but I was just with his wife and son—they haven't seen him either.

Yun said, He has a wife and son?

Jake tried not to show any reaction, but he silently cursed himself for revealing this. He said, They stayed at my house last night.

Why?

Because Sam is missing.

Koman and Im exchanged glances, and Koman said, Start at the apartment.

Wait, Jake said. You might scare his wife and son—

Fuck them, Yun said. I am going to find your cocksucker brother and—

Quiet, Koman said.

Yun stopped and glared at Jake.

Jake said, Let me find him and talk to him. There's no need for this to get out of hand.

Im said, It's already out of hand. Your brother fucked up. I bet you know where he is.

No, Jake said. I haven't seen him since you and he were at my club.

You are fucking lying.

Jake said to Koman, My brother can be impulsive. But he eventually sees reason. He is probably trying to figure out how to fix this. Let me find him and talk to him. He will listen to me.

Yun was about to speak, but Koman gave him a hard stare that shut him up.

Jake asked Yun, Did the girl go willingly?

That's not the point and you know it, Koman said.

Im asked Koman, How do we know he is not hiding him right now?

Koman stared at Jake while he answered, Because he knows that his relationship with Mr. Oh is in danger. He knows that lying to us now will jeopardize his ties with us later.

I am not hiding my brother, Jake said.

Then find him, Im said.

Koman didn't break his gaze from Jake, and said, You have until tonight.

What do you mean?

You have until tonight to bring him to us.

267

Jake said, But I don't know where he is. He can be anywhere.

Tonight, Koman said. After that Im and Yun will look for him, and there is nothing I can do for your brother. Or for you.

I would like to talk to Mr. Oh about this, Jake said.

That's not possible, Koman said. I am your main contact now.

When Mr. Oh gets back—

Mr. Oh is back, Koman said. I am your main contact now.

Jake kept still. This meant that Mr. Oh was already distancing himself from this. Jake stood up slowly. Is that all? he asked.

Tonight, Koman said.

Jake went to his car and sat there for a while. Was this Mr. Oh's way of punishing Jake, or was it the dismantling of their partnership? Maybe Mr. Oh expected Jake to protect his brother, so he was giving Koman license to deal with Jake however was necessary.

Jake started his car, but remained in the lot. He pulled out his cell phone and called his brother's apartment. It rang five times, and then Yunjin picked up.

Has Sam shown up? Jake asked.

Yunjin paused, then asked, Is he in trouble?

Yes. Is he there? He is in danger.

Yunjin said, He just left.

With a woman?

Yes. She was beaten badly. She could hardly walk.

This stopped Jake. His brother probably felt like he had no choice but to save her. He said, Where did they go?

I think to your house.

My house? Jake almost groaned. This would implicate him further. He put his car in gear and drove out into the

268

street, heading for the Bay Bridge. He said, You and David might be in danger. I will come and get you. Don't go anywhere. Don't go out.

I was about to get David.

No. Stay. I will come and pick you up and we will get David.

Why?

Just do as I say.

What is happening? Yunjin asked. Who is the woman?

Jake was distracted, looking at his rear-view mirror. He couldn't be sure, but he thought a car might be following him, an older model Porsche. He said to Yunjin, Stay there.

He hung up. He turned down a side street, and the silver sports car made the same turn. He said aloud, What did you do to me, Sam?

37

Sam kept asking Unha if she was all right, and she kept replying that she was fine. But as they were driving up into the
hills she nodded off to sleep, then jerked awake with a small
gasp and winced in pain, sucking in air through her teeth. She
breathed heavily but finally leaned back, relaxed, and dozed
off. Sam hoped she would stay asleep. She was still in shock
and seemed to have trouble focusing on anything, answering
his questions in a distracted far-off tone. Yunjin had tried to
talk to her at the apartment, but Unha barely registered the
questions. Finally, after Yunjin helped bandage her feet and
disinfect the scratches on her arms and face, Sam packed
some of his clothes and told Yunjin he was going to find
somewhere safe and then return for them.

Yunjin had shaken her head.

What do you mean? he asked.

I am not going with you.

He noticed Unha was listening. He thought about
this, knowing how hard he had made life for her, and said, I

understand, but what about David?

I will take care of him until you are ready.

What about money—

I will figure it out. I always have.

He felt the sting of this. He said, There might be people looking for me. It is not safe here. I will give you money for a taxi. Go get David and then go to my brother's.

He pulled out the cash he had taken from Yun and his men and counted out fifty dollars.

Where did you get that? she asked.

I need to get supplies for Unha. I will meet you at my brother's, he said. I think we will be safe there for at least a night. Then I will go.

Where?

He hadn't answered her because he had no idea, and now, as he drove up toward his brother's house, he knew he was going to ask Jake to look after Yunjin and David, and Jake would be furious. And Sam would need more cash. He had about three-hundred dollars left from Yun, but how long would that last?

Maybe he and Unha should head down to L.A. He could find work, save money, and then he could send for David. Im once mentioned that Mr. Oh's businesses were limited to this area, and Yun's seemed to be in the South Bay, but he wasn't sure how hidden he'd be with other Koreans, so maybe L.A. wasn't good. While he was doing carpentry work up here, someone had told him of a building boom going on in the suburbs of Los Angeles, farther south. Maybe he could find work there. No, maybe head north, to Portland or Seattle. He wasn't sure what kind of work he'd find, but surely there'd be something.

The more he thought about this, the more worried he became. He wondered if he should go to the police and get Unha protection with them, but this meant she would be deported. Wouldn't that be better than this? But he could imagine them getting away and hiding out. They could change their names and start new lives. He could get back into carpentry. He could make furniture.

He drove up a steep, narrow road, his engine shuddering as he shifted into a lower gear. Unha stirred. She turned to him, confused, and their eyes met. She gave him a half smile, but the pain of this made her grimace. He felt a tug of affection for her, an unfamiliar desire to protect her, to hug her. He thought, There was nothing else I could have done.

He parked his car in his brother's driveway, and helped Unha out. He said, We'll go in back. I know where he keeps an extra key.

She limped next to him as they walked down the slate steps, the house set in a hill so that the back was propped up on large wooden columns. Upstairs there was a balcony overlooking the valley below, but down here there was a door leading into the basement where Jake had built the sauna. The key was hidden under a large stone. Sam let them in and helped her up the steps to the main floor. She looked around and said, This is nice.

Sit down, he said, pointing to the sofa in the living room. Rest. I am going to wash up and then we have to figure out where to go.

Where is your brother?

I am going to call him in a minute. I just need to think.

She eased herself down onto the sofa, exhaling in pain. She said, I need...I need to sleep.

Sleep, he said. We will be safe here for a while.

Thank you, Sam.

He moved toward her, and she shrank away. He stopped.

She said quickly, I'm sorry. I am still...I can't think clearly—

It's all right, he said. I understand. Let me find you a blanket.

No, I just need to lie down for a minute.

She curled up on the cushions and closed her eyes. Sam felt an uneasy pulse of panic, of everything tumbling out of control, and the unsteadiness in his chest made him take a big breath of air. He steadied himself. He watched over Unha as she slept.

38

David was startled to see Yunjin and his uncle appear at the dojang, and had to step out of the line while the practice was still going on. The teacher, Muk, a black belt who taught some of the children's beginner classes, motioned David to get out of the way as he began to get them ready to practice their forms.

David was wearing his uniform, and Uncle Jake gave him a small smile. He said, Very professional. I am sorry we have to pull you out of practice, but we have to go.

Where?

To my house, Jake said.

David went into the back to change, and when he came out he saw Yunjin nodding to Mr. Kim. They didn't talk, but Mr. Kim smiled in familiar way. David found this strange and when they walked to the car he asked her what was happening.

Many things, she said.

What is going on with Sunsengnim Kim?

Yunjin hesitated. She said, We will be working together at his new studio.

Really?

What? Jake asked.

I will explain later, Yunjin said. But I am going to get
a job with him.

David said, How—

Doing what? Jake asked.

Office manager.

David tried to make sense of this, and was about to ask more
questions, but as they drove up into the hills, he began to get
nauseous; the sudden inactivity after all the punching and
kicking was already disconcerting, but now the steep turns
and twists were making him dizzy. He said, I'm getting car-
sick.

We're almost there, Jake said. I had to take a different
way.

Why? Yunjin asked.

We were being followed.

She whirled around.

Not anymore, he said. I know these confusing roads
well.

I feel really sick, David said.

Do you need to throw up? Uncle Jake asked.

I don't know.

He said, Open your window. Get some air. We're almost home.

While David stuck his head out, he heard Yunjin ask,
How bad is it?

Bad, he said.

They fell silent. They drove up to Jake's house, David's
face cooled by the breeze, and he saw his father's car parked
out in front. When they walked into the house he saw a
woman with a bruised and puffy face lying on the sofa. She
pulled herself up, and even through her injuries David saw

the similarity to his mother. He stopped in the doorway. His father walked out of the kitchen. He said to Jake, We have to talk.

Unha introduced herself to David, and while his father and uncle went into the kitchen Yunjin and David sat in the living room with Unha. He felt the tension even though he wasn't sure what it was. Yunjin asked if Unha was feeling better.

Unha said, Thank you for helping me earlier.

Yunjin said, Where will you and Sam go?

I don't know, Unha said.

David thought, Go? Go where? He couldn't stop staring at Unha. Somehow the puffiness in her eyes made her look even more like his mother.

Unha touched her face and said to David, I must look very bad.

What happened to you? he asked.

She hesitated, and Yunjin said to him, You should take a shower.

Can I use the hot room?

Ask your uncle.

David moved toward the kitchen and heard his father say, This is the last time.

It is always the last time. Here is two hundred dollars.

He walked closer to the kitchen entrance. His father said, They were going to kill her. I had no choice.

Bobby Yun has Mr. Oh's help. Do you understand what you have done?

I understand.

It will be a matter of honor for Mr. Oh to turn you over to this Yun. You are his employee.

I am no longer his employee.

Stupid thick-headed idiot! You have also put your family in danger. And you have gotten me involved. Don't you know that I will have to answer for you! What have you done to me!

I need a place to hide. I can't hide here. Do you still have that condo in Santa Cruz?

David stepped forward and the floor creaked. His uncle peered around the corner and asked what he wanted.

Can I use the hot room?

It's not on right now. Later. Go to Yunjin.

David walked to the living room, where Yunjin and Unha were sitting without speaking. He stared at Unha again, and wondered if she was related to his mother. He asked her how she knew his father.

She said, I used to work at Club Saja, where your father also worked.

Really? Yunjin said. He worked at Club Saja?

Uncle Jake yelled, That's it! I can't help you anymore!

David's father came out of the kitchen, and stopped at the sight of the three of them sitting on the sofa. He said to Unha, We are leaving.

David stood up.

He turned to David. No, you stay here with your uncle.

He was confused, and asked where his father was going.

Away for a little while. I will send for you when I'm ready.

Where? When?

He shook his head. I don't know, he said.

But...? David didn't know what to say.

It will be all right, Sam said.

David glanced at Yunjin.

Jake came out and said to David, I'll get the sauna started for you.

His father came up to David, kneeled down and put his hands on David's shoulders. He said, You listen to your uncle and to Yunjin. You be a good boy, okay? His hands were large and callused. David felt one of his calluses catch the fabric of his shirt.

But where are you going? David asked.

Just to take Unha to somewhere safe. Okay? It won't be very long. You just listen to your uncle.

He squeezed David's shoulders. David would never forget that feeling of his father's strong hands tight on his bony shoulders. He released David, patted his head and stood up, cracking his knees.

Jake said to David, Come on. I'll get you a towel.

He pulled David along. David looked back at his father, who was saying to Yunjin, I am sorry but I have to go.

Go, she said. It's fine.

Jake hurried David along.

David sat in the sauna by himself, wrapped in a towel and listening to the muted voices of Yunjin and his uncle. Everything was confusing to him, but at the same time he liked the excitement of it. He had been in the sauna only once before, shortly before his mother died, and being here, seeing Unha, and feeling the upheaval of major changes had a disturbing effect. He remembered his mother with startling clarity. He could almost hear her voice amidst Yunjin's and Jake's.

He felt dizzy from the heat, his head pounding. He still felt the squeeze his father had given his shoulders. He heard more voices. His mother opened the door and walked in, wearing a black dress and pearl necklace. She sat down next to him, the wooden bench creaking. She asked him why he liked the sauna so much.

David was too surprised to answer. He asked what she was doing here.

Seeing you, she said.

She had all her hair, which fell loosely over her shoulders, and her cheeks were pink. She looked healthy and happy. She gave him a soft, kind smile. He lay down on his side, watching her, still not believing what he was seeing, and she stood up over him and touched his hair, stroking it as she used to when he had trouble sleeping. Sweat dripped into his eyes, and he closed them. He wanted to tell her how much he missed her but couldn't find the words.

Then his uncle rushed in, picked him up and told him that he should never sleep in here; it's too dangerous. David said, My mother... My mother was here.

Uncle Jake paused. Who?

My real mother.

Uncle Jake sighed. David felt the cool air over his skin.

Yes, Uncle Jake said quietly. Your mother is everywhere.

39

Sam explained to Unha that they would spend a night at his brother's condo in Santa Cruz, and from there they'd drive down to L.A. He and Unha would then figure out where to go next.

Sam added, It's a condo he hardly ever uses.

He wondered how many other properties his brother had sitting around, apartments that Sam could've stayed at instead of struggling with the rent for a dirty, small apartment on a busy street. How difficult would it have been to let Sam use the condo to save money? He could have maintained it. He could have even renovated part of it.

Right before Sam left, his brother said, I hope you know what you are doing.

Sam hadn't replied. He was thinking about David. He didn't want to leave him behind, but he knew he had little choice.

Now, as he drove south on 880, he began having doubts. He was about to go on the run from Mr. Oh and his debt; he had abandoned his wife and son; he had stolen Unha from Bobby Yun. When he thought about his situation, he felt hopeless.

The freeways were oddly quiet for the middle of the afternoon, and as he was driving through the South Bay on the way to Santa Cruz he wondered if it was some kind of holiday. He asked Unha how she was feeling.

Better, she said.

You should try to sleep. We have another hour or so.

She leaned back in her seat and closed her eyes.

Sam really didn't know Unha very well, and he had just ruined his life for her. No, he had ruined his son's and his wife's lives. He could turn the car around, and show up at Club Saja. He could explain everything, and hope for Mr. Oh's forgiveness.

But he couldn't give Unha over to Bobby Yun.

Unha said, I am sorry that you had to leave your son.

Sam glanced at her. Her eyes were still closed. He said, When I feel like everything is safe, I can send for him.

Not for her?

No. She does not want to be with me.

She opened her eyes. I am sorry for that, too.

No. That is not your fault.

She said, Can you tell me about your late wife?

Her name was Sunny.

Sun-ne?

Yes, but she liked the American version. Sunny.

How did you meet?

In Seoul. Her parents worked at the same factory my parents did. Her father had a big birthday party, and we were invited.

And then?

We went on dates. Once I began apprenticing with a carpenter we were married. Then my brother sponsored me to emigrate so we came over here.

Your brother never married?

No. He doesn't seem interested in having a family.

They fell quiet, and Sam found it strange to be talking about mundane things after all that had happened. He took a deep breath and asked, Did you know a girl named Minji?

Unha sat up. Yes, I did. Where is she? Did you see her?

Sam asked, How did you know her?

She came with me from Seoul. We flew into Mexico together. Where is she? I was worried about her. She is so young.

Minji. Skinny with big eyes?

Yes, yes. How do you know her?

Sam said, I am very sorry to tell you this.

Unha stared at him, and without his saying anything she seemed to know. She covered her face and shook her head. I can't take this, she said quietly. I can't take any of this.

He wanted to touch her arm, but was too shy. He said, We are getting away from it all.

How did she...?

A customer did it.

Unha asked, How do you know?

I was working for Mr. Oh and Hyunma. We had to bury her.

Did the customer get arrested?

I don't think so.

That is not right.

None of this is right, Sam said. You should rest.

She leaned back and stared out her window.

The condominium was off Seabright Avenue, only two blocks from Twin Lakes Beach, and Sam stood on the balcony that had a sliver of an ocean view between two other homes. He heard the clanging of a railroad crossing. The bright afternoon sun reflected off the buildings, making him squint. Sam felt the cool sea air chilling his bare arms, but he inhaled the saltiness, the freshness, and was struck by how clean his lungs felt here.

He heard Unha walking across the floor and she stepped out onto the balcony. He turned. She had washed up again and had draped a blanket over her shoulders. She said, Come, we should eat.

Laid out on the living table was their lunch—club sandwiches from a nearby deli—and Sam sat down. He watched Unha eat slowly, wincing when she opened her mouth too wide. He said, We will leave here tomorrow.

Tomorrow morning?

Yes. I will buy some maps today, and check the car.

What about money?

I have some.

This is a nice apartment.

Sam agreed, looking around at the practically unused furniture, and was envious. Jake's vacation apartment was better than Sam's full-time one. How could they be so different? He wanted to believe it was luck, that his brother was in the right places at the right times, but he knew better. His brother was smart, and worked hard. Sam never seemed to make the right decisions.

Like this. Was this the right decision? They ate in silence, and Sam found he had little to talk about. His uncertainty grew as he thought about the enormity of what he was doing. He was giving up everything for a woman he hardly knew.

As if she were reading his mind, Unha said, If this is too much for you, I can stay here by myself for a few days and then leave on my own.

Why?

You have done so much for me. Thank you. But I can take a train to Los Angeles by myself.

Do you know anyone there?

No.

What would you do?

I don't know.

Sam shook his head. We go together. Anyway, Yunjin wants to leave me. You and I can start over together.

Will we be safe?

Yes, Sam said.

Sam bought maps of California and Los Angeles and spread them on the living room floor. Although he was tempted to drive into Koreatown he worried about Mr. Oh's and Bobby Yun's connections there, so thought again about going farther south, into Orange County.

Unha came out of the bedroom and sat down on the floor next to him. She asked, Don't you want to rest?

Soon, he said. I want to have our route planned out.

I don't know how I can thank you.

He sat up. You don't have to.

She looked down.

Sam didn't know what to do. He reached out and touched her hand, and her body stiffened. He pulled away. I'm sorry, he said.

No, no. It's me. I don't…I'm not sure…

He said, I just want to be near you. That's all.

She sat closer to him. He said, Don't you want to rest?

I will stay out here with you until you're ready, she said.

They sat there quietly together.

40

Jake sat at his kitchen table, sipping coffee and planning how to deal with Mr. Oh. His brother kept taking and taking, and now he had jeopardized Jake's career, his livelihood, and it had to stop. He had given Sam the keys to his condo in Santa Cruz. This was all he could do for him. Sam had agreed to leave the condo tomorrow morning, and that would be the last time Jake would hear from him until he sent for David.

He heard Yunjin talking quietly to David up in the guest loft. David asked a question and Yunjin replied in a whisper. Jake would let them stay here for a few days, and then set them up in a cheap apartment. He'd give Yunjin a job at the Shilla.

Tonight he'd tell Koman that he had talked to Sam, urging him to come in with Unha, but that Sam had fled. He would then wait until tomorrow and tell Koman that Sam had used the Santa Cruz condo without Jake's permission. If he had to, Jake would pay back all of Sam's debts, including paying for the girl he took. This would mean holding off on the new restaurant in Berkeley, but he had to placate Mr. Oh.

Sam had once claimed that Jake liked being the more responsible one, liked having Sam always ask for help, but it wasn't true. Maybe when they were young he relished the praise he received over Sam, especially when Sam bullied him, but once they grew older Sam's dependency was exhausting. Part of it was bad luck, as with Sunny's illness, but even bad luck can be controlled. If Sam had read the health insurance details, he wouldn't have signed onto a lower premium but lower lifetime cap health plan. That had been sloppy, and his finances were in ruins after Sunny's death.

Now this. Jake had a brief, guilt-ridden thought that maybe Sam would be better off dead.

Yunjin walked into the kitchen and asked, Can I walk around the neighborhood?

How is David?

Sleepy. He will take a nap.

No more saunas for him.

He said he saw his mother.

Jake nodded his head. He said, I have to get back to work. Let me give you an extra key.

Jake found another door key, and told Yunjin to help herself to the food in the refrigerator. He added, I'll bring something back tonight for dinner.

Yunjin left the house. Jake sat at his desk, and went online, checking his e-mail. The doorbell rang, and he thought it was Yunjin not being able to use the key. He walked to the door and opened it.

Im stood there, shaking his head. He pointed down the road and said, That's his wife, right?

Jake said, What are you doing here?

Bobby tried to follow you, but lost you in the hills. I called Koman and got your address.

I was just about to contact him. I haven't found Sam yet—

Stop lying. You must have talked to him. He left his wife here with you. Is his son here?

They haven't seen him—

Im pushed Jake back and forced himself in. Jake stumbled, and said, What the hell—

Shut the fuck up, Im said. I'm going to take a look around. Sit down and shut up.

Mr. Oh is not going to like this—

Im swung his fist. Jake's vision exploded and blurred, a yell of pain caught in his throat as he fell to the floor. He held his cheek and looked up. Im said, Koman told me to find Sam. That's what I'm going to do. First I'm going to search this house, then you and I are going to talk. Stay right there and don't move. Do you understand me?

Jake nodded. His son is upstairs. Don't scare him.

I don't care about his son, Im said.

He began walking through the house while Jake sat there, his cheek stinging.

41

David sat up as the man whom his uncle called Im searched through the house, and then walked up to the loft. He saw David and said, Where's your father?

I don't know, David answered. The man's face was pale, his eyes and teeth strangely large and frightening.

He said, When did you see him last?

David didn't know what to say, so kept quiet.

Im studied him. Are you stupid?

I'm not.

He said, Come downstairs.

Jake called up, He has nothing to do with this.

Im reached for David, who backed away. Im lunged forward, grabbed David's shirt and yanked him off the bed. Go, he said.

David hurried down to the main floor where Jake pulled him closer to him and said to Im, What the hell do you think you're doing! My brother isn't here!

So where is he?

I told you I don't know!

Where did the woman go?

Who?

The tuigi.

She went to explore the neighborhood, Jake said.

You know I have to find him, Im said. He was my responsibility. I am not leaving here until you tell me.

I don't know.

Im slowly put his foot on the coffee table, pulled up his pant leg, revealing a leather strap. He drew out a long, thin knife. He said, Your relationship with Mr. Oh has been damaged. Yun will cause a lot of problems if we do not make amends. Koman has given me permission to do whatever I have to. Do you understand?

David turned to Uncle Jake, whose forehead was sweating. My brother doesn't tell me anything, he said.

That's too bad, Im said, grabbing David's arm and pulling him away from Jake.

Wait, Jake said, but Im raised his knife.

David was too stunned to react. Im held the knife to his throat and said to Jake, Don't make me do this. Tell me what I need to know.

You would hurt a child?

Im nodded his head. Of course, he said.

David felt the blade on his throat, and it was warm.

Jake said quietly, I…I can't…

David smelled Im's sour sweat. Im gripped David's shoulder tighter and said to Jake, Sooner or later I will find him. How many more people will get hurt? What will happen if Mr. Oh decides to put you out of business? What will happen if Mr. Oh decides to ruin you?

Jake stared at him.

Your brother has done this to himself, Im said. Tell me the last time you saw him.

Jake shut his eyes and, after a long pause, said quietly,

A couple of hours ago.

Im relaxed his grip on David's arm and said, Where?

Here.

He was here? Im lowered the knife.

Jake nodded his head, but kept looking at the floor.

Where is he now?

Jake whispered, He is my brother.

You can still repair the damage with Mr. Oh, Im said. You can help us and Mr. Oh will appreciate it. You know this to be true.

But he's my brother.

He did this to himself, Im said. Where is he? This is the last time I'll ask you. Where is he?

Jake said quietly, Santa Cruz.

42

Sam filled the gas tank and checked the oil. The tires were worn but would last another few thousand miles. He made sure the car was locked and walked back to his brother's condo, savoring the chilly evening air. He loved the smell of the ocean, the saltiness lingering in his nose. He fantasized about staying here in Santa Cruz, rent free, finding some carpentry work and living with Unha by the beach. The apartment seemed unused; it was just waiting for him to live here.

He walked into the condo now and imagined it was their home. Unha had fallen asleep on the sofa. The maps were still spread out on the floor, but Unha had cleaned up the crumbs and wrappings from their quick dinner. He noticed that she had also dusted the tables and closed the curtains. Sam smiled to himself. She liked everything to be neat and orderly. In that sense she was the opposite of Sunny, who often forgot to clean the apartment until they had guests coming over. Dishes piled up in the sink, and when they ran out of plates Sam and Sunny would wash the dishes together.

He remembered how, after working with his hands all day, the act of drying the dishes sometimes hurt. Sunny would see him trying to hold the dish towel, and she would tell him to rest. But he insisted on helping. He liked standing with her while she washed the plate and then handed it to him. They would talk about their day. Sunny would lean into him affectionately.

Unha woke up and watched him. She said, Are you all right?

Sam nodded and asked if she wanted to go to bed. He said, It is more comfortable than on that sofa.

She began to sit up, and winced. He hurried over to help her. She said, Everything hurts.

I can buy some aspirin.

No. I just need to rest.

He walked with her to the bedroom and when she lay down he pulled the cover over her.

She said, Will you sleep soon?

He said, I can use the sofa.

No, there is room here.

Let me wash up first.

Goodnight, Sam, she said. I am very sleepy.

He leaned over her and touched the top of her head. She put her hand over his. He pulled away slowly, and she looked at him with wide, worried eyes.

He couldn't stop thinking about David and tried to use the telephone to call Jake's house, but the line here was disconnected. Sam knew that his brother always had his cell, so there was no need to have this phone working. He considered walking to the corner store to use the pay phone, but he was too tired. He took a long shower, and when he realized he had forgotten to bring a clean change of clothes, he washed his underwear and shirt in the sink and then used an old hair dryer on them.

He put his warm clothes on, and checked Unha. She was curled up, breathing deeply. He debated crawling into bed next to her, but didn't want to scare her. So he went into the living room and lay on the sofa. He kept telling himself that everything would be fine, that once they got to Los Angeles they'd be safe and would figure out what to do.

Sam didn't realize how tired he was until he relaxed into the cushions and felt his limbs loosening. His body had been clenched, his joints stiff from tension. He tried not to think too much about his situation, because he felt the unsteady panic growing within him. He told himself that he just had to get to L.A. and everything would be fine.

He hated leaving his son behind. He should have said something better than, Be a good boy and listen to your uncle. He should've told him how important he was, how happy he and Sunny were. He trusted that Jake would tell David this.

Despite his protests and grumblings, Jake always helped Sam, and maybe Sam was too used to it. He disliked asking his brother for money and jobs and now the use of this apartment, but at the same time he knew Jake wouldn't refuse him. Sam was good at reading his brother. Today, for example, when Sam mentioned the use of this condo, he could see that Jake hadn't thought of it; a brief glint of recognition passed across his face, and then Jake closed it off. Sam knew that his brother had considered it a good idea, but didn't want to give in too easily. It was the way he tried to cover up his hesitation with an immediate refusal. As soon as that had happened, Sam knew he would get to use this place.

He felt himself relaxing, sleep approaching. Tomorrow they would leave. He had a total of five hundred dollars—the additional two hundred had come from his brother—and a full tank of gas. They would find a place in Los Angeles. He didn't think it would be too hard to get work, if not as a carpenter then in a restaurant. Unha also had enough experience now to find a waitressing job. He suddenly envisioned their lives in the future, married with David living with them. Maybe another child on the way. He would eventually get back to making furniture, maybe even open his own shop. He thought about what kinds of chairs he would make, and fell asleep soothed.

43

Jake tried calling the Santa Cruz condo, then remembered he had disconnected the phone months ago. He hung up and tried to think of another way to warn his brother. Sam's cell phone didn't work. Jake didn't know any of his neighbors. There was the maintenance number, but that was for an off-site property manager, hired by the condo association. He could try to drive out there first, but if Im saw him, Jake would be in more jeopardy with Mr. Oh.

He sat down and thought, What have I done?

He heard Yunjin upstairs, telling David to sleep. Then he heard the sofa creaking as she got comfortable.

There was no way to warn Sam. There was nothing he could do, but hope that Sam would leave the condo before Im showed up. Im had called someone, probably Yun, as he left the house. Sam's odds of escape worsened with every passing minute.

Jake heard the clicking of the sauna heater. He went downstairs, stripped off his clothes, and sat down in the sauna. He thought of David hallucinating in here, seeing his mother.

Once or twice when Jake had been dehydrated and sitting in here for too long, he had heard voices. He had never seen anything, but he remembered when he heard children laughing and he thought some kids had trespassed in his yard. The second time was when he heard an older man's voice, possibly his father's, talking in Korean in a confused, rambling way. He had sat up abruptly, his heart thumping. At first he had thought he had left the TV on, but when he walked through the house he found it off and everything silent. He went back to the sauna, shivering. The voice returned. He wondered if there was an acoustical trick that somehow allowed him to hear a neighbor. But he had no Korean neighbors. He recognized his father's voice, and kept still. The voice soon faded away.

Later that night he had called Korea and asked his mother where his father was. She told him he was in the hospital for kidney stones. He had been delirious with pain and was now sedated. Jake didn't tell her that he thought he had heard him. She wouldn't have believed it.

So now, as he sat there naked and sweaty, he wondered if maybe David had seen the ghost of Sunny. This rattled him. If she was here, then she would see him naked.

He laughed this off. He was baking his brain in here.

But then he said aloud, Sunny? I am very, very sorry about Sam. Please forgive me.

He waited for an answer, but all he heard was the clicking of the heater.

He leaned forward, burying his face in his hands.

44

Sam woke up in the middle of the night, his chest and back sweating. He had been dreaming about Sunny marching down a well-worn path. She had glanced back at him, waiting impatiently. He rubbed his eyes and sat up. He listened carefully. He thought he had heard something. He looked around, momentarily confused as to where he was. A strange living room sofa. His brother's. He hurried to the bedroom to check on Unha, who was deep asleep. Creeping across the floor he stopped at the window and stared down at the quiet, dark street. One streetlamp was flickering, sending pulses of light onto the sidewalk. His thoughts were muddled, and he tried to shake himself awake.

Then, slowly, as he remembered all that had happened, his body grew heavy with worry. He glanced at the nightstand where his wallet lay. He had about five hundred dollars now. Some of that would be needed for gas and food to get to L.A. Then what? A cheap motel? Sleeping in the car?

What the hell was he doing?

He heard another sound, a clicking at the front door. He tensed. Moving quickly across the floor he went into the kitchen and found a carving knife. More rattling. Someone was checking the door handle. He crept to the security hole and peered through, and recognized Bobby Yun. He had a small white bandage over the bridge of his nose. Sam gripped the knife tightly.

The deadbolt was in place and the sliding chain secure. Sam doubted Yun could get in. He wasn't sure how Yun had found the apartment; it must have been through Jake.

He hurried to the bedroom and gently woke up Unha. She peered at him, confused.

He said quietly, Get dressed. Bobby Yun is out there.

She bolted upright. Out there? Right now?

He shushed her and nodded his head. He thought quickly. They had to get out without Yun seeing them. He went out to the living room and listened, then peered through the security hole; the hallway was empty. Maybe Yun was waiting nearby?

Sam crept to the balcony patio doors, but couldn't see the street from inside. He slid the door open slowly, and crawled out onto the balcony where the low concrete wall hid him from the street. He had parked his car a few houses down, and he needed to know where Yun was waiting.

Over the top of the ledge, he saw his car on the quiet street. He moved slowly toward the other end of the balcony and peered down. There. It was same silver Porsche Sam had followed in Mountain View; someone was sitting in the driver's seat, waiting. The person was hidden in the shadows, but it must be Yun.

Sam crept back inside and closed the patio door. Unha was standing there, waiting anxiously. He said, Bobby Yun is outside, probably waiting for us.

How did he know we are here?

He might have gotten it out of my brother.

Unha said, What are we going to do!

Sam asked, Can you drive?

No.

He said, We passed a bus station. It's on Front Street. Let me show you where it is on the map.

Why?

I think we should split up. You take the half the money and take the bus to L.A. I will try to distract Yun, and lead him away.

I don't want to do that!

We have to. He's waiting for us down there. I will make sure he is alone. But you should go without me.

Unha whispered, I'm scared to go alone. I don't know anything about the U.S. I don't know how to take the bus.

It's very easy. As long as you have money and can speak English, you will be fine. Let me show you the map.

She shook her head quickly.

He grabbed her hand. It will be okay, he said. You will be fine.

And you? What will happen to you?

He said, I will distract Yun, then lose him. Then I will meet you in L.A. At the bus station. We will figure this out. Come. Look at the map with me. Come.

He pulled her toward the maps, and she followed him reluctantly.

45

The low murmuring carried up the stairs and bounced off the ceiling and encircled David. It was completely dark, and although he knew he was still in his uncle's loft, he thought his father was drunk and mumbling downstairs. The voice had the same kind of rambling quality to it, and his first thought was, He's back. David jumped out of bed.

But then as he climbed down the steps, he continued listening and realized that it was his uncle, and he was in the basement. There was no slur of alcohol, no erratic exclamations, just a low, steady, monotonous murmur. David moved closer to the sound, and heard it coming from the sauna.

Uncle Jake was speaking in Korean, reciting something, and the language was difficult to understand. David heard him say, Search me, know my heart. Know my thoughts. See if there is anything wicked, and lead me to better paths.

David realized his uncle was praying, and after a moment of shock, he backed away, a chill in his neck. He hadn't been to church since his mother died, and hadn't heard his uncle pray since the memorial service.

He stepped up into the stairwell. His uncle let out a long, shaky sigh and swallowed. David heard the sorrow and held tightly onto the wooden banister, which creaked. His uncle stopped praying. David heard him move inside the sauna and he tried to run up the steps but Uncle Jake opened the door too quickly. He was naked, sweating, and crying.

David averted his eyes.

Uncle Jake said, I'm sorry if I was too loud.

David shook his head.

Uncle Jake grabbed a towel hanging on a hook next to the door, and wrapped it around his waist. He wiped his eyes with the back of his hand and said, Did you hear me?

David said, Praying?

I was reciting the Psalms that the minister read at your mother's funeral, he said. Your father and I had to memorize them when we were children.

Why?

He hesitated. Why did we memorize it?

Why were you saying it?

I like the sound of it.

He shivered and flipped a switch near the door. The heater inside the sauna clicked loudly. He asked, Do you want something to drink?

No, David said. What's going to happen to my father?

He shook his head. I don't know.

He led David back upstairs, and he put on a silky robe. He pointed to the photos on the fireplace mantle, and said, I showed you the picture of me and your father as kids, yes?

David took down the photo, which he had glanced at before, but never very closely. Black and white with a white border, the photo showed them at about his age, maybe younger, posing in front of a low table covered with food. David hadn't noticed the food before, and asked his uncle what was happening.

It's the tolsang of a neighbor. A baby's first birthday. Jake pointed to the table and said, You see the scroll, the paint brush, the book, and the bow and arrow?

David nodded.

Everyone waits to see what the baby grabs first. It's a sign of what might come.

What if he grabs the food?

Noodles mean long life. Rice means wealth. There are other things, but I forget.

Did you and my father do this?

Of course.

What did you choose?

I don't remember. You did this.

I did?

And you grabbed the book of Chinese characters. It means you're going to be a scholar.

David was disappointed he hadn't chosen the bow and arrow.

How come there are no pictures of my mother?

Jake said, They're hidden away. They upset your father. Come on. You should go back to sleep.

He guided David toward the loft stairs, and said, Everything will be all right. Your father will be fine.

David heard his voice catch in his throat. Before that moment David hadn't really thought about the danger his father was in, and the fact that his uncle had been crying in the sauna now scared him. Uncle Jake gently pushed David toward the stairs, and he climbed them slowly. He turned back and saw his uncle's thinning hair plastered to his head, his cheeks and forehead flushed and sweaty, and on his uncle's face was a sad, helpless look that he would never forget.

46

Sam walked quietly down the stairs, through the lobby, and checked the front door, finding the lock broken, the metal plate bent and the wood cracked, probably from a crowbar. That was how Yun had gotten into the apartment building. He waited until he heard Unha walk down into the basement garage, the heavy iron door slamming behind her. He took a deep breath, and then burst out of the front entrance and hurried down the street toward his car.

He heard a car door close, but he didn't turn around. Instead he quickened his pace and jumped into his car. He started it, and saw Yun walk in the middle of the street toward him, but not in any hurry. This confused Sam, but he began to pull out of the parking space.

The steering was sluggish, a rubbery slapping sound coming from under the car. He tried to accelerate, but the car only jerked forward, and he heard the tires moaning and warping. He looked down the street. Yun was still approaching, his thin jerky figure moving steadily.

Sam opened the door and peered down—the tire had been slashed. He got out and saw that both tires on this side were flat.

Yun called out, You think I was just going to let you get away?

Sam turned and ran. He heard Yun following him.

He crossed the railroad tracks and ran for the beach, trying to lead Yun in the opposite direction of Unha. He ran past a row of beach houses with rickety shutters and over-grown lawns, then past a series of small apartments similarly neglected with the lights on in scattered windows. His lungs hurt. He smelled something burning, smoky residue mingling with sea air. He glanced behind him—Yun ran down the block, slowly gaining. Sam cut through a yard, between two small houses, ending up on another street closer to the ocean. He ran toward the sound of waves and found himself high up over the beach—a concrete ledge fenced off, with a path running parallel. He saw a large bonfire on the sand below, and people sitting around it. How was he supposed to get down there?

A gust of wind blew sand up around him. He covered his eyes.

Then he saw the concrete stairs a few yards ahead, and ran to them. Yun wasn't far behind. Sam hurried down the steep steps, the grit of sand beneath his shoes, grabbing the pipe handrail for support. He found it almost impossible to see below him. Then he had an idea. He stopped and crawled under the pipe, scrambling on the dirt and rocks. He scraped his knee. He lay still. He heard Yun grabbing the fence, and then walking down the stairs, his shoes slapping the cement. Yun muttered to himself. Sam leaned back and held his breath, his lungs aching.

When Yun walked by, Sam grabbed his legs and tack-led him. Yun grunted, and grabbed onto the handrail, but the force of Sam's tackle sent both of them tumbling down the steps. The concrete edges slammed into Sam's back and side, and he heard a clunk against the pipe and Yun yelled in pain. They hit another pipe, and Sam lashed out in the dark, not sure what he was hitting, and Yun grunted.

Yun hit Sam in the groin, and he gasped. He let go of Yun, who kicked his leg and tried to scramble up. Sam lunged forward and grabbed him again, pulling him down. Yun tried to kick him off, but Sam reached forward and grabbed Yun's face, tearing off the bandage and hitting his nose. Yun cried out and kicked furiously, and then after a moment Sam felt him trying to pull away. There was a click and a loud shot. Sam felt a sharp pain in his side, near his waist. He leapt forward, and grabbed Yun's hand, and felt the warm metal of the gun. He yanked it up, aiming it away from him, and with his other hand clamped his fingers around Yun's throat.

Yun kicked and thrashed, but Sam had a strong grip from years of carpentry, and only tightened his hand. He felt the ridges of Yun's throat and crushed it under his thumb. Yun wheezed, and let go of the gun, which clattered on the concrete, and he tried to scratch at Sam's face, but Sam brought his other hand to Yun's throat and squeezed with all his strength. The throat collapsed in his hands, and Yun gurgled. Sam kept squeezing. Yun flailed his arms and legs, his body jerking. After a minute he stopped moving. Sam kept his grip strong and finally began breathing. He let go of Yun's throat. Yun lay still.

Sam saw a flashlight approaching from the camp fire. A young man's voice asked, Is everything all right over there?

Sam stood up, the pain in his groin ricocheting through his body. He trudged up the steps, not looking back. He heard another voice say, What's going on up there? Hey! You!

He ran.

47

Unha read the street signs and followed the route Sam had drawn for her on the back of an envelope; she had to go three blocks, then turn left, then right, then cross a bridge; the bus station should be right there. She was afraid of getting lost, so she often read the street signs aloud to herself to make sure she wasn't mistaken. Her feet hurt so badly that she had to stop every block and rest.

He had told her to make sure no one was following her, that Yun didn't have someone helping him. But Unha saw no one. The streets were empty, quiet.

Sam had given her half of his cash, and when she felt the small folded wad of ten- and twenty-dollar bills in her pocket, she felt safer. With this she could go almost anywhere. She thought about taking a bus somewhere else, and not meeting Sam. She could call him and tell him that she knew he had given up so much for her, and she couldn't accept this. She thought about his son, his wife, his brother—because of her they were all angry with him.

She remembered that a girl from her village, Munya, was supposed to be in Los Angeles, though now Unha wondered if it was a lie. Maybe Munya wasn't even alive anymore.

She turned another corner, and saw the bridge—a small highway running over a wide stream. She hurried along the walkway and onto Front Street. The bus station should be up ahead. Warehouses and boat supply shops sat on both sides of the large, quiet street. Buses were parked on the side streets. Reading off the address numbers she approached Love Transportation Services, and saw a Greyhound sign in the window. She hurried to the depot, but the sign said it was closed. The ticketing hours began at 6:30 in the morning. She peered at a clock inside. It was 2:30.

She sat on a bench near the entrance and lay down. A faint ringing in her ear grew louder, the ringing pulsing with her heartbeat, and slowly it became the urgent breathing of the man on top of her. She hugged her legs. She sat up and remembered what had happened at the Mountain View train station. So she walked around the side of the building and sat on the ground, leaning against the concrete wall. She hummed to herself for a minute, pushing away the ringing in her ear. She then listened for any sounds, but all she heard was the wind blowing across the tall, dead grass.

48

Slowly, as the adrenaline wore off, the wound in Sam's side began to throb with an insistent, pulsing ache. When he touched the tender area he felt the blood soaking his shirt, his skin sticking to it. The bullet had entered above his waist, but he wasn't sure if it was still in. He had to check the wound in a mirror. He hurried back toward his brother's apartment, prioritizing his concerns—this wound, Unha, the car tires, the police—and felt a moment of gleefulness that he had killed Yun. One less thing to worry about. He had a surprising lack of remorse. He had never killed anyone, and yet Yun's death was a huge relief.

He stopped and bent over, his groin still hurting. Would he need a doctor? A hospital? What about his car tires? But he was running out of cash. Could he get more money from Jake? The logistics of this overwhelmed him.

He heard a police siren nearby, and stood up quickly, too quickly, the pain searing his side. Doubling his pace, he trotted down the street, and saw his car angled out of the parking space. He checked the other side. All of the tires had been slashed. He cursed.

When he checked the front lock of the apartment building again, he saw that the edges no longer lined up, and the door stuck open.

In the light of the foyer, he could see all the blood he was losing. His shirt and pants all along his right side were stained dark red. He suddenly felt weak. Panic welled up in him as he hurried to the stairwell. His vision blurred.

On the second floor, he staggered down the hall toward the apartment. Losing too much blood, he thought. He had to staunch the bleeding. He remembered seeing gauze pads in the medicine cabinet. He needed to clean the wound, change his clothes, and get the hell out of here.

He pulled out his brother's keys, and fumbled with them. He swooned. He could feel his strength ebbing, and he tried to control his panic.

He heard footsteps down the hall, and turned.

Im appeared at the top of the stairwell.

Sam blinked and stared, not sure if he was hallucinating. But then Im approached. Sam tensed, about to run, but Im said, No, don't.

Sam asked, What do you want?

I see Bobby got to you, Im said.

Bobby Yun is dead.

Im smiled. Good. He was an asshole. Now, let's deal with you. Go ahead inside.

Sam put the key in the door, but before he could open it, Im moved quickly behind him and said, Don't do anything stupid, Sam. You are already in enough trouble.

Sam said, I have to tend to this wound.

Go in.

He opened the door, and Im pushed him in. Sam stumbled forward, losing his footing, and fell heavily to the floor. He cried out in pain and tried to protect his wound. Im closed the door behind him and said, You've done too much damage to get out of this.

Im stepped forward. Sam tried to get up, but Im raised his foot and jammed his heel into Sam's chest, forcing him down. Sam was too weak to fight back.

Im said, You are such an idiot.

Wait—

But Im dug his heel harder into Sam's chest. He kept his shoe there and reached down to his other leg and pulled out his knife. Sam tried to roll away, but Im was too fast. He plunged the knife into Sam's chest. Sam fell back in shock. He looked up at Im, who pulled the knife out.

Sam said, Oh.

Im stood up. Sam stared up at the hanging lamp, one of the lightbulbs out. He tried to tell him to leave Unha alone, but he couldn't form the words.

Im said, Stupid fuck. He shook his head and stabbed him again. He then wiped the blade on Sam's shirt, and stared down at him. He watched calmly as Sam's strength ebbed.

Sam thought of Sunny as he closed his eyes.

49

Unha paid the forty-eight dollars for a one-way ticket to Los Angeles, and sat in the back of the bus, waiting for others to board. There were only a few passengers, and the driver, a large black woman reading a paperback book, told one of the people boarding that they would be leaving in fifteen minutes.

Unha had woken up cold this morning, her clothes damp, and her body so painfully stiff that she had trouble straightening her limbs. She had searched for Sam as the ticket office opened, but he wasn't there. She remembered his instruction that if he didn't show up, she was to go on without him and meet him in Los Angeles. She worried that Yun had found him.

Now, as she studied the piece of paper Sam had given her with the address of Choi Storage—a back-up just in case he couldn't get to the L.A. bus station—she suddenly had the feeling that Sam wouldn't be meeting her. Something had happened, and she was on her own. She didn't want to go to Choi Storage. What if Yun knew about it? Yun had found them in Santa Cruz. Why not Los Angeles? She needed to hide.

She had two hundred dollars left in her pocket, and she would use this to find a job. She could start with restaurants and factories where there were other Koreans. She had heard of a large Koreatown in Los Angeles, and she could find it once she arrived.

After a few minutes the driver said, All right. All aboard. We're heading to L.A. We'll have three rest stops. Settle in.

The driver closed the doors and started the engine. Unha sat back in her seat. As the bus pulled out onto the street, she again looked down at the address. She knew what she had to do. She had money. She could speak Korean and English, and knew how to be a waitress. And she was free. That was all that mattered. She was free.

EPILOGUE

Jake searched for his brother the next day, finding the broken lock and the bloodstains on the carpet, the maps and the sandwich wrappers, but there was no clue as to where Sam had gone, if he was even alive. His car, the tires slashed, had been ticketed for parking in a street cleaning zone, and Jake had it towed and repaired, and eventually gave it to Yunjin.

From the way Mr. Oh resumed their normal business relationship with no mention of Sam, Jake suspected the worst for his brother. He finished the Seoul Silver, continued his partnership with Mr. Oh until Mr. Oh died of a heart attack a few years later, after which Jake severed all ties, paying Hyunma for Mr. Oh's half of the club. Hyunma soon sold off all of the businesses and retired to Korea. Jake opened up three more restaurants—two in Berkeley, another one in Oakland.

Yunjin worked for Mr. Kim and Kim's Fitness, first as his office manager and then, with his encouragement and night classes, as his bookkeeper. She learned more about accounting, helping Mr. Kim expand his two studios into a chain of exercise gyms, and she now runs the Bay Area office of Kimco Corporation, the umbrella company. She bought a condo in West Berkeley, and David lived with her until he left for college in Boston.

David became a professor of sociology. Sometimes he wondered if the fact that he had chosen the book of Chinese characters during his tolsang had predicted his future or had actually directed it.

David never stopped thinking about his father. This naturally led to his curiosity about Unha. Even though he had spent only a few minutes with her, had glimpsed her only through his shyness and confusion, he knew that somehow she was the key to understanding where his father had gone. He learned more about the trouble his father had been in from Uncle Jake, but there were many, many gaps.

David once hired a private detective to search for his father and Unha, and although this intrepid investigator couldn't find any trace of Sam, he did manage to locate Unha's mother in Korea, but she had not heard from her daughter since Unha left for the U.S. The only clue about Unha's whereabouts was an unsigned, typed postcard from the United States, a postcard of Malibu Beach with no message or return address. It could've been from anyone, but Unha's mother and grandmother always believed it was Unha telling them she was all right.

David's father was in all likelihood dead, but with no body, with no news, with no evidence of any kind, David would harbor a fantasy that his father was still alive. It was the most optimistic of scenarios, and perhaps at his core David knew the truth, that his father wouldn't have kept silent for this long if he was indeed alive. Still, David never gave up hope. He imagined even the remotest of possibilities.

Was it so impossible to imagine them right now, in fact, his father working as a cabinetmaker somewhere down near Los Angeles, Unha a waitress at a Korean restaurant? They have no children, and live an anonymous, placid life. They go on hikes on their days off. They visit the beach. They talk of their uneventful days and relish the quiet. Perhaps once in a while Sam thinks about his former life, but worries that the debts he owes and the trouble he has caused will never be forgiven, so he must stay hidden for a long time. But one day he will find his son.

This is one possible ending, one with an epilogue set in the future in which David's father contacts Uncle Jake, and then contacts David. Then what? Then they meet in person. Perhaps in L.A. Perhaps over coffee. The reunion in David's fantasy is muted, awkward, but slowly his father tells him everything he wants to know. Slowly they reestablish all that they lost, and David finally understands why his father had to leave him.

No story is ever truly finished, so David waits patiently for news from the dead.

ACKNOWLEDGMENTS

Thanks to my dedicated and intrepid first readers, Frances Sackett, Eli Brown, Tonya Hersch, Susan Taylor Chehak and Jen Ames; to my editor of fourteen years, Jerry Gold; to my supportive, loving and long-time rockclimbing friends who kept me sane, including but not limited to Melissa and Brian Quiter, Ben Khoo and Unhei Kang, Julie and Rob Bailis, Anna Rosenbaum, Ashley Holt, Anne-Cécile Laudon, Seth Joseph and Jodi McMahon, Dave Watkins and Kathryn Tillett, Jen Atkin, Amelia Chenoweth, Brian Crockford, Isabelle de la Fontaine, Jess Liberman and Pete Alagona, and the usual Berkeley Ironworks and Oakland Great Western Power Company crowd; to Nat Sobel and Judith Weber; to Tom and Susan Chehak for their generous hospitality; and to Gaylord's Café in Piedmont, Groundwork Coffee in Hollywood and Literati Café in Brentwood.

ABOUT THE AUTHOR

Leonard Chang was born in New York City and studied philosophy at Dartmouth College and Harvard University. He received his M.F.A. from the University of California at Irvine, and is the author of five previous novels. His books have been translated into Japanese, French and Korean, and are taught at universities around the world. His short stories have been published in literary journals such as *Prairie Schooner* and *The Literary Review*. He lives in the San Francisco Bay Area and Los Angeles, and teaches at Antioch University. For more information, visit his web site at www.LeonardChang.com.